"Are you afraid of me?"

Sebastian asked, his usually cold eyes suddenly brightening.

"Should I be?"

He lifted Danielle out of her chair, pulling her close against him. She was indeed afraid of him, but she couldn't bear to move away.

"Perhaps you are afraid of what your grandmother told you—stories of intruders walking through her rooms at night . . . noises in the walls and ceilings."

"I did poke around the house, but I didn't see or hear anything unusual," Danielle told him.

Sebastian frowned and moved away from her. "I would advise you not to go *poking* around where you have no business. Some of the railings on the balcony need repair—you just might fall." That said, he walked away.

Dear Reader,

Winter is truly here, so you'll really need to bundle up as you read our newest Shadows, because both the weather and fear will have you shivering if you're not careful.

Regan Forest takes you to Wales in *Bridge Across Forever,* an eerie tale that combines a touch of the past with the present to create a story unlike any you've ever read before. This one has an ending that will truly surprise you.

New author Carrie Peterson checks in with *The Secrets of Sebastian Beaumont,* a marriage of convenience tale with a scary twist. You'll never think of the traditional plot line in the same way again.

In months to come, look for more spooky reading from such great authors as Helen R. Myers and Lindsay McKenna here in the shadows— Silhouette Shadows.

Yours,

Leslie Wainger
Senior Editor and Editorial Coordinator

CARRIE PETERSON

THE SECRETS OF
Sebastian Beaumont

SILHOUETTE® Shadows™

Published by Silhouette Books
America's Publisher of Contemporary Romance

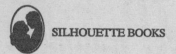 SILHOUETTE BOOKS

ISBN 0-373-27022-4

THE SECRETS OF SEBASTIAN BEAUMONT

CARRIE PETERSON

enjoys writing songs, poetry and novels, working in her garden and reading everything imaginable. Born in Arizona, she and her photographer husband have lived in Florida, Mexico and Alaska, and have now settled near Yuma, Arizona, where she also takes pleasure in the company of her friends, two cats and a dog named Daisy.

To my husband, Andy, and my sister, Donna—
always there for me

CHAPTER ONE

As the pilot began the descent, Danielle Beaumont closed her eyes, thinking of the crumpled letters on her desk, the delicate, spidery writing. Maybe she should have brought the letters with her instead of leaving them at home. What if her grandmother was senile and denied sending her the one-way plane ticket and begging her to come with such urgency?

The Gulf of Fortuna lay below, a brilliant turquoise, calmly translucent all the way to the bottom. Boats of all sizes and shapes cluttered the seaport as far as she could see along the shoreline. She could even make out some people below, dressed in shorts, their arms sleeveless. Only a few days ago she wore a heavy coat and still felt the New York cold.

Oh, Lordy, what was she doing here?

"Is this...your first visit?" A woman in the next seat tried a halting English. They hadn't spoken since the passenger had boarded at the last stop. Danielle had assumed she didn't speak English and the woman probably was put off by the irritation in Danielle's expression. She was ashamed of herself for feeling so anxious; Howard and her grandmother weren't worth it. She was finished with letting people manipulate her.

"Yes, I've never been out of the United States before. Can I practice my rusty Spanish on you a little? I may have need of it where I'm heading."

"*Por supuesto.* Of course, but first let me see where you are going. May I see your ticket?"

Danielle pulled it out of the bag at her feet.

"Ah, if you are going to LaCeiba, you will have to take another plane to go there," the woman said. "After that it is not far to King's Ransom. I have heard of it, a big plantation in a little country.''

Great, another plane. The closer she came to meeting her grandmother, the more she wished she had never left New York.

''Do they have ah—political problems in LaCeiba?'' She pictured guerrilla soldiers sneaking through jungles.

''No, no, *señorita*. I have heard my husband call La-Ceiba the Central American Switzerland. It is—how do you say— Neutral.''

Well, that was a big relief, but still she couldn't be sure.

There was the Sierra de San Pablo, a chain of rugged mountains, just as she'd read about, pushing its way almost to the coastline.

She didn't have long to wait in the airport before a small plane taxied up and the customs officer directed her to board. She was the only passenger and in spite of her interest in the tropical terrain below, her thoughts kept turning inward.

What was she getting into?

Danielle rubbed her tired eyes. The old woman had no right pulling her strings after all these years. The only recollection she had of her grandmother was the years of pain and heartbreak the woman had caused Danielle's mother.

At the second airport, she tried in vain to make herself comfortable on a scarred wooden chair and waited hours for someone from the plantation to claim her. No one approached the rickety old building except a few workers who nodded politely, but didn't try to speak to her.

She ran her fingers through her unruly red hair. She hated the curls, but unless she let it grow long, it insisted on curling and she didn't like the way long hair looked on small women like herself. She smoothed down her beige knit skirt and suddenly thought of Howard. He liked her in beige, said it matched the gold of her eyes. Howard. She wrinkled her nose and shook her head in denial of the pain and anger. He had wanted to live with her, sort of a trial marriage. To her way of thinking, it was all or nothing.

''Señorita Danielle?''

She almost jumped out of her chair. She turned to look
at a short, swarthy man with a wide mustache and grin to
match. In a charming mixture of English and Spanish, he
introduced himself as Ramon, the gardener from *Tesoro del
Rey*—King's Ransom.

"Is this a Land Rover?" she asked about the vehicle when
they started on their way. How odd to ride in such a car; she
tried to imagine it on the streets of New York.

"*Sí, señorita.* We have heavy rains here and very few
roads. Sebastian, he brought this from England." Ramon
spoke proudly.

As they drove, annoyance settled upon her along with the
light coating of dust from the road. Sebastian. Every other
word coming from the gardener's mouth was Sebastian,
spoken with respect bordering on reverence. Already she
was tired of the name and she hadn't even met the man.

When she could stand it no longer, she interrupted his lo-
quacious monologue.

"Who is this Sebastian person?"

His dark eyes showed surprise as he turned to her and he
nearly landed them in a ditch. He pulled the car back onto
the roadway or what passed for one.

"*La Chaparrita* never told you about Sebastian?"

"Who is *La Chap Chaparita?*"

"Oh, it is a name we have—with much respect—for Doña
Mercedes, your grandmother. It means—let me think in
English—it means short little woman."

"Short?" Odd to think of her grandmother as short. She
always pictured her as very tall and formidable.

"*Sí.*" He nodded happily. "About like you, I think."

Danielle frowned. Everyone she knew politely overlooked her shortness. When she first started in the designing end of the garment industry, she had become
accustomed to six-foot-tall models looking down at her, and
she'd tried to rise above that with the sheer force of her
personality. It didn't always work.

"And this marvelous Sebastian of yours?"

He grinned in innocent acknowledgement of her description. "Oh, *sí,* he is marvelous. Very good word. If not for

Sebastian, *La Chaparrita* would have lost plantation many times. We have big *huracan* come to this place—'' His arm swung wide to indicate the surrounding area while she held tightly to her seat in an effort to stay inside the car.

"Sebastian, he work beside us, harder than anyone, to save crops. Day and night he work so *Tesoro del Rey* can again make money.'' He interrupted his speech long enough to point a finger at some flying parrots, at risk of life and limb. He continued as if he had never interrupted himself.

"Once we have terrible union trouble. Big, ugly men come from far away, tell workers must all join union. Burn many plantations, hurt many people, but Sebastian keep them away from here. They afraid, know Sebastian mean as they are.'' He laughed loudly at his joke.

Danielle couldn't help but join him, relieved that this Sebastian character had a major flaw. So he was mean. For a while she thought he must be the Paul Bunyan of the banana belt.

"Is your Sebastian married with a big family?'' she asked, not really caring but wanting to keep Ramon talking. His speech was quaint, his accent charming and his cheerfulness helped keep her worries at a manageable distance.

He turned and for a moment looked grim. "Señorita Contreras has him like this.'' He held up a tight fist in front of his nose. "He make promise with Doña Mercedes to not marry until the old woman die.''

He crossed himself and she grabbed for the wheel just in time to miss a large rock. "Poor Chaparrita, not feel very good now. Ah, *señorita,* you will meet them both soon.''

She grimaced. Between a grandmother she detested and a man who was beginning to irritate her before she'd even met him, doubts piled upon doubts.

To take her mind away from her problems she tried to concentrate on the scenery passing by so quickly. It was difficult to focus, with the Land Rover bumping up in the air all the time. Ramon paid no attention to either potholes or boulders. She held on for dear life and suddenly felt an unfamiliar zing of pleasure course through her body as she began to enjoy the lush jungle along the road, the flash of bright birds and the smell of loamy soil and vegetation. No wonder my mother found New York a cold and strange place, she thought. But suddenly the verdant richness of the landscape flashing by made her edgy—uneasy. It seemed unnatural, somehow surrealistic like a Gauguin painting.

She tilted her chin and straightened her shoulders, determined to treat this as an adventure. No more, no less. Before she could change her mind again and regret her impulsiveness, the vehicle screeched to a halt in front of double iron gates.

Once inside the gates, Danielle stared in wonder at the house before her. The house looked as if it had chosen to ramble off horizontally as well as vertically, all on its own. The haphazard additions were charming in a way, if overwhelming. The edges of the east and west wings vanished into a maze of greenery.

Ramon had been chattering on as usual, but suddenly broke off in midsentence.

"Ah, Sebastian," he breathed.

Danielle was at once conscious of her rumpled, dusty appearance. The man striding toward them was well groomed from his shiny boots up to the white shirt open at his tanned throat. She stood watching as he ignored her, speaking in Spanish to Ramon. With a courteous bow, Ramon hurried away and she was left to face Sebastian alone.

From the looks of him, he was a man who had worked outdoors all his life. She tilted her head back to look up into his face and was startled to see greenish hazel eyes fringed in thick, black lashes staring back at her.

His hair was dark as a raven's wing. His nose was straight with just the slightest hawklike curve. His lips—when her gaze reached his sensuous mouth Danielle turned her head away and felt a blush coming on as if she were a silly schoolgirl.

Suddenly conscious of the silence, she spoke with as much dignity as she could muster.

"I am Danielle Beaumont. Of course you're Sebastian." She almost said *the great Sebastian* and stopped just in time.

He looked intimidating enough without any help from her sardonic sense of humor.

One black eyebrow shot up and he smiled, although the smile did not reach his eyes. She began to wonder if he spoke English when he replied without a trace of accent.

"Welcome to *Tesoro del Rey*. Doña Mercedes is expecting you. Did you have a comfortable journey?" His words were polite, but she felt the coldness beneath them.

Why would this stranger be so cool to her?

"This is so—so different." She gestured toward the house and surrounding gardens. How awful to feel like a complete idiot and even worse have him tower above her so. She moved away to give herself more space.

"You don't feel comfortable here?" He sounded hopeful.

"No—that is, I didn't exactly say that. My home is in New York. Have you ever been there?" That ought to take him down a peg or two.

He shrugged wide shoulders and a grin edged across his lips. "No. I don't have any desire to go there, either. *This* is my home." He leaned toward her and brushed his big hand across the back of her neck.

She jumped away, startled.

"A small spider, Miss Beaumont. I did not think you would care for his company."

"Thank you." Her voice sounded stiff to her own ears. She wasn't afraid of bugs, but then neither did she like them, especially the idea of wearing one.

"New York is filled with crime and urban decay, I have heard."

"Maybe. However, we do not have soldiers skulking through the jungles blowing up innocent villagers."

He looked pained. "If you had bothered to get your facts straight, you would know that LaCeiba is—"

She held up her hand. "I know, it's neutral. Why?"

He smiled, some of the edge gone from his voice. "We are a small country, tucked away in the middle of Central America. In the past we have been overpowered by more ambitious countries, but now we have a stable government and we are respected as neutral. There have been no political problems here since I was born."

"I apologize for my prejudgment of your country, but you shouldn't try to fit mine into a pigeonhole, either. New York is many things, not only the negative."

He bowed low with a graceful sweep of his arm. "Then I owe you two apologies, Señorita Beaumont. For maligning your home and for my lack of manners as a host. You must be exhausted. The maid will take you to your room and when you have rested a little, Doña Mercedes will see you."

It was like a dismissal and it irritated her, but there was no way she could come back at him without sounding touchy.

When they entered the house, a small man came rushing forward. He looked to be in his seventies, but well preserved in a cherubic fashion.

"Ah, Miss Beaumont, what a delightful surprise. We didn't think you would really come."

"This is Peter, he's been here from the start. Doña Mercedes wanted to retire him, with a piece of the property for his home, but he wouldn't hear of it."

"My lands, no, Don Sebastian. What would I do all day?"

"That's true, he rules this house." Sebastian and the little man smiled at each other like old friends. So, the big guy could unbend if he wanted to, only not toward her. Why was that?

Sebastian handed her over to Peter as if glad to be rid of her company. Before he could leave, a maid came from upstairs and whispered something to Sebastian. They argued for a moment and then he turned back to Danielle.

"Doña Mercedes is aware of your arrival and wishes to see you immediately." His lips tightened with barely repressed anger.

"I'll escort her," Peter offered. "You go about your business."

What was wrong with the man? The long, exciting day began to catch up with her. She thought longingly of a hot bath and a cool bed.

But first her grandmother's summons.

She walked through the spacious rooms, captivated by the high ceilings and the overhead fans moving slowly, even in winter. Or what was winter in New York. Here and there maids worked silently, dusting, polishing, everyone busy. How many people worked here? Did they live on the plantation or come from a village nearby? So many questions. In spite of her exhaustion, the exotic spell of all she had seen and felt and imagined coursed through her body, invigorating her, renewing her.

Instead of dreading it, she started to look forward to meeting her grandmother, if only to get the long-harbored grudge off her chest once and for all.

Danielle heard the imperative ring of a bell, the querulous voice that rolled off Spanish spoken like a native. She took a deep breath and pushed into the room.

Her grandmother had written that she must see her granddaughter once before she died. If Danielle expected to see a frail, delicate old lady, she was wrong on several counts.

Doña Mercedes held court from the middle of her bed like a dowager queen. Her tiny body barely raised the covers under which she lay, but her presence filled the room. She was tanned and wrinkled from the sun with skin resembling brown parchment paper, and her eyes shone out of the deep sockets like two golden marbles. Her voice was strong and she called out across the room.

"Come, come, child. Let me look at you. God knows I've waited long enough."

A woman, probably her nurse, stood in the shadows at the back of the room. Peter had backed out and closed the door behind him, as if he hadn't wanted to intrude.

Danielle could feel the vitality, the strength emanating from the old woman even though it was plain to see she was very ill.

The two regarded each other in silence for a long moment. No endearments expressed between them, no pretended familial sentiment. Danielle felt relieved with only a small twinge of disappointment.

In spite of not wanting to like her, a smile tugged at the corners of Danielle's lips as she moved closer.

"Ah! You have *his* hair. But you have the Beaumont eyes." She leaned back on the pillows to study her grand-daughter. "Thank you for coming."

Danielle swallowed against the tightness in her throat. "I didn't want to," she said truthfully. "My mother finally forgave you for your cruelty, but I never did."

Doña Mercedes nodded. "It took me years to realize that I shouldn't have sent her away like that. But we had such plans for your mother! She was the apple of your grand-father's eye. I'm quite certain he loved her even more than he loved me. He wanted to send her to the best schools in Europe, to marry from the cream of society."

"I guess she had other ideas," Danielle managed to say.

Her grandmother brushed Danielle's words away as if she hadn't noticed anyone speak. "It wasn't as if we asked her to marry without love. If she had waited, she would have found someone suitable."

"My father—"

"Your father was a scoundrel and a ne'er-do-well. Henry and I knew it from the first moment we saw him. He wanted to get his hands on King's Ransom and I couldn't let that happen."

"I have to agree with you there, he wasn't much. He took off—left my mother pregnant with me in a strange city. She never saw him again."

"Oh, no! I feared that, but by the time I regained my senses, it was too late," Doña Mercedes said, her eyes losing their light.

"To this day I'll never know how she managed to survive. Still—that doesn't excuse your part in it, does it? You could have asked her to come back."

"If only she had written after I got down off my high horse. I would have sent for her, even if I was bitter. The shock of her leaving killed your grandfather, you know."

She hadn't known. Her mother never spoke of him. Not ever. Toward the end, all she ever wanted to remember was King's Ransom, she missed her home so much.

Danielle stared at the woman she wanted so badly to hate. "Do you expect me to believe you'd have sent for her? I read her diary after she died and saw the returned letters that you never opened."

"But of course. I admit that. Did you also notice the dates? Before you were born, am I not correct? She only wrote to me once after that, to tell me of your birth, and left no forwarding address. Over the years I became frantic with worry. I had no idea if your father was with you, but I was ready to accept him—even let him share in King's Ransom, if that was what they wanted."

The old woman sounded sincere but Danielle was wary. "How did you find me?"

"I cannot take full credit for that," Doña Mercedes admitted. "Several years ago, my old friend and advisor, Paul LeFarge, thought of hiring a private detective."

"Several years ago? What happened to that notion in the meantime?"

"I didn't want to have anyone know—it might have gone badly and . . . more has happened lately that made me feel I had to find you."

"You couldn't admit to failure, if you hadn't found me," Danielle finished for her.

The old woman nodded. "Something like that. Peter contacted a private detective for me. We wanted to find you so much."

We. Did that include Sebastian?

Never one to skirt around edges, she asked the question.

Her grandmother's eyes lit for a brief moment at the mention of Sebastian, the look quickly displaced by a pained surprise. "No. I have not confided in Sebastian, which is a pity. I wanted time to smooth things out a bit—"

"Smooth things out! He's only. . ." She started to say *a worker,* but stopped. Obviously, he was more than that here.

"Sebastian is like a son to me. My husband adopted him and gave him our name."

"A son? Is he the reason you didn't need my mother or me?" Danielle didn't try to keep the bitterness from creeping into her words.

"Oh, never!" Her grandmother sounded shocked. "It had nothing to do with you. We brought him to King's Ransom as a boy of nine or ten. His mother disappeared, he never knew his father."

That made two of us, never knowing a father. "He isn't from here, is he?"

"Yes, well, we found him in the city, near the beach. He is of mixed parentage and the people were not kind to him then. He took care of himself for years—barely staying alive, I suppose." Her voice registered pride.

It must have seemed like a godsend, gaining a son after losing a daughter. In spite of her bitterness, she could understand what had to be her grandparents' extreme sorrow and guilt.

Sebastian must be in his mid-thirties, Danielle calculated. This was his home now. He'd told her that in no uncertain terms.

"We sent him to Oxford. I wanted him to have the chance your mother refused."

No wonder he wasn't impressed by her New York background. He had taken full advantage of her grandmother's generosity. The old woman had lavished her attention on a stranger and ignored her own flesh and blood all these years.

She thought of the many privations her mother had endured. The blurred ink from her tears on many of the diary pages was silent testimony to her mother's grief. All that sorrow and pain—just because she had done the unpardonable by falling in love with a handsome soldier of fortune who had stopped a while at King's Ransom.

"If it was not for Sebastian, I would have lost King's Ransom several times over," Doña Mercedes was saying. "The year of the big hurricane, he worked harder and longer than anyone. When union organizers came here from the city to cause trouble, he kept them away. They burned several plantations, but not ours."

The more she extolled the virtues of Sebastian, the more Danielle disliked him. He sounded like an opportunist, taking advantage of a lonely old woman. A woman with a fixation for this place, who would sacrifice her own family to keep her property from harm.

"Why did you send for me as if were a matter of life and death? You seem to have all the family you need." She didn't bother to hide the resentment.

"Oh, don't say such a thing!" Her grandmother leaned forward, holding her arms across her chest in a protective gesture. "Just because I loved and cared for Sebastian took nothing away from my feelings for your mother. I *did* try to find her."

"I believe you," Danielle conceded, alarmed at the old woman's sudden agitation. "But I still don't see why you want me here now."

"Of course you would wonder, child. It seemed like something I had to do, but now I am not so certain. That is not to say I'm not glad we found you." She took a deep breath and leaned back, regarding Danielle intently. "You look delicate. I doubt you would flourish here," she murmured as if to herself, changing the subject abruptly.

"Nobody has ever accused me of being delicate before. Besides, what has size to do with ability? You are smaller than I. Anyway, I have no intention of flourishing here." Danielle felt her temper rise at the old lady's calculating scrutiny.

Doña Mercedes smiled, the worry disappearing from her eyes. "You sound just like your great-grandmother. A more cantankerous, obstinate woman never existed. I was afraid you would be soft like your mother."

"What's wrong with that?" Danielle bristled. "It would make me proud to be like her."

Her grandmother's expression softened. "Perhaps. Your mother was sweet and gentle, but had no backbone. The only time she ever stood up to anyone was when she ran away with your worthless father."

"Who do you think raised me alone in a strange city without anyone's help? She never married again—she was too busy taking care of me and staying alive." Danielle's cheeks flushed, her body quivered with unexpressed anger.

"What did she do? How did you both live?"

"She cleaned offices first and then started sewing for different people. Someone who admired her work found her a job in the garment district. It was hard work, but I think she liked it."

"But she must have put you through school and—"

"Of course. She brought work home sometimes and I learned to help her. I never got to go beyond two years of college—she died then, and there was no time or money."

"Ah, if I had only known to look for you then."

"We survived. She taught me her craft and from that I went on to designing." Made a good name for herself, too. She was in much demand as a free-lancer.

Doña Mercedes closed her eyes wearily and patted the bed for Danielle to sit down.

"I'm saying everything wrong, my dear child. Forgive an old lady for her rudeness. I've always said exactly what I thought and sometimes—no, often—I've regretted the impulse. But I can hardly change now, can I?"

As her grandmother smiled, Danielle saw traces of the beauty she must have been in her youth. She also saw her own impulsive nature mirrored in that tiny person.

"The detective told me you are very successful in your work. I suppose you young people call it a career. It must be a great satisfaction to do something well. That is all we wanted for your mother. To do something with her life."

The nurse reached hurriedly for a carafe of water near the bed and placed two white pills into Doña Mercedes's shaking palm. After she took the pills, she leaned back, face beaded with perspiration.

"*Señora,* you have talked long enough." The nurse spoke in Spanish, yet Danielle was able to understand. "Perhaps it would be better to continue tomorrow?"

"Nonsense. Stop bossing me." She waved the nurse away and turned back to Danielle. "Tell me more about yourself while I collect my poor old body together," she commanded.

Danielle carefully veered away from discussing her life with her mother and instead told her grandmother about her work. Naturally Howard's name came up a time or two. She listened to herself and wondered why she tried so hard to make her life sound rich and full. Hadn't it been? She had always believed so until lately.

"You mention Howard. Who is this man?"

"A very nice person, really. We had plans to marry eventually—when things were right for us."

"Nice?" The old woman shook her head. "Did you say nice? What a pitiful way to describe a fiancé! And why *plans* to marry? You either marry or you don't."

Danielle flushed. "What's wrong with a nice man? Do you prefer a man like my father?"

"Nonsense. I loathe his kind of vain uselessness, but I can't abide 'nice' men, either."

"It seems we can't talk without biting each other's ears off. Were you like that with my mother, too?"

"No. She wouldn't argue with me. I wish she had. We might have understood each other better."

Her grandmother reached over to touch Danielle's arm. Without thinking about it, Danielle held the tiny hand inside hers. She felt a stab of pity for the wasted years of not knowing her grandmother. They would have argued plenty, but it never would have been dull.

"I must rest now, my dear. Please stay at King's Ransom a while. Try to get to know us. Later, when I have more strength, there is something I want to tell you. Something important."

There was that "us" again. "If 'us' includes Sebastian, I don't think he likes me."

The old woman made a face. "That is my own fault. I did not confide in him—he did not know until yesterday that you were coming here."

"Why should it matter to him?"

For once her grandmother did not seem so sure of herself. She looked away. "I—I don't want to go into that now, perhaps later. But as a favor, please don't mention that I sent for you. Not until I explain it all to him. You see, I never expected to be successful in finding you, much less bringing you here. I was going to tell him—but it all happened so quickly. If the matter comes up, will you wait until I speak to him?''

Danielle nodded reluctantly. She always hated subterfuge, but her grandmother was very adamant about it.

Much later, as Danielle was halfway through her bath, she realized the question of why she was here had not been answered.

CHAPTER TWO

The following days drifted by slowly, lazily. For as long as she could remember, Danielle had never had time to just do nothing, and after she replaced the guilt with pleasure, she began to enjoy her vacation.

Visiting with her grandmother once in the morning after breakfast and once in the evening before dinner had become the routine, and she even began to look forward to her conversations with the quaint, irascible woman. She had tried to avoid the moody Sebastian but when she decided that he in turn was ignoring her, it became an embarrassing situation. He must have been avoiding Doña Mercedes, too, yet her grandmother was too proud to speak of it. Danielle could see she was hurt and puzzled by his absence.

This morning, Danielle put on her comfortable old jeans, which she had packed in her luggage at the last moment. It was time to go exploring. Perhaps she could talk to Ramon.

She found him in the rose garden. "Ramon. *Buenos días*. The garden is so lovely. Did you do it all?" She knelt by his side as he worked painstakingly trimming the wayward shoots of a new plant.

"*Sí.* Doña Mercedes, she loves roses. She can see them from her window. She used to sit here hours and hours."

He spoke half in English, half in Spanish when he became excited, but she did not interrupt, allowing the words to flow around her like petals from the roses.

Suddenly Ramon leaned back on his heels. "Ah, it is Sebastian."

Danielle noted that all of the servants and workers called him by his first name but the reverent tones more than made up for any implied familiarity.

At the other end of the garden she saw two people, a lovely woman with long black hair and the tall, broad-shouldered Sebastian, walking side by side in a way that said they were on very familiar terms.

Danielle stood, brushing the loam from her knees in an absentminded manner, unable to stop watching. The woman was dressed in a white pants suit that showed her slender figure to perfection. She stood only a scant head shorter than her companion. As Danielle watched, Sebastian doffed his hat in her direction, a mocking gesture that told he had seen her watching them.

As the couple walked toward her, she reached up to smooth her windblown hair and thought of the freckles visible without her usual light touch of makeup.

"Permit me to introduce our charming guest, Danielle Beaumont," Sebastian said, after he had spoken a few words of greeting to the gardener who promptly disappeared. "Teresa and her brother, Raoul Contreras, own the next plantation, a few kilometers away."

Danielle knew Ramon didn't appreciate Sebastian's interest in this neighbor, but she wondered what her grandmother thought of Ms. Contreras.

The tall, willowy Teresa inspected her with narrowed eyes and then, as if Danielle were not worthy of a second thought, dismissed her with a toss of her dark head.

Danielle flushed, speaking with strained politeness. "Good morning. How did you find Doña Mercedes this morning?" she asked Sebastian, knowing full well that he hadn't been in to see her.

She was rewarded by his brief loss of composure. Their gazes locked and she felt disturbed by the sudden flow of energy between them. Teresa must have noticed; she tugged on Sebastian's arm possessively. He ignored her as he regarded Danielle with a steady stare. She was the first to turn away, retreating to the safety of the house.

Later in the evening, Danielle waited alone in the study for her meal, which had been her custom after the first night of dining alone in her room. Her grandmother never received visitors between breakfast and dinner. Danielle didn't mind—their discussions had to be tiring to the old woman; they could never agree on anything.

As she sat waiting in front of the fire in the comfortable room, rare and expensive books lining the walls, she began thinking that perhaps it was time to leave. Whatever had possessed her grandmother to bring her here, the obvious disruption between the old woman and Sebastian had cast its shadow.

As if the name conjured his person, Danielle looked up to see Sebastian leaning against the doorway of the study, watching her. When he entered the room, it became somehow smaller as he filled it with his presence.

"Ah, I thought to find you here, perhaps showing the maid how to dust properly."

She flushed and stood, not wanting him to tower over her if she was in a seated position. It didn't help, so she moved back toward the fireplace and stepped up on the little brick ledge that circled it. "I wasn't showing the gardener anything this morning, out by the roses," she said, clearly understanding him. "I wanted to see what he was doing. By the way, there's something I want to ask you. I'm curious about the electricity. When I arrived, I saw no utility poles and . . ."

He smiled. "No. We're too far away from civilization for such niceties. We provide our own with generators."

She looked puzzled. "Wouldn't there be the sound of motors running?"

He shook his head. "Henry was quite emphatic about that, he wanted nothing to destroy the peace of King's Ransom. He had an underground tunnel built behind the stables. It houses the generators so that very little noise escapes."

"Generators? More than one?"

"My, my, you *are* curious, but Doña Mercedes always claimed curiosity was a sign of intelligence. Yes, we have separate generators for each wing of the house and the main portion, as well as for the stables and gardens. If one goes out, the others will keep working."

"Organizing such a system took a lot of thought."

"Henry liked nothing better than to ponder possibilities unendingly. As I grew up, I began to appreciate his thoroughness."

Odd how one took such things as electricity for granted in the city. Being here gave new insights to the way other people lived, that was for sure.

"Peter said you took your meals here. Alone. We have a dining room, you must know. We are not completely uncivilized."

"Oh? I hadn't noticed," she said sarcastically. "It seemed pointless to sit at that long table all alone." Golden eyes clashed with hazel-green ones. She observed that he had changed from working cords to a pair of slim dark trousers and a white shirt unbuttoned at the neck. The white of the shirt contrasted with his tanned skin. She looked away before he could catch her gazing at the hard planes of his jawline, the mouth...

"I came to see if you would care to dine with me tonight."

She felt disconcerted by his sudden change of tone. The firelight glinted on the top of his hair as he bent to look in her eyes as he asked the question.

"You have her eyes, don't you?"

"If you mean my grandmother's, I suppose I do. My mother's eyes were blue." She had always envied her mother for that, hating the oddness in her own.

Why did he show such hostility toward her? She knew exactly why she disliked him—he was a leech, hanging on to his good life, which was granted to him by her grandmother—at the expense of her own family. She felt certain that if Sebastian had not occupied his favored position all these years, the old woman would have tried harder and sooner to find her daughter and granddaughter.

"I prefer that you dine with me every evening that I am home," he said stiffly. "It would seem more presentable."

To impress my grandmother with your courtesy? she wanted to ask. Instead she sat down and curled up her legs in the big chair that she had just vacated. "Thanks but no thanks. It's much more cozy to eat here. Alone." She started to pick up a book from the table beside her but was stopped by the look of anger deepening in his eyes.

He bowed in a low, mocking sweep. "Very well, but if you should change your mind, we dine at eight o'clock." He turned on his heel and shut the door firmly behind him.

She sat for a while, waiting for Peter. He had brought her dinner promptly at seven every evening so far. A strange man, he always acted as if he wanted to speak but changed his mind at the last minute. She turned to look toward the door, hearing his discreet cough.

He entered, empty-handed. "Good evening, Miss Beaumont."

"Good evening to you, Peter. Am I not eating tonight?"

He started to speak, looked uneasy but plunged on. "I hope it is no inconvenience, but other plans have been made."

Why, that impertinent oaf! How dare he assume that she would bend to his will and dine with him even after she'd refused.

Seeing her frown, Peter began to back out of the room.

She laughed, in spite of her indignation. "No, it's nothing against you, Peter. I know you are just the messenger." It was obvious the man equated her red hair with a fiery temper such as her grandmother must have.

"Can we talk a moment?" She sensed that now would be a good time to encourage him to open up.

He smiled, relief plain on his round cheeks. He reminded her of a chipmunk, pale and fidgety—at odds with his gray hair and stooped back.

"You're like family, aren't you, Peter?" No use asking him to sit, she knew he wouldn't. He had an old-world formality about him that none of the other servants had.

"Oh, yes." His voice came in puffy little gasps, as if he were out of breath. "Henry Beaumont brought me from England, hired me before he ever built King's Ramsom. He envisioned the entire house and hired me to oversee it when it was finished." He smiled in remembrance and pride.

"What was my grandfather like? You must have been here when my mother..."

"Oh my, yes. I was here for her birth. Such a tiny, fragile baby. Your grandfather sat by her crib night and day for a while. He was a kind man, a philosopher, soft-spoken, one of life's dreamers. We all loved him as we did the *señora.*"

"They were exact opposites," she said.

He smiled. "Of course. Their marriage was full of ups and downs, it was delightful to watch. Your grandfather had been so afraid he had lost both his wife and baby during the delivery, so after that they were very cautious, very protective of her."

Danielle had always wondered how her mother could have left home, severing all ties. She didn't give the impression of being that strong a person, but she had to have been. Perhaps leaving here had seemed like the one chance of freedom to a young, innocent girl. Maybe her parents' love and concern was smothering.

"We are most happy to have you here, Miss Beaumont. I know your grandmother is overjoyed to have found you at last."

Overjoyed was not a word she would apply to the crusty old woman supervising her domain from her bedroom, but Peter must know her better than anyone.

"You helped her to bring me here, didn't you?"

He looked uncomfortable for a moment, as if wondering just how much she knew. "I'm glad to have been of assistance," he said. "She didn't think you could be found, you know, a marriage, name changes, that sort of thing."

"Is that why Sebastian is so rude? Just because she didn't confide in *him* about this?"

"Oh my, no. It's more like he might think—well, he could think—"

The light finally clicked on as to why Sebastian was so out of sorts with her. "That I came here to put in some kind of claim for a share of King's Ransom? That's absurd! I live in the States—I have no interest here, outside of curiosity to know what sort of person would turn her own daughter out."

"You shouldn't judge, Miss Beaumont," he said stiffly, regaining his former coolness.

"No, I shouldn't. I'm sorry, I realize you and my grandmother are old friends. Yet I can't talk to her about it, and I needed to talk to someone close."

"I'm honored, ma'am. As I said, it isn't good to judge too harshly. The circumstances were different twenty-three years ago—it was the first time your mother wouldn't listen to reason and perhaps it shocked Doña Mercedes. Poor Henry never accepted the fact that your mother left. He waited until the day he died for her to turn up again at those big iron gates."

Danielle heard the heavy sorrow in his voice, sorrow for his old friend Henry, sorrow for her grandmother and most of all, sorrow for the wasted years.

"You're right, I have no call to judge anyone. I'm honored to visit King's Ransom. I will prize the days spent here for the rest of my life."

Peter's eyebrows shot up into his receding hairline. It was obvious her words had shocked him, but why? Before she could ask him, the imperative sound of Doña Mercedes's bell echoed through the house and he excused himself hastily.

Funny, she hadn't missed home yet. Was it that things were so new and exciting here? Shouldn't she miss Howard a little, even if she had decided to break it off with him?

Before they started going together, when Howard was only known to her as a co-owner of one of the major chains of dress shops in the city, he claimed her impetuous nature fired her creativity, made her a top designer. Afterward, when they began dating seriously, he disliked that side of her, called it pushy, unfeminine.

If only he had offered a genuine commitment instead of the wishy-washy living arrangement he proposed. She had seen what a one-sided love had done to her mother, and she wasn't about to take a chance on it with anyone, even if she never married.

Danielle went upstairs to change for dinner with Sebastian. It wasn't so much giving in gracefully as it was curiosity, she assured herself.

At precisely eight o'clock she walked down the curving staircase to see Sebastian waiting, which gave her a twinge of irritation she tried to hide.

"Ah, you left your charming jeans in your room. I'm delighted to know they are not permanently attached to your body," he said lightly as he took her arm.

What did he know about what she wore? Had he spied on her while she roamed around the house and grounds? She smiled up at him sweetly and said nothing. She'd be darned if she let him have the satisfaction of knowing he annoyed her.

They entered the dining room and he sat at the head of the long, mahogany table in a matter-of-fact way that irritated and impressed her at the same time. The table gleamed beneath an exquisite crocheted tablecloth, which was the soft warm color of eggshells. The chandeliers glowed with a soft light behind delicately etched glass. How could she ever have thought this room formidable and cold?

They ate in silence for a while. A not uncomfortable silence, as the food placed in front of them absorbed their interest. First they were served a shrimp salad with a savory dressing that glided over the tongue and nipped at the taste buds. Then followed a fillet of pork loin basted in apricot sauce, so tender it cut easily with a fork.

"I can see you enjoy good food," he remarked, his expression amused and almost friendly as he watched her for a moment.

She nodded. "It appears my grandmother provides a bountiful table. Pity she can't be here and share it with us."

His eyebrows pulled together in a scowl as he put his fork down carefully on the edge of his plate. "Perhaps it is time you realize that *I* belong here. Doña Mercedes has treated me as a son and I have tried to repay her at every opportunity over the years." He glared at her under dark lashes. "What I do not understand is why *you* are here."

"Why don't you ask her, since you are so very close. I haven't a clue as to why she invited me."

"She invited you? I don't believe that for a moment."

"And why not? All you have to is—" Oh, Lordy, here she was just about to blurt out *ask her.* She had promised her grandmother that she would not say anything to Sebastian about the invitation.

"I needed a vacation, maybe that's why I'm here. As soon as she feels a little better, I'll—"

"'Feels better'! *Dios mio!* You must know Doña Mercedes is dying. Isn't that why you are here?"

Danielle gasped in shock at his tone of voice, the words not sinking in yet. Then she began to realize what he had just said. "I don't believe you. That's a cruel thing to say." Against her wishes, Danielle had begun to admire her grandmother. It wouldn't take much to become actually fond of her.

Looking into his eyes, she saw the truth reflected. "Does she know?"

"But of course. She is much too intelligent not to know. We never speak of it—there is no need. The doctor tells me she cannot last the month."

Danielle started to rise, but now sat back weakly, trying to absorb the news.

"Of course I assumed you knew. Why else would you be here now, so precipitously. A coincidence I find hard to believe," he said.

She pushed back her chair and stood, flinging the napkin onto the table. "Of all the rude, insolent—I don't give a damn about your moldly old plantation, if that's what has your back up."

"Why wouldn't it have my back up, as you so quaintly put it? I am the only person alive who can make this plantation survive. Dozens of families depend on us. I care for this land just as she does, and have put as much of my heart and soul into it as she...but you wouldn't know about that, would you?"

"No, I wouldn't know. While you were in England going to Oxford, my mother and I managed to survive because she worked day and night as a seamstress in a sweatshop and I helped when I came home from school. How different it might have been for both of us if my grandmother had taken the trouble to find us back then.''

He looked disconcerted for a moment and then stiffened his back. ''I am sorry for your mother's hardships, but you can hardly blame that on me. I didn't know you existed until you showed up on our doorstep. Doña Mercedes has always fretted about her daughter but nothing was ever mentioned about a granddaughter.''

Our doorstep. Always *us* or *our*, both he and Doña Mercedes excluded everyone with those little words. Danielle turned on her heel and ran up the stairs.

Safe in her room, she slammed the heavy door shut behind her and fell on the bed. What an insensitive jerk! As if she cared about his dumb plantation. She *did* care about her grandmother, though. How could she hold a grudge against the only one left in her family? She rolled over and looked up at the high ceiling, absently noting that it hadn't been painted in a long time. She supposed her grandmother had lost interest in things like that.

She got up and walked to the big bay window, examining the workmanship on the drapes. Beautiful, but old and fading, needing a renewal. Well, perhaps Teresa Contreras had that in mind; she seemed quite at home here. Funny, though, her grandmother had never mentioned the woman and Danielle kept forgetting to ask about her. Not that she cared one smidgen who Sebastian was seeing.

Danielle realized she didn't even know what kind of plantation this was. Did they grow bananas? Coffee? She hadn't been curious enough to ask before and now realized there were many things she would like to talk about with her grandmother before...

Her room overlooked a huge jacaranda tree with feathery, fernlike leaves and clumps of gigantic purple flowers. Beyond the tree lay the rose garden with the full moon shining down on the fountain. The moonrays turned the tumbling sprays of water into molten drops where they lay shimmering at the bottom of the pool.

Doña Mercedes wanted her to stay a while, that was why she hadn't sent a return ticket. Did her grandmother choose this room for Danielle imagining how full of wonder it might be to her? How she might compare it to the noisy, smog-encrusted city streets that her own apartment looked down upon?

She shook her head, denying that the maneuver was working. She was a city girl, with the spirit and spunk that it took to survive there. Surely the view here would grow tedious and bland with time. Surely, despite what Sebastian said, Doña Mercedes's health would improve and Danielle could go home.

Go home. How hollow the words sounded now. Her career suddenly did not seem so important, especially working in proximity to Howard every day. In the past, that had been a major attraction. Of course she liked creating, but it came to her that Howard had been slowly stifling her more whimsical, unconventional works along with her eager zest for life.

Perhaps that was why she was drawn to Sebastian. He had a zest for living, for surviving, more so than anyone she'd ever met. Danielle squirmed uncomfortably, thinking of how much she'd begun to look forward to seeing him every day and the quick stab of disappointment she felt when he was out in the fields and she missed him. This unwelcome attraction made it even harder to face the wary look of mistrust in his eyes. A mistrust she could understand even while knowing it was unjustified and unfair. Was it only that she saw Howard in a true light, as a selfish despicable cheat that made her feel so alone and susceptible to a man like Sebastian?

She had better leave here soon before the slow seductive quality of this place took over, leaving her with nothing to fight with when she returned to the city.

Because sooner or later, that was something she must face.

CHAPTER THREE

The next morning Danielle entered her grandmother's bedroom as usual. She stopped short, seeing Sebastian seated near her bed, her tiny hand engulfed in his. If Danielle thought he might indicate embarrassment at showing his feelings so openly, she was mistaken. He did not seem to think holding the matriarch's hand and smoothing the wispy hair away from her forehead was anything out of the ordinary.

"Ah, Danielle. Come, sit down, child. I wish to talk to both of you while I still am able to."

A protest started from Danielle's lips but she checked it. No need to pretend; Sebastian had said her grandmother knew she was dying. Danielle moved toward the bed, and eased herself into a chair beside it.

When the old woman began to speak again, her voice was so soft that they both had to lean forward to hear. "I can see you do not like each other. It was my dearest hope that..."

As her voice was swallowed by a spasm of coughs, Sebastian shook her hand gently. "Nonsense. Of course we like each other. Why would we not?" A dark eyebrow shot up as he looked directly at Danielle, challenging her to disagree. It was as close to an appeal as he would ever come, obviously because he wanted to spare Doña Mercedes any unnecessary anxiety.

Danielle cleared her throat. Her normal instinct was for total honesty, but her mother used to chide her that there were exceptions to every rule. This may be one of the times.

"We take our main meal together and have long talks," she said. "We are beginning to know each other quite well, I assure you." The old woman did not recognize the sarcasm underlying her innocent words, but Sebastian did. She almost laughed out loud at his sudden frown.

Doña Mercedes's expression eased and she opened her eyes.

"Let me have your hand, too, child," her grandmother said, her voice gaining strength with her enthusiasm. "You don't know how happy that makes me." She turned to Sebastian. "Did you see to Princessa? I want Danielle to have my horse. If she doesn't know how to ride, I'd like you to instruct her."

"Do you think that wise under the circumstances?"

"Thank you," Danielle interrupted. "I do ride some, but..." She wanted to say she would not be at King's Ransom long enough for any lessons on riding, but she caught the words in time. If it made the old one happy, let her believe what she wanted. What could be the harm? Why was Sebastian so selfish?

Doña Mercedes patted Sebastian's hand, his long brown fingers holding her tiny hand as if it were a butterfly, his palm slightly curved to encase hers.

"Do you like it here, child?" she asked. "Do you feel the pull of King's Ransom in here?" Letting go of Danielle's hand, she patted her chest with curved fingers pointed inward.

In the silent room, the question struck Danielle as more than just a polite query made by a solicitous hostess.

"Why, yes, yes I do." Surprised, she heard the truth in her words. "It's almost like..." She couldn't finish; Sebastian was frowning and she really didn't know what she wanted to say anyway.

"Like coming home?" her grandmother finished for her.

Danielle turned away, toward the window that was open to the breeze in spite of the morning nip in the air. Yes, she *did* feel that way; her mother had talked about every nook and corner of King's Ransom until Danielle felt she knew everything about it. Nothing much seemed to have changed in the more than twenty years since her mother left.

Sebastian stood up abruptly, carefully placing Doña Mercedes's hand on top of the cover. "It is obvious we are tiring you." He put a finger against her protesting lips. "Hush. We will talk more tomorrow." He bent forward and brushed her cheek lightly with his lips, then standing up, he moved toward the door.

"I want my granddaughter to stay with me now a little longer, if you'll excuse us, Sebastian."

Doña Mercedes called Danielle closer and whispered, "I don't trust Teresa Contreras! I despise her and her brother. I don't want her here after I'm gone. She and Raoul are—are not good for Sebastian. He deserves better."

Danielle knew her grandmother must be whispering to avoid gossip, for the nurse was in the corner, reading a book. Did the nurse also speak English, then?

"What can I do about it? I've only just met Teresa and have never seen her brother." Maybe it would make her grandmother feel better to know she and Teresa had disliked each other on sight, but she said nothing.

Doña Mercedes made a wry face. "Their father died when they were very young. Later, the mother took another husband. I know it is uncharitable of me, but the mother and I—we never got along, argued every time we met, so we seldom visited. It was her dream for Sebastian and Teresa to marry—to combine the two plantations."

"But then how did the stepfather...?"

"I'm coming to that, child. Forgive an old lady for trying to catch her breath from time to time."

Danielle felt a guilty stab and leaned back in the chair, waiting as patiently as she could for her grandmother to continue.

"The mother died several years ago—bad heart perhaps. No one knows. They just buried her, without really knowing the cause of her death. We are so far from doctors here. Then the stepfather was killed in a fire they say was set by the union thugs."

"*They say?* You sound as if you don't believe that."

Doña Mercedes waved her hand imperiously to stop Danielle's line of questioning. "Doesn't matter what *I* think. The point is, he is gone and *they* own the land now."

"Ramon told me a little of the— Would you call it an uprising?" She needed to move the conversation away from the brother and sister, which seemed to agitate her grandmother.

"No! Our workers had no reason to revolt. The strangers from the city forced the field workers to go on strike. I could do nothing—your grandfather had passed away and I was helpless for a while."

Her thin voice swelled with pride as she continued.

"Sebastian kept them away from King's Ransom. He fought with the ringleader and broke the back of the strike. He has a terrible scar on his arm to show for his valor—the ringleader just missed his throat with a machete."

"What was so terrible about a union?"

"You'll have to go into that with Sebastian. I don't have the energy to explain. The point is, I don't trust those two. They scorned their mother for marrying again, putting someone before them. And now she's dead. They hated their stepfather, and so too is he conveniently gone. They are greedy and selfish—their workers are not happy and sneak over here to work for us. We cannot hire them all."

"But if Sebastian trusts her— You must give him credit for not being stupid."

"Pah! Hormones, male hormones. I don't think he even wants to be with her—ah—permanently, but he thinks she waited for him when he was in England. I know better."

"She must have been resentful that you sent Sebastian away."

"Oh, she was more than resentful, she was wild! Parading her lovers in front of everyone. She guessed that if I wrote and told Sebastian, he would blame me and we'd lose him forever. She might have been right, but I'll never know because I never told him. I couldn't take that chance."

"Then you must trust him now. He'll see the light sooner or later."

"You sound like a priest. They never gave me much solace, either, always patting my hand and saying, 'tsk, tsk, my dear, don't tire yourself.' I tell you it was the mother's—and now their dream—to make King's Ransom and their plantation one. The largest in the country—maybe in this hemisphere. I can't *bear* to think of Teresa here after I'm gone!" She turned her head away from Danielle.

Were those tears escaping down the worn cheeks? Danielle resisted the impulse to make a comment or offer consolation; the old woman would be too proud to accept solace.

"Maybe they aren't as close as you imagine. Surely Sebastian can see through her if she is not—not good for him." Her words sounded childish and naive to her own ears. With a body and face like Teresa's, what man need look further?

Doña Mercedes reached for Danielle's hand, holding it with a surprising strength. "I know I've made a frightful ruin of our family. I've had to live with that since Henry died, although, bless his heart, he never offered the slightest accusation to me over the years."

Doña Mercedes looked down at their entwined hands. Danielle wondered if her grandmother was seeing her own hands again without the age spots, supple and strong like her granddaughter's.

The woman's next words came with difficulty, as if she wasn't certain she should speak. Highly unlike the dominating woman Danielle had come to know.

"There is more to it. I've tried to tell Sebastian but he laughs at me. Even that cow over in the corner knitting doesn't believe me. Why should she? She sleeps like a stone. Never hears anything."

Danielle looked over at the nurse sitting oblivious to her employer's contempt. She hoped the poor woman didn't understand English.

"That is why I doubled my efforts to find you. I'm very worried, child, very worried. My workers tell me of strangers poking about, visiting the cantina in the village, talking and asking questions about King's Ransom. It was that way before the big union fight, too."

"And Sebastian isn't concerned?"

She shook her head. "I don't think so, although he promised to look into it. There's more."

"More?"

"I've seen someone in this house at night. I think it is Teresa. I've heard voices in the night, coming from somewhere."

Goose bumps rose on Danielle's arms, and the back of her neck felt chilly, as if a presence breathed against her skin. As she held on to her grandmother's hand, she felt the pulse in the old woman's veins jump like worms beneath her fingers.

"Could it be the servants walking around at night?" That sounded logical enough. They had their own wing behind the kitchen.

"No! The servants have their own facilities, and besides, the people who work here are frightened of this place after dark. They are silly—they think Henry's ghost is walking about. How ridiculous! Even if his spirit were here, he would never harm anyone."

"Maybe his spirit is trying to warn you." Danielle meant it as a mild sarcasm, but her grandmother nodded.

"Yes, child. I thought of that, too. Henry was as obsessed about King's Ransom as I or Sebastian."

"There's another thought." Danielle hesitated only briefly before continuing. "If Sebastian and Teresa are— ah—" She wanted to say *lovers,* but somehow the word wouldn't come out in front of her grandmother. "Maybe Teresa comes up to visit Sebastian sometimes. That wouldn't be unusual, under the circumstances."

"Impossible!" Doña Mercedes sat up straight, her eyes narrowed with anger, her mouth a tight line turning her lips white. Her earlier fright was forgotten. "Sebastian wouldn't lie to me. He promised never to have her in my house while I am alive."

"Then who..."

"I don't know! That's why no one will believe me, but I saw her—Teresa—standing at the foot of my bed more than once. Staring at me. I've never feared anything in my life, but I had the feeling she'd like nothing better than to put a pillow over my face. Oh God, it's mortifying to be a helpless old woman. I never thought this day would come."

"And what did Sebastian do when you told him about all this?"

"He patronized me just as you're doing, said I must have had a dream. It was no dream. My body is weak, but my mind is perfect."

"Okay, let's say that you did see her. Why would she be here? What would she come here for if not to meet Sebastian?"

In spite of the hormonal weakness her grandmother ascribed to Sebastian, Danielle didn't think he would stoop to bring his paramour in under the matriarch's nose. It was obvious he had a lot of respect for Doña Mercedes.

"*That* is the part that alarms me. She doesn't appear when Sebastian is home, always when he is on a trip to the city. It's as if she is looking for something. She must have bribed someone for a key to the house and my room."

Danielle leaned back to take a deep breath.

"Remember I asked you not to tell Sebastian I invited you here?"

"Yes, and I don't understand. That has put me in a very awkward position."

"I'm aware of that, child. But Sebastian has a very sensitive nature he hides beneath that layer of bravado. If I could do it all over again, I would never have sent him away from us to a foreign land for schooling. He thought we abandoned him. Now that I am dying...." She pushed away Danielle's protests with a shake of her head. "Now that I am dying, I can't bear to have him think I turned away from him to call on a 'stranger'."

"A stranger?"

"Please, let me finish before I become too tired." The old woman's words implied that she never knew when it would be their last conversation, and that made Danielle very uneasy.

"I need a promise from you—more than just the one about not telling Sebastian I wrote you letters to invite you here. You can tell him that after I'm gone if I don't have time to explain it to him."

"A promise?"

Her grandmother nodded. The old woman's grip was weakening; she was growing weary of the talk and the emotion expended. "Soon I shall be buried next to Henry, near the roses. Please say you'll stay here a while—just to see if I've been a suspicious old lady for nothing. I feel as if King's Ransom is in real danger."

"But it's only a house."

"I don't just mean the building, the house—I mean the *place*. There is danger to this place. I feel it."

"Shh. Shh. If you don't calm down, the nurse will come over and make me leave. Please don't get so agitated."

Her grandmother lay back against the pillows, her wrinkled forehead wet with perspiration. "Yes, my dear, you're right. It's just that I could die in peace knowing that my flesh and blood might come to understand some of what possesses me about King's Ransom. God knows, your mother never did."

Danielle doubted she'd ever come to that, either; time wouldn't help. It was just a *place*, for heaven's sake.

The old woman managed a slight raise of her hand, willing Danielle to listen carefully. "Don't trust *anyone*, child. Keep your own counsel. I tell you, there is danger here, I feel it closing in."

Suddenly, tears rolled from out of the sunken eyelids and her grandmother turned away. Danielle beckoned for the nurse to hurry over. "I promise to stay a while, Grandmother—please don't cry, it isn't good for you."

Danielle, suddenly chilled to the bone, let herself out of the door, closing it softly behind her. That was the first time she had called her "grandmother." She hoped Doña Mercedes had heard it.

Outside, Sebastian waited. "Long conversation. Do you think it's wise to tire her?"

Danielle felt weary and drawn-out and uninterested in fencing with this man now. "I stayed as long as she wanted me to."

"Thank you for cooperating in there—about our so-called burgeoning friendship," he whispered. They walked away from the bedroom door, knowing there was nothing

rong with Doña Mercedes's hearing. "Even if you might
ave overdone it in spots."

"I assure you, it was not for your benefit," she said
oldly. "If a few simple lies help ease the mind of a dying
oman, then I don't mind."

"Oh? Am I to presume that telling lies is against your
thics?"

She stiffened. "I don't know about my ethics, that's a
tuffy word. Let's just say it goes against my principles."
Vhat a prig I sound like, she thought, but how he does rile
e until I say all the wrong things. She understood now that
e perceived her as a threat to Doña Mercedes giving him the
lantation. An opportunist pushing herself in for what she
ould get. What an absurdity, a degrading insult. All her
randmother wanted was to ease her own conscience and say
oodbye to her only relative. Anyone could see the planta-
on belonged to Sebastian, his mark was everywhere.

"What else did she say in there?" Sebastian wanted to
now.

"She's worried. She thinks King's Ransom is in some
ind of danger."

"Ah, that again." Sebastian smiled engagingly, showing
er for a flashing moment the boy he used to be. "She is
verwrought from having to stay in her bed. It has been a
ear now since her fall from Princessa. Injured her back.
he hates the confinement and has come up with all sorts of
eird imaginings."

"I thought she was an accomplished horsewoman. Why
ould she give me her horse if it nearly killed her?"

"There's absolutely nothing wrong with Princessa ex-
pt she's a spirited horse and Doña Mercedes wouldn't have
ad her any other way. Something went wrong, maybe a
ake lying in the grass, a small animal—something stared the horse, and she reared. When your grandmother fell
ff, the horse fell on top of her legs."

"Oh, my God. What a terrible thing!"

"Yes, doubly so for her, she was always so active. Paul
eFarge, her friend and attorney, wanted to bring in a

wheelchair and one of those little electric carts, but she wouldn't hear of it. Now she's too weak."

"Has she seen a doctor?"

"Of course. Raoul has a plane, and he flew a specialist in from the city. The doctor said it's her heart." He looked away and cleared his throat. "I assume that you will tire of this boring life soon," he said, looking straight into her eyes.

Danielle was on the verge of assuring him that she was no threat to his safe little haven, but she paused, considering. He jumped to all the wrong conclusions, so let him stew a while.

The next morning, while she sipped coffee on the terrace outside her room, Sebastian called up from below.

"Ah, you are awake. Doña Mercedes insisted this should be the day for your first lesson, and I had nothing going that Manuel, the overseer, couldn't do today, so..."

She set down her cup and leaned over to look at him. He was dressed in his working cords, shirt open at the throat as usual. He appeared intriguingly bold, a bit too macho for her taste.

"Lesson? Oh, you mean the horse. Thanks, but I've ridden before. I have other things to do."

He laughed, teeth white against the warm tan of his skin. "Such as? Come on, I dare you. Besides, it was at La Chaparrita's request and none of us care to oppose her wishes."

"Oh, I suppose I could," she said. "Since you insist on standing down there raising such a hullabaloo," she added under her breath. "I'll be down as soon as I change."

"Try to dress appropriately," he called up as he walked away whistling.

Why that arrogant... What did he mean by that crack? Of course she knew what to wear horseback riding. Didn't she?

When she faced him downstairs at the stables, she could barely keep the grin from spreading her lips. He looked bewildered at her delicate white blouse and plaid skirt that came long enough to touch the tops of her fine leather boots.

"Here I am, appropriately dressed and all. Of course, you hate those jeans I wear so I just assumed . . ."

She thought at first he was going to turn on his heel and walk away in a huff but instead, a smile broke through his frown of vexation and together they broke into wild laughter.

When they could get their breaths, he took her hand and pulled her toward the stable. "I want you to meet Princessa. Doña Mercedes loves this animal. I've always been a little jealous."

Once inside, Danielle's eyes quickly became accustomed to the gloom of the stable. She didn't know much about horses; she'd only ridden once in Central Park, but she didn't mention that to Sebastian. He was far too smug already.

In the back stall, a horse reared on its hind legs and let go with a tattoo of hooves against the door, almost springing it from its hinges.

Oh, no, could that possibly be Princessa?

Before she could ask, Sebastian pulled her along in that direction. "Princessa, meet Miss Beaumont."

The horse was splendid in a wild, uninhibited way that appealed to Danielle immediately. She climbed upon the two-by-fours that made up the stall until she could lean across to offer her palm.

"No!" Sebastian had looked away for a moment to talk to one of the workers, turning back just in time to see her move forward.

He grabbed her waist as if to pull her away from harm just as the horse snorted and gently touched her muzzle to Danielle's hand. Sebastian let go immediately and stood back to watch, along with the stable hands.

"She's a beauty!" Danielle had felt the hard warmth of Sebastian's hands almost crushing her waist—that was what had put her out of breath, surely. Had he felt her heart beating so rapidly against his chest? She stepped down. "I'd like to ride her now."

He looked down at her and then at the horse. The workers had drifted off and they were alone again. "You say you've ridden before. As you can see, this one is quite spirited. I don't know how you managed to charm her so quickly."

"It was mutual," Danielle said.

Outside in the sunlight, he attended to her saddle and bridle personally while a stable hand saddled up Sebastian's black stallion. "Her coat is the same color as your hair," he remarked. "She even has a freckle or two across her nose like you."

Danielle smiled. It was good to have him behaving decently, not acting surly with the anger he had been harboring since her arrival.

He gave her a lift up and as she paused, trying to decide what to do with her skirt, he laughed. "Want to go back to the house and change?"

She tilted her chin. "Nope. This will do fine." She pulled the full skirt up to give her freedom and spreading her legs, lifted one over the horse and pulled the skirt demurely around her knees again. "See?"

He shook his head, still laughing. "You are your grandmother's all right." He lifted himself gracefully into his stirrups and onto the saddle, reining the horse forward. "Two things I must insist on—go easy at first, this horse is not used to the feel of your hands. And never go out on Princessa alone. You don't know this place and if you get off into the jungle, you may never find your way home."

Feeling certain he was just trying to scare her—probably his outdated idea of how to keep a female in line—she didn't bother to argue. It was enough to trot along, enjoying the sunlight on her body, feeling the rhythm of the horse under her. She couldn't help admiring the way Sebastian sat on his horse—as if he owned the world. Her skin still felt warm from his touch.

They had ridden for at least a quarter of an hour, Sebastian remarking on how natural a rider she was, when they both stopped the horses and turned at the sudden sound of galloping hooves. Two riders emerged from the edge of the forest and Sebastian made a low curse.

"What is it?" she asked, alarmed.

"Teresa and Raoul. I don't like the way they use their horses. Running them to the ground is no way to treat animals. I'd never do that to Diablo, or any of ours."

They waited until the brother and sister rode up in a cloud of dust. Her gaze was drawn to the brother who was exceedingly handsome—too handsome for her taste.

Raoul was the first to speak, disregarding Sebastian's disapproving scowl.

"Ah, such beauty lights up the heavens!" Raoul exclaimed, doffing his wide-brimmed hat in a sweeping gesture. He turned to his sister. "Why did you not tell me the *señorita* was . . . ah, words fail me."

Danielle doubted that very much. Something about the man felt smarmy, false. Perhaps it was just that she was not accustomed to such blatant flattery. She had worked with tall, lean, exquisite models for so long, hearing the adulation heaped on them, she suddenly realized that people usually accepted her for an artist and left it at that.

What were they saying now? She tuned back in to the present, leaving thoughts of her old life behind.

Sebastian and Teresa had their heads together, talking quietly with their horses pulled up close to each other.

"My sister was remiss in describing you, else I would most certainly have been here sooner," he fairly purred.

Danielle wondered how Teresa had described her and then decided it was better not to know. It angered her somehow to see Sebastian and Teresa excluding her—them—from their company.

"When your horse is rested, want to race?" Danielle pointed across the pasture toward the grove of huge trees from which the brother and sister had just emerged. Surely Sebastian would be furious, but riding came naturally to her, he'd said so only minutes before, and Doña Mercedes had said she wanted Princessa to be her grandaughter's.

"Don't worry about my horse, *señorita*. Let's go!" With that, he gave a shout and turned to race. She followed right behind him and soon began to gain on him. To her dismay, Raoul was hitting his mount while Princessa seemed to become more and more excited, not galloping straight as Danielle directed her, but half rearing from time to time.

Suddenly Raoul stopped short just in front of her horse, and as Princessa reared, pawing the sky, Danielle soared over the animal's rump, landing with a thud on the soft turf. Before she could get her breath, Sebastian was kneeling at her side, a scowl narrowing his eyes, but still she saw concern there.

"*Por dios,* you might have been killed. Or worse, killed poor Princessa." The last he offered when he saw Danielle's eyes open. He lifted her to her feet lightly but carefully, still not certain if she was hurt. When she stood without falling, he walked over to examine the mare. The whole incident probably brought back the unhappy memories of her grandmother's accident.

"I'm sorry, Sebastian." The words sounded inadequate, but what could she say with Teresa watching and Raoul galloping up in his usual cloud of dust and mangled vegetation.

They stared at Raoul's horse, its sides bellowing out in a desperate attempt to catch a breath, foam coating its muzzle. Sebastian looked as if he wanted to say something, but was stopping himself.

Teresa's brother leaped down, grace in motion, and peered into Danielle's face, his gloved hand supporting her chin. "Are you hurt? Should you send a car for her?" He directed the last bit toward Sebastian.

He was a little late to express his concern, and why had he stopped his horse so short just in front of Princessa?

"No, she'll be fine." Sebastian picked her up with one swoop of his powerful arms, holding her closer than necessary for a moment. "The best medicine is to get back on the horse."

Danielle started to protest, feeling sore and achy all over. It would be easier to walk.

She felt the loss of his closeness when he lifted her up onto the saddle, calming the horse with a low, soft voice as he did so.

With a flurry of excited conversation between them, both laughing like naughty children, Teresa and Raoul shouted their goodbyes and galloped off toward the edge of the clearing.

When it was quiet again, Sebastian swung up on his mount and regarded her for a long moment, the expression on his ruggedly handsome face pensive, not angry as she expected.

He reached forward, lightly brushing back the flyaway hair against her cheek as a parent would do to a child.

"What happened?" he asked. "I looked up to see you both stop suddenly, and then your horse reared up."

No use causing trouble between neighbors. It had been a silly accident. She shrugged her shoulders without speaking.

"I hope you learned something from this. You might have broken your neck showing off to Raoul that way."

"I was not showing off to him!" She felt foolish, which made defensiveness rise up in her. If she cared to admit it, she had raced her horse to try to get Sebastian's attention away from Teresa, but she was grateful he didn't realize that.

She thought his expression softened around the edges just a tad. "I've done foolish things in my life—everyone has— but the important object is learning from those things."

He sounded so pompous. Didn't he ever take time out for fun? Then she chided herself for criticizing him when he was only trying to help her and save Princessa and...oh, she had botched things up royally.

It was she who had never grown up. The thought came suddenly from nowhere, striking her with unexpected ferocity. She had always thought of herself as an achiever, a go-against-odds sort of person, but was she? She had always wanted to sculpt, but stayed in fashion design because it was something she knew and it made her a comfortable living. She had fallen into a relationship with Howard—because it was there and it was comfortable.

The introspection had reached the point of discomfort. He had probably thought her frown directed at him and had wheeled his horse around, cantering toward home.

Still groggy from her fall, she followed close behind.

CHAPTER FOUR

A week later Doña Mercedes died peacefully in her sleep. During the time Danielle had had with her grandmother, they had grown to respect and care for each other, although the crusty old woman wouldn't have told her so in so many words.

Danielle felt there was much more her grandmother would have liked to discuss, but neither of them was used to sharing their feelings.

The workers became subdued and quiet; servants shuffled through the long, dim halls without the customary banter and laughter. Danielle could see they all cared deeply for the gruff, demanding little person that had been Doña Mercedes.

"Are you going to make the burial arrangements?" Danielle asked Sebastian the next night, after dinner was almost finished. She hadn't seen him since her grandmother had passed away. He had taken his meals elsewhere, probably wanting to be alone with his grief.

"No. I'll leave that to Peter. Next to Paul LeFarge, Peter was her oldest friend."

"You're going to miss her, aren't you?" Danielle wanted to touch the hard, brown hand that held the water goblet, but she was afraid of being rebuffed.

He didn't answer for a long moment and then looked at her directly, holding her gaze so that she couldn't have turned away if she'd wanted to.

"Yes. We were all we both had for a long time. You look so much like her when she was younger. Even as a boy who didn't care about such things, I knew she had a special beauty."

Danielle wondered if her grandmother had ever allowed herself to be emotionally demonstrative to the young boy he had been; to show by a kiss or a hug that she loved him. She must have, because there was a closeness between the two of them that could only have come with a mutual respect and love.

Sebastian had a lot of her mannerisms—a sudden burst of cool reserve, a hands-off-don't-come-too-close feeling. Yet from some of her own conversations with Doña Mercedes, she knew her grandmother to be fiery and passionate about many things. She wondered if Sebastian had this in common with her grandmother as well.

"There's another matter we must talk about." He sounded reluctant, as if the words came without his consent.

She waited for him to continue.

"It was Doña Mercedes's wish that you stay. At least for the reading of the will."

Danielle stared at him, this time not lowering her gaze when he stared back. "I don't think so. This will reading is private, having nothing to do with me. How many times must I tell you I didn't come here for any devious reason?"

"I'd like to believe that, Danielle. For her sake, I'd like to believe that."

"For her sake?" She suddenly needed it to be for more personal reasons but felt certain that was out of the question.

He shrugged, his wide shoulders pulling the throat of his white chambray shirt open wider, and she saw the deep tan of his chest. Suddenly a picture of him flooded her imagination. She saw him astride the big black stallion, his shirt off, his upper body tanned and muscular, his long legs tight against the horse's round sides.

Danielle looked down, playing with her napkin to stall for time until the audacious picture inside her head disappeared.

"Have I offended you in some way? Or are you bored and not paying attention?"

"Oh, for goodness sakes, must you always demand everything your way?" The accusation was uncalled for; she realized that the moment it was out. She always had the bad form to become defensive when cornered.

He laughed at her discomfort, angering her more.

"Damn me for admitting it, but you're even prettier in a tantrum. But you could trip on that luscious bottom lip, the way you're sticking it out."

She had to laugh with him then. Her mother used to tease her about pushing out her bottom lip and pouting when she was a little girl.

"I can imagine what kind of little girl you were like." He looked pensive, his expression opening up something inside her, some reserve she always kept to herself.

She fought against it, not trusting him or the feeling that was sweeping over her body, the warm flush she could feel all over as she absorbed the sea-green light from his eyes.

"I can imagine you as a boy, too. You must have been very lonely here on this big place with only older people around you."

He looked away for a moment and she felt bereft as the enveloping warmth was removed.

"It was lonely, but it was a splendid place to grow up. I had love on all sides of me, everywhere I looked. For the first time in my life I had someone to care if I woke up in the morning or not."

"But when they sent you off to school, did you resent that?"

"Of course. I carried a grudge for awhile, a chip on my shoulder, I guess you'd call it. Finally I realized what they had done for me. They wanted me to be near them too, yet they sacrificed this need for *my* benefit. It's just that I missed them and *this* so much." The words were wrung from him as he splayed his big hands across the shiny table and then picked up a fragile cup as if he were holding all of King's Ransom in his hands.

"I—I think I understand." Oh, Lordy, what had she stepped into? That he would mistake her loneliness, her desire to be near something that belonged to her people as mere greed was so overwhelming, it was as if it struck her for the first time.

The spell broken by her tentative words, he shoved back his chair and moved quickly to her side. "Ah, Danielle, why have you made me go on like a teenager? You don't care about us here in this provincial hole-in-the-wall. Mercedes told me about your career in the big city."

He was so close, standing behind her chair, she could see them both reflected in the gold-veined mirror at the other end of the room. If she leaned her head back only slightly, her hair would touch him. The idea sent a warmth creeping upward that didn't stop until it reached her face.

He bent down and touched his lips lightly to the top of her head and then he was gone.

During the next few days, there were other surprises. Danielle had assumed that her grandmother had led a sheltered, isolated existence, but her perceptions soon changed. Merchants, bankers, carriages with old ladies and older men, Land Rovers and trucks of every description, men riding horseback—people by the droves came to pay their respects. Her grandmother had supported an orphanage near the capital city, and the entire group of children with all of their teachers came in a bus that must have been held together by bailing wire and their combined prayers.

Peter made the arrangements for burial and the funeral services. The gathering stood under the overhanging trees on the clipped lawn beyond the rose garden where the heady scent of roses and honeysuckle filled the air.

Danielle looked over at Sebastian; his expression was stony, his mouth set in a grim line. She felt the need to comfort him, but she knew he wouldn't accept it from her. In the shade of the huge trees, she could see a marble marker and make out the last name, Beaumont. That must be her grandfather's grave. Bordering the serenity of the soft grassy spot, the harsh color of raw earth for the new grave made an unsightly intrusion. Beyond that, the outlines of a wrought-iron fence covered in a patina of soft green surrounded the area.

She had been introduced to the parish priest from the city; Peter had sent someone for him, not taking any chances of the local village priest being unavailable. Now the priest intoned the service and she listened with half of her attention, while watching Sebastian and the others. She recognized servants and what must be field workers mingling with the out-of-town guests without so much as by-your-leave. Very democratic. She hadn't thought it would be that way here, somehow.

It was clear they had all respected and cared for Doña Mercedes.

When the ceremony was over, she stayed behind, wanting to be alone with her thoughts. When she saw Sebastian had also remained, she started to leave, not wishing to intrude.

His lips moved as if he were telling Doña Mercedes goodbye one last time, and then he turned to Danielle.

"Are you all right?" He touched her lightly on the shoulder and then dropped his hand quickly as if regretting the impulsive gesture.

"Yes, thank you." How generous of him to think of her at a time when he was obviously hurting. "But it's you who has lost the most. She was your whole family."

"Family and a damn good friend. I'll miss her."

Danielle and Sebastian stood close together, silent for a long moment. For the first time their differences disappeared.

"Have you seen the other grave?" He spoke into the silence as if regretting their sudden closeness.

"You mean my grandfather's?"

He shook his head. "No, that one." He pointed toward the other side of the big tree.

Curious, she walked forward and knelt, gently brushing aside the wildflowers in front of the marker. There was her mother's name and birth date; the space for the last date was blank.

She leaned back, looking up at him. "They expected her to return. All these years they waited."

He nodded. "It hurt your grandmother, especially when Henry died. She figured he gave up waiting and died of a broken heart. I never thought so, privately, but then no one ever argued with Doña Mercedes."

"My mother's buried in New York. It's smoggy and noisy and there aren't many trees, but if she's in heaven, she knows about this place set aside for her."

"I imagine so," he said quietly, studying her for a long moment. "We'd best get back to the guests," he added.

Even after the funeral service, people continued to come and pay their respects. Sebastian took over as head of the household, which seemed perfecty normal under the circumstances. What irked Danielle was that Teresa stood at his side, assuming the role of hostess. Her grandmother would have had a fit.

Teresa knew everyone, of course, putting Danielle at a disadvantage. Half of the time, when Sebastian was elsewhere, Teresa didn't bother to introduce her to the visitors.

Disgusted, Danielle entered the gazebo in the rose garden and sat down to gather her thoughts before this afternoon's luncheon. It was time to leave. She felt strange staying in the same house alone with Sebastian, even though it was so big they could go for days without seeing each other if they wanted.

"Ah, here you are hiding, Señorita Beaumont. I was searching for you." Raoul made a low, courtly bow and sat down beside her. He and Teresa could have been twins, they looked so much alike. Maybe they were twins, but she didn't want to show enough interest to ask him. He didn't need any encouragement.

"I am not hiding. And you may as well call me Danielle."

"What a pity I have wasted so much time in not visiting you. My sister was sadly remiss in not telling me of your beauty." He took her hand lightly in his and though she suddenly felt the need to distance herself from him, she held still, not wanting to be rude.

She could feel Raoul's eyes raking her body and she tried not to squirm under his steady gaze.

"It seems your sister is right at home here," she said to take the spotlight away from herself. She nodded toward the couple standing at the edge of the garden talking earnestly to a little group of guests.

He accepted her statement as a compliment, ignoring the sarcasm she intended. "But of course. Teresa is efficient to her very core. I notice you also have a flair for making people comfortable. I have seen you speaking with the Rodrigues couple. They seldom venture from their plantation and never speak to strangers. Yet they chatted with you like old friends."

She looked for a hidden agenda beneath his words but found nothing but admiration. He wouldn't be half-bad if he didn't try so hard to be charming.

"They're a sweet pair, with a lot of interesting stories about my grandparents. They invited me to visit them anytime."

She almost laughed out loud as his eyebrow shot up into the dark curve of hair that lay just so on his forehead. Apparently he and his sister were not exactly welcome at the Rodrigues plantation.

Teresa had moved away and Sebastian stood alone, towering above all the guests. Any other time she would have admired his rugged good looks, but his effortless command of the situation, his take-charge attitude put her off. But then why shouldn't he have smooth edges? she thought meanly. While he'd gone to Oxford, she had attended the school of hard knocks.

She was about to excuse herself to go upstairs to freshen up, when Sebastian called out to her. Raoul bowed low and brushed a kiss across her hand that felt remarkably like a procession of ants. He left before Sebastian and the man he brought with him reached the gazebo.

"Ah, I see Raoul found you." Sebastian's voice sounded strained. It was so obvious he didn't like Teresa's brother. Why?

The man with Sebastian took hold of her hand and bowed low over it. The gesture didn't feel smarmy the way Raoul's had. She smiled in greeting.

"This is Paul LeFarge, Doña Mercedes's attorney and one of her oldest friends," Sebastian said.

"I would know you at once, child, even without an introduction. You have the look of your grandmother when I first met her. My God, could that have been forty years ago!"

"If you knew her forty years ago, you must have met her in England, before she came here. Did you know her before she met Grandfather?"

LeFarge sat near Danielle and took her hand in his. "Call me Paul. The truth of the matter is, your grandfather and grandmother came here by mistake. They were supposed to stay in what was then British Honduras, now renamed Belize. England was encouraging colonization at that time. The ship overshot its mark in a storm and landed here. But I'm a boring old man repeating himself. I'm certain your mother told you all of this before."

She shook her head. Her mother had refused to talk about her family; she would speak only of King's Ransom itself.

"Please go on, I'd like to hear it."

He exchanged a smile with Sebastian. "She's like her grandmother with her curiosity. In many other ways, I think." He sighed, continuing. "They were made very welcome in this country. I had settled here previously, practicing law—that's quite another story—and offered my assistance with Spanish and the land purchases. Ah, but your grandmother was so beautiful. A tiny woman but so confident, even at such a young age." He smiled at his recollection. "I loved her from the moment I first saw her and have never stopped. Alas, she never had the slightest interest in anyone but your grandfather."

Danielle felt the love in his words and wondered how many years it had taken him to arrive at his present tranquil acceptance.

She wanted to ask the attorney what her grandmother had said about her irrational fears for King's Ransom, but Danielle wouldn't inquire in front of Sebastian. He had already put her in her place about that subject.

She lapsed into her own thoughts as LeFarge and Sebastian reminisced for a moment or two. Then, something the attorney said made them both laugh. She looked up, liking the sound of Sebastian's laughter. Across the garden, her gaze met with Teresa's who also must have heard him.

Teresa looked exceptionally lovely today, her tall, well-proportioned figure encased in tissue-thin layers of some exotic black material. A black widow, that was what she reminded Danielle of, and she smiled at her fancy. Someday Teresa would be a big woman, Danielle tried to console herself.

Two suitcases had not allowed much in the way of clothing changes and suddenly she felt dowdy, like an intrusive country-bumpkin cousin, a distant relative who wasn't really welcome.

Just then, Danielle was saved from more unsettling thoughts by the announcement of lunch being served. Sebastian excused himself to mingle with the guests as Danielle was seated between a couple who spoke nothing but Spanish. At first she tried a few hesitant words but when they began to speak too quickly, she lost her concentration. The words flowed around her as she started to eat.

Doña Mercedes would have been proud of the feast set out for her guests. There were many varieties of fish, lobster and shrimp from the Pacific Ocean, several beef roasts, one a huge standing rib roast, crispy and crackly on the outside, pink and full of juice inside. The cook had made fillets of pork and all sorts of delicacies, the names of which Danielle could only guess at. In spite of being in the presence of all this plenitude, she pushed the food around on her place listlessly.

Sebastian shot her a searching look but she refused to meet his eyes. Something was depressing her, something more than her grandmother's death. She made an excuse as soon as it was polite to do so, retreating to her room.

She had no more than slipped out of her shoes when a knock sounded on her door.

"Come in."

Danielle was surprised to see Teresa, for once tentative and undecided, standing in the doorway. "Come in," she said again. What could Teresa want?

"I wish to talk to you." Teresa's gaze roamed the room and came to rest on the glass doors leading to the terrace overlooking the rose garden.

Danielle had the uneasy impression that Teresa had been in this room before. But when? It had been forbidden by her grandmother to allow Teresa into the house, and she didn't think Sebastian would have gone against Doña Mercedes in this.

"Please sit down." She forced a politeness she didn't feel. Her grandmother's disdain aside, why didn't Danielle like this person?

Teresa ignored her for a moment, looking out into the garden. "This is a beautiful place—ours is more masculine, more ordinary. My father and mother had no time for gardens. They started their plantation from nothing."

Now that your mother and stepfather are dead, you can change your place, Danielle wanted to say, but refrained. It was none of her concern.

"I wanted to—I needed to tell you of my feelings," Teresa said after a lengthy silence. "Sebastian and I have had an understanding since we were children. You are not staying long, are you?"

"I don't know. What has my staying to do with yours and Sebastian's understanding?"

Teresa's full lips turned down in repressed anger. She really was a beauty in an earthy, exotic way; only her constant sullen expression marred her perfection.

Teresa shrugged. "It is only that your presence here detracts from—ah—from our relationship."

"Shouldn't Sebastian be the judge of that?"

"He is a man. Men do not think with their brains sometimes."

"I'm flattered, but I have no romantic interest in—" Liar! Even as she spoke, the words sounded false, hollow. In spite of not wanting to, of fighting hard against it, she definitely had developed a physical and emotional pleasure in Sebastian's company. Would he ever feel the same toward her? She doubted it very much, he was so certain she was here to get what she could and she had no way to prove him wrong. Before Teresa could say anything to match her uplifted eyebrow, Danielle spoke.

"Regardless, for some reason, my grandmother found your—your relationship, as you call it, unacceptable. Why is that, I wonder."

Danielle felt the full flash of fury in Teresa's expression for a brief moment. She didn't back down, continuing to look steadily at Teresa. She'd fielded a lot of guff from difficult people in her lifetime.

Teresa looked away first. "Who can say? Jealousy? She never wanted Sebastian out of her sight."

"I can't believe that. She sent him to England to school."

"To get him away from me. It worked for a while—I thought I would marry someone else, but then Sebastian returned and—"

Never one to beat about the bush, Danielle interrupted. "Another thing, as long as we are speaking our minds, my grandmother thought you only wanted King's Ransom."

Teresa's expression was one of exasperation that she didn't bother to control. "My mother wanted that. She wanted it so bad, to combine the two plantations to make one of the largest in this country. I don't know why. That doesn't appeal to me."

Danielle thought Teresa was lying. "Then you would live on your own plantation if you married Sebastian?"

"Of course not! King's Ransom is the most beautiful place I have ever seen. It's no wonder Sebastian loves it beyond anything—except *her,* of course, your grandmother. I would renovate it completely, make it even more beautiful so that we could entertain friends from the city."

"You sound as if everything is settled. Why are you telling me this?"

"Because I have plans for Sebastian. He is such an excellent businessman, but it is wasted here. With my help, he could do more, much more, perhaps even become governor of this department and—"

"Department?"

"That is what you might call a county of a state in your country. We have nineteen departments in our country." She gestured impatiently with her hand, obviously annoyed by the interruption and having to explain.

"But is this what Sebastian wants?"

"Who cares? Men have no idea what they want or need or what is good for them. Women are the stronger sex—only, men do not know that. We must control our destinies through them."

"We—I don't believe that. Iron fist in a velvet glove, surely that went out a hundred years ago."

Teresa gave a shrill laugh that raised the hairs on Danielle's arms. "Perhaps in your country, but not always in Latin America. Sons come first here. Women must do what they must to survive."

Danielle motioned toward the door. "I need to rest for a while so that I can return to the guests. If our conversation is over..."

Teresa's dark eyes showed a restrained anger that she obviously kept in tight control. "Very well. I just thought we might as well talk, at least once before you leave King's Ransom."

She sauntered through the doorway without looking back.

Toward evening, when Danielle felt a little renewed, she came downstairs again. Paul LeFarge and Sebastian had been standing near the fireplace talking when LeFarge saw her and pulled the younger man along, reluctantly, she noticed, toward her. Arm in arm, himself in the middle, Paul steered them outdoors to a bench in the rose garden.

"You must tell me about your exciting life, child. I have always wanted to visit your country's greatest city."

It had been an exciting life, or she had thought. Now it seemed empty and shallow. Earning money to live well, to wear nice clothes and eat in fine restaurants—was that all there was? She squirmed, as if Sebastian read her thoughts and mocked her with that tilted eyebrow.

"Ah, you blush. You have a beau, do you not? Someone so lovely as yourself must have a beau."

She smiled at Paul's old-fashioned gallantry. "No. As a matter of fact, I do not." It was all over between her and Howard; that was part of her depression, she guessed. Not a depression because they had broken up, but that she hadn't done it sooner. He had been unfaithful, and distance from him gave her perspective to realize there had been signs she had ignored. He had seemed to think it no big thing, especially since she wouldn't live with him. But it was important to her.

"Still, I must leave soon," she said. "I have imposed on everyone's hospitality long enough."

"Nonsense, my dear. You are family, after all, are you not? Doña Mercedes's only family. Ah, except for this young man here, who is like her son," he hastened to add. "You must stay for the reading of the will."

She lifted her chin defiantly. "Yes—Sebastian informed me of that. However, I don't see what I have to do with the will. No one will miss me, I assure you."

The attorney glanced at Sebastian and then back at her. "I thought I told you Miss Beaumont *must* be present."

Sebastian shrugged wide shoulders. "I do not have control over Miss Beaumont."

Sebastian turned to her. "I wasn't aware you were planning to leave us so soon. Are you not enjoying our company here at King's Ransom?"

She wished it had been a real question instead of his brand of subtle sarcasm. For a while he had seemed gracious, but the hostility had returned since the attorney showed up and reminded him of the will. What was wrong with the man?

"It's just that now, without my grandmother here, it seems hardly appropriate..."

Sebastian smiled. "In other words, you feel compromised? Staying in this big house with me? I am honored."

"Compromised? That word went out with hoop skirts," she retorted, stung by his mockery. "I just mean that it does not seem fitting for me to stay any longer."

"In other words, you accomplished what you came for? But how can you be sure until the will has been read?"

The attorney drew in a sharp breath, and Danielle said angrily, "I don't know what you mean by that. Frankly, without my grandmother here, I do not feel welcome." That ought to hold him.

She was rewarded by his flush of discomfiture and a flicker of something in his eyes. At least she had touched some nerve there.

"My children, this is such a sad day. Leave your quarreling alone for a while. It is most inappropriate. These days, with all kinds of people living together, all manner of uncivilized carrying on, you are a delight to worry of impropriety, my dear," Paul said to Danielle, pointedly ignoring Sebastian.

She squirmed guiltily. It hadn't been impropriety she was thinking of, merely that she was uncomfortable around Sebastian and his suspicions without the protection—no, *buffer* was a better word—of her grandmother.

"I wish you would stay, a few more days at least, if it pleases you to do so, of course," Sebastian said stiffly. "I am certain, although Paul has not seen fit to confide in me, that Doña Mercedes included you in her will. Perhaps some jewelry, old books, we do not have much capital lying about in banks."

Paul cleared his throat, putting a hand on Sebastian's arm as if to stop him.

Sebastian continued, unchecked. "If by some chance she neglected to mention you, I could see that you receive a settlement or monthly stipend, whichever you prefer."

She looked at him steadily, the two of them ignoring the presence of the attorney as if they sat alone on the garden bench. "That is more than generous of you, but I neither want nor expect anything from my visit to King's Ransom. I thought I made that perfectly clear to you from the first."

Paul stood up, touching both of them on the shoulders. "This is not a matter for discussion," he reprimanded them. "Doña Mercedes would not appreciate your antagonism toward each other. As I've already said, it is especially unseemly at this time." He looked sad and Danielle was sorry for that, but why did Sebastian insist on trying her patience?

"I must check on the horses, one of them hurt his leg yesterday while performing his—ah, duties as a sire." Sebastian stood up to leave. "Doña Mercedes wanted her to have Princessa, she told us both that," he said to Paul. "Although what she thought her granddaughter would do with a horse in New York City is more than I can imagine." He regarded her for a long moment, his expression that of puzzlement and speculation.

With that he strode away, and they watched him go.

CHAPTER FIVE

The big, sprawling house seemed more than unusually empty now that the last guest except Paul LeFarge had gone home. Danielle ignored the first shocked, then amused glances from the servants as she rolled up her sleeves and pitched in to help with some of the cleaning.

"But Miss Beaumont, this is unseemly!" Peter protested.

"Nonsense. I've never been pampered with servants waiting at my every call, why should I now?" She hoped Sebastian was within earshot and suffered a little discomfort at her jibe. "Besides, these uncomplaining people have had a lot of extra work thrown on them. Even you were helping put away the china, I saw you," she accused.

He smiled, turning his back to the listening servants. "Very well, whatever you say. May I offer some suggestions of what needs doing?"

After some time passed, the workers unbent and some tried a little tentative English, at first self-conscious and shy. She felt surprised at how fast her Spanish came back to her. They laughed at her attempts sometimes, but it was good-natured and comfortable and she enjoyed it.

"My grandfather had an odd idea of how to design a home, didn't he?" she asked Peter when they stopped to rest.

"Oh my, yes. King's Ransom was quite intriguing to everyone when he first built it. People came from the capital to look. Someday I'll show you the secret rooms beneath the house, if I can locate the keys."

"Secret rooms? Keys? You're teasing!"

"No, not at all. When the Beaumonts first came here, there was a lot of political unrest in nearby countries. Your

grandfather provided a safe haven for his family and workers in the event thugs burned down the house. He never had
to use the rooms of course, and not many know of their
whereabouts."

"Of course, Sebastian does."

"I imagine so," he said dryly. "When he first came here,
the underground gate and door had no locks. Sebastian
went exploring—he disappeared while we searched for days.
Doña Mercedes became quite frantic with worry."

Danielle thought of the young Sebastian, lost underground in darkness and silence. How frightened he must
have been, a stranger in a strange place and suddenly the
world closed in on him. She imagined her worried grandparents—had they thought perhaps he ran away, into the
jungle? Did he call out as he wandered below ground? Did
he cry? Instantly she knew he had not.

Suddenly it was important for her to know more about
Sebastian. Too bad she had not spent more time with her
grandmother talking about him, it would have no doubt
pleased the old woman, too.

"Was he hysterical when they found him? I would have
been." She waited for Peter to finish his story.

"No. Matter of fact, he was a very quiet little boy for a
few weeks. Let me tell you, he never ventured underground
again, won't even check the generators. Ramon or Manuel
has to do that. Only thing I've ever known Sebastian to
fear—the dark underground."

"Well, don't bother to look for the keys on my account,
I'd expect the place to be taken over by bugs and snakes
and . . ." She shivered.

"You're quite right. Once I thought of turning it into a
wine cellar but since we have very little company, it wouldn't
be worth the bother," Peter said before disappearing into
the kitchen.

It seemed her grandfather had planned on an ordinary
enough house, building two stories like a proper estate.
Then, instead of staying tall and stately, the house ram-
bled, wandered off on fascinating tangents like an old person telling a story. It had charming nooks and corners, and

each room had its own distinctive flavor. She imagined it must have been a joy to decorate.

Sebastian entered the room as Danielle bent to put some books back on the shelves and dust them. She felt his presence first and turned to face his raised eyebrow.

"Are we short of servants?" His expression was not that of annoyance for a change, but of amusement.

"I don't suppose so. I just needed to do something. Can you understand that?"

"Perhaps. It is a very admirable trait. I wanted to tell you that after lunch Paul will have the will reading. You may want to change." He grinned at the apron that almost wrapped around her slim body twice and the head scarf one maid insisted she wear.

She made a low curtsy. "Oh, perhaps I will, perhaps I won't, Master Sebastian," she teased.

After lunch had been served, Paul called Sebastian and Danielle as well as Peter into the study. The attorney's expression was solemn as he waited for them to sit down.

When he finished reading the will aloud, he removed his glasses and looked from one stunned face to another, waiting for the response.

Sebastian was the first to move, leaping to his feet, his fury barely contained. "I'll contest this, of course!"

LeFarge shrugged. "That would be a costly, time-consuming mistake. This represents Doña Mercedes's last wishes and I'm afraid you will either abide by it or—" He broke off, then continued. "At least think about it, think about what her intensions were. We both know she was sharp as a tack to the end. You've never gone against her before, why should you now?"

"I can tell you why," Danielle exclaimed, coming out of shock and leaping to her feet as well. "This is a terrible thing to do to Sebastian. I would never have thought my grandmother capable of—"

"You didn't know her that well, child," Paul gently reminded her. "She had such a fierce love for King's Ransom, and that passion controlled every judgment she ever made. When she lost your mother and then her husband, King's Ransom was all she had except for Sebastian."

"And this is how she repays my loyalty? By preposterous demands?" His anger filled the room to bursting point.

Danielle felt as if she couldn't breathe and was glad when he turned on his heel and left the room.

When he had gone, Paul took her arm and pushed her gently back down in the chair. "Do you understand what has happened here? The terms?"

She nodded. "I suppose so. Both Sebastian and I inherit equal shares of the plantation provided neither of us sells our portion until a time period of two years has passed." Of course she remembered it word for word, it was burned into her consciousness forever.

"Yes. And even then you are only permitted to sell or transfer it to the other heir. If either of you refuses the terms, the property will be given in trust to the LaCeiba Orphanage in the capital. You will both receive a yearly stipend the rest of your lives—or for how long the plantation survives."

His voice told her he didn't hold much hope for that.

"Excuse my bluntness, but I don't want the damn place. I only came here at her request, although Sebastian won't believe that. Under the circumstances, I suppose the timing of my arrival does look suspect."

"Nonsense, child. You couldn't have known she was so ill. You wouldn't have known she would take to you, or put you in her will. Besides, there are not that many detectives in the city. I could find him, if you say she hired one. Although why she didn't confide in me, ask me to help her, I can't for the life of me say."

"You see how funny it looks. Maybe she took a detective's name from a magazine ad, who knows?" Danielle offered, knowing she couldn't involve Peter in this until he was ready to talk to Sebastian about it. Maybe her grandmother swore him to secrecy and he never would talk. She didn't want to be the one to damage the relationship between the old servant and Sebastian.

"The real point is, Sebastian thinks I'm some money-hungry schemer and—"

"But of course he doesn't think that! He is overwrought by Mercedes's death. None of us thought she would ever go—she was always the strong one, held everything together. He'll get over it. He'll have to."

"What do you mean?"

"I mean that this is going to prove very difficult, especially if you persist in leaving so soon."

"But why on earth would I want to stay now? I only came to see my grandmother."

"I know, I know, my dear. But Sebastian could lose everything, if you leave before I get this all thought out. He can't run King's Ransom with an absentee partner, it's just not possible. All the legal documents he has to sign, just to export his bananas—and the vanilla! What a paper trail that leaves behind."

"But I won't be an absentee partner! I don't want anything to do with this place once I'm gone."

Paul held up his palms in a gesture of conciliation. "Understood." He smiled. His sharp blue eyes crinkled at the corners and she was afraid tears were going to pop in them any moment.

"You are so like her—you'll never know how much you remind me of her when she came here. You even have her temper, although you obviously try to restrain yours. She never bothered, everyone loved her for that, too."

Danielle stood and walked over to the desk and touched her hands across the papers, the journal, the musty old set of books that were so inadequate for keeping track of finances. This was Sebastian's domain, she could feel him here, smell the faint odor of vanilla and good loamy earth that always lingered when he came into a room.

She turned to face the attorney. "I don't want to hurt anyone, I hate it that I've disrupted everyone's life here. But what can I do? I didn't have anything to say about what she put in that damned will of hers."

"I know that, and so will Sebastian, when he stops to think of it. He's just feeling abandoned, I suppose. She was his only family. You must remember how it was when you lost your dear mother?''

How could she forget? She had bitterness toward her mother for a long while after she died, for leaving her alone. Which only added guilt to the bereavement. Then she came to realize that the love her mother had left behind would always be with her. In time, Sebastian should be able to work that out.

She had to give him time. She now realized she needed time, too; she wasn't ready to go back yet.

After telling Paul she would stay a while, she excused herself and went outdoors for air. Sebastian stood in the garden. She caught a glimpse of Teresa's bright dress through the shrubbery as the woman left in a hurry. So, Teresa waited like a vulture for the will to be read. It must have been a bitter disappointment. Danielle's compassion for Sebastian faded away.

She turned to leave but he saw her. "Please, don't allow my presence to detract from your share of the garden." His voice was deceptively soft.

"Sebastian, I must talk to you." She walked forward, unmoved by the beauty of her surroundings for once.

He regarded her with narrowed eyes, but waited for her to speak.

"This is as much a shock to me as it is to you," she began, not knowing how to explain this to him. "I don't know what my grandmother could have been thinking of—why she would do such a thing."

"Don't you?" He towered over her and the muscles in his jawline clenched and unclenched in his effort to contain his anger. "It was expeditious of you to suddenly appear to meet a dying relative whom you've never had the courage to try to contact in all these years. She didn't know your whereabouts, but surely you knew hers. Not even a letter from you!"

She understood his furious resentment. He couldn't have been closer to her grandmother than if he were her own flesh and blood. She knew how much the plantation meant to him; it wasn't just land and a home to him, but like part of the family he never had as a child. Then there was Teresa and her ambitions.

"We should be able to work something out," she said. "We have anger on both sides. Why would I try to get in touch with a person who treated my mother in such a reprehensible manner? That my grandmother regretted it later is beside the point, since my mother never knew that."

He smoothed down a piece of sod absentmindedly with his boot. "You're right. I suppose you must see her side though. Doña Mercedes was fair but she had certain rules one did not break. She neither liked nor trusted your father, yet your mother turned her back, disobeyed and ran away. As you Americans say, 'she made her bed,' wouldn't you agree?"

She had to admire his loyalty; even with his resentment toward Doña Mercedes, he defended her.

"The point is, she did write and ask me to come here."

"Yes, well, I only have your word on that, don't I? Perhaps you might show me the letters sometime?"

So, the old conniver never did get up the courage to tell Sebastian or Paul about the letters and the detective. How uncharacteristic; she would have thought her grandmother was always in complete control. She must have loved Sebastian very much and feared losing his love or hurting him. Yet she couldn't take the chance of telling on Peter and causing a rift between the two. They needed to pull together, especially now.

"I bore the brunt of her will, many times," he went on, pacing up and down the garden. "At first, I did not want to leave this—my country—and go alone to a cold, forbidding land across the ocean to attend school. At the same time, I know it hurt her to send me away. But I went because it was her decision. Later, I understood the wisdom behind it." He walked closer and stood looking down at Danielle, his long, sensuous lips curled in derision. "This, though—I do not understand. How she could tie us together, knowing we both have plans..."

"Yes, of course we do." She should probably pack—leave tomorrow. Never mind her promise to stay on a while, the old woman was a manipulator right up until she died. Danielle didn't owe her anything, did she?

"Well, now that you've won your little victory, what are your intentions?"

Of all the arrogant, rude... Her temper began rising. She struggled for control.

"Perhaps you should return to New York. Before you leave, we can work out some agreement—on contract naturally—so that I can send you a share of the profits until the time limit has been reached."

"And then?" She was burning up, but repressed her desire to lash out at him in angry denial.

"I will buy you out, of course."

She turned away from him and sat down on a slatted bench in a corner of the garden. "You are anxious for me to go so you and Teresa can set up housekeeping without a moment to spare, I suppose." Why should that disturb her? She blamed it on her grandmother. "*She* didn't like Teresa, you surely were aware of that."

He shrugged. "I know, I never understood why. She refused to talk about it. However, Teresa has her own plantation to run, and it is none of your business at any rate."

Of course, that was true enough. Suddenly her life in New York was too much to think about. She had made her grandmother several promises, she should try to keep at least one.

"I might remain here for a bit. Grandmother wanted me to know King's Ransom, otherwise she wouldn't..."

She was unprepared for the hard hand that clenched her arm, pulling her to her feet. Angrily she stared up at the lean dark face, as eye to eye they glared at each other.

"So, you *did* scheme to get your hands on King's Ransom!"

"Don't be absurd. I told you, she sent for me."

"I don't believe that for a moment. She would have confided in me."

"But it's true! She was going to tell you, but I came without much warning and she wasn't prepared." At least that was what her grandmother had professed. Had she lied to them both? If not lied, misrepresented—was it the same? Why?

"I don't believe you. She didn't send for you at all. You had access to the old letters she mailed to your mother. You knew how to find us anytime you wanted to."

There was that "us" again. Her lips tightened in righteous indignation. If only she had brought those letters to show him. It did look bad. But he had no right to accuse her. It made her lash out in anger at him.

"You may be forgetting one important thing. *My* name has *always* been Beaumont."

The quick flicker in his eyes reflected the hurt her words caused. She was sorry the moment she uttered the ill-considered words; that was hitting below the belt.

Danielle always knew that was her main fault, never considering her actions or words, but operating on guts and emotion. It had helped her get ahead in the fashion world of a big city, but she knew it was not one of her endearing qualities.

"Oh, Sebastion, I'm sorry. I shouldn't have said that. My grandmother, Peter, Ramon, Paul LeFarge—all of them have told me over and over how you kept this plantation going in the face of nearly every adversity known to mankind." She tried to lighten up the conversation.

He didn't speak for a long moment, he just looked off into the distance toward the jungle that constantly infringed on their tenuous clearing.

Reluctantly she broke the silence. "Let's call a truce. We can work this out, I know we can. Meanwhile, I *need* to stay here. I can't go back just now. I'd like to explain but..." She raised her palms in a helpless gesture. Right from the first, her feelings told her to turn the plantation over to him. But Paul said that would contravene the terms of the will, that they would both lose it then.

It would serve him right if she kept him doubting her intentions for a few days.

She needed time to think.

CHAPTER SIX

As the days stretched out, Danielle had felt the servants' resentment toward her; they were offended that a foreigner should usurp Sebastian's rights. But since Sebastian seemed to accept the situation as gracefully as he could, she could see them warming to her again as before Doña Mercedes's passing.

She knew they called her the young Chaparrita behind her back. The small one.

Although Sebastian had declared a truce, his noncommittal politeness had become a strain. She almost wished for a return of his old arrogant, openly skeptical self. At least she didn't have to see him often; he stayed out of sight for the most part, sometimes not eating in the dining room. She suspected he might be at Teresa's.

Danielle had been in the stables all morning, grooming Princessa and talking to the workers. Instead of doing what she wanted to do, which was to take a ride, she'd stopped to consider her tenuous cease-fire with Sebastian and decided not to antagonize him by riding the horse alone. Although his anger might be preferred to his ignoring her.

"Ah, *buenos días, mi querida.*" Raoul said, startling her as he swooped off his horse and threw the reins to a waiting stableboy.

"*Buenos días,* Raoul. Lovely day." He had never looked more dapper and handsome, standing partly inside, partly out, the backlight shining on his black hair. She wondered if he'd struck the pose deliberately and then scolded herself for being uncharitable. He didn't fill up the doorway the way Sebastian did.

"I see you are brushing your horse." He barely refrained from wrinkling his fine patrician nose.

"Yes. I enjoy being with her." For a while, Princessa was the only one, human or otherwise who had tolerated her presence.

"I feared you had left without saying goodbye."

"Didn't Sebastian tell you I was staying a while?"

He shook his head, carefully she suspected, so that the stray curve of dark hair fell just so.

"I haven't seen Sebastian since the funeral."

"But I thought..." Her throat constricted with happiness that she tried to fight away. "I thought he visited your plantation often."

Raoul laughed. It wasn't a generous laugh like Sebastian's, merely a token that didn't call for joining in. "You have a lot to learn about us. Sebastian never comes to our place. He and my stepfather had words—he suspected the old man of instigating the unions down here. How droll. Even Teresa has tried to explain that was foolish. They killed him, you know, the unions."

"Yes, I heard about the fire. I'm sorry—that must have been a jolt to lose your father so soon after your mother."

"*Step*father," he corrected. "And their deaths were years apart." He looked down at his immaculate boots to see if he'd stepped in something. There had been no flicker of emotion on his face when he spoke of his parents. Perhaps because his mother had died so long ago, she reasoned. Yet his nonchalance was hard to understand; Danielle still felt a sadness and loss when she thought of her mother.

"Did you go off to school like Sebastian?" Raoul was obviously educated, yet no one had ever mentioned how.

"Of course. We all had to. However, we were not as fortunate as Sebastian—we could not go to Europe to study." He shrugged. "No matter, school was wasted on Teresa, and I certainly did not enjoy it."

What a pompous ass. Very little pleased him, it seemed.

"Would you care to walk?" she asked politely. If he insisted on visiting, they might as well move along.

It was difficult not to continually compare Raoul with Sebastian. They were so different. It was like comparing a sleek, elegant panther to Sebastian's tigerish, rugged virility. Danielle smiled at her thoughts and Raoul noticed.

"Ah, my lovely, your smile lights up your face. You should not be so serious as you are most of the time." He moved closer, holding her elbow as they walked up the grassy slope toward the house. "Does anyone ever call you Danni? That sounds more like you. Short and to the point." He laughed at his joke, which of course she had heard before.

"Yes, I've had friends call me that." Howard had occasionally.

How odd. Suddenly there seemed to be more than the normal number of workers about. Yardmen and gardeners she had never seen before worked here and there, busy at their tasks.

"I see our host provided for his absence," Raoul remarked dryly. "Apparently he doesn't trust me or you or either of us."

She paused and looked at the yardman not twenty feet away, trimming a hedge that looked perfect.

"That's absurd. In the first place, he doesn't care what I do and in the second place, that would be a terrible invasion of privacy, wouldn't it?"

"Do not leap to criticize so harshly, my dear. Ours is a different land with different customs. Perhaps he is old-fashioned enough to place value on your, ah...your unmarried state."

"What about Teresa?" she countered. "I don't see her riding around with a *dueña* in tow."

Raoul laughed. "Teresa is a law unto her own, I'm afraid. Although I am the older, I would never presume to instruct her." He held her elbow as they turned back toward the stable, away from the grassy slope toward the house.

"It is so crowded here, perhaps you would join me in a ride?"

She thought a moment. Something didn't feel right about Raoul, and she didn't especially care to be alone with him, away from the safety of the plantation. But if Sebastian was keeping a watch over them, it was out of line and he had no right. Even without that idea, it would be nice to get out into the open and the horse did need exercise.

"That might be nice, I haven't ridden her since the last time we were out." They were inside the stable now, her eyes getting accustomed to the gloom.

"Fine. I'll call the boy to saddle her."

She didn't like the way he gave orders, curt and sharp. There was no need for that; workers at King's Ransom seemed to enjoy what they did and were treated like family.

He moved closer to her in the darkness, ignoring the presence of the workers until he was distracted by the stableboy's hesitation.

"I am sorry, *señorita*," the young boy directed his speech at her alone. "*El Jefe,* he say no one rides Princessa without his permission."

Danielle had had about enough of Sebastian's high-handedness. First he has me watched and embarrasses me in front of a guest and now he forbids me to ride *my* horse, she thought, her anger growing. She threw her head back in frustration. Her eyes must have flashed their indignation at the poor stableboy, who backed away in alarm.

Pity for the boy brought her show of anger and frustration to a halt. It wasn't his fault.

"I am going to ride Princessa. I will be certain to tell *El Jefe* that you tried most valiantly to stop me."

"That won't be necessary." Sebastian's figure blocked the light sifting through the doorway.

"What are you doing here?" His voice was cold, his eyes fastened on Raoul.

A warm feeling had flooded her body when she heard his voice, causing her to become infuriated with herself as well as with him.

"We were about to go for a ride, what does it look like?" She retrieved her outrage, wrapping it around herself like a cloak to stave off the chill of his gaze.

"I cannot forbid it, but there are reasons that it would be in your best interest not to, ah...not to ride Princessa without me." His voice was soft, not so his expression.

Raoul glanced from Sebastian to Danielle and raised his palms in a gesture of surrender that didn't coincide with the look of implacable fury banked in his eyes and directed toward Sebastian. "Good day, *señorita*," he said politely and pushed by Sebastian still standing in the doorway. They could hear his galloping horse as it receded into the distance.

"You are the most arrogant, selfish, tyrannical...oh! You have no right to interfere, to spy on me and forbid me as if I were a child!" She drew up to her full height to look him square in the eye.

To her surprise, the cold had left his expression and his eyes showed, if not an apology, something akin to regret.

"Come, let us sit in the garden and talk. That is, if you can shut your pretty little mouth long enough."

He turned to go up the path, expecting her to follow. Once she walked too fast, and he too slow, and they bumped; she pulled away as if the touch had burned her. He turned to look at her but said nothing. In the garden, they chose a secluded bench and sat, not speaking for a while, listening to the fountains and the birds. She was determined not to make it easy on him and waited for him to begin.

Raking his hands through his thick hair, so unlike the meticulous way Raoul made the gesture with a quick flick of his head, Sebastian cleared his throat uneasily.

"I have no right to tell you what to do, but in this case, you are a guest of this house and I owe you protection. It is our way," he added.

"Protection? From what?" she blurted out. "If you mean from Raoul, please give me some credit. I'm not naive." She hoped to see one of his rare smiles but he remained serious.

"It's a touchy situation, Danielle. I am not at liberty to speak openly, because of my friendship with Teresa. Suffice it to say, Raoul is probably different from any man you will ever meet. He is completely amoral and unpredictable. Those are his good points."

She rolled her eyes and touched her palms to her cheeks in an exaggerated gesture of dismay. "Sir, you are too kind, however, I am not a sheltered innocent from the provinces. I assure you, I can take care of myself. Have for years." So what if she had never been with a man, he needn't know that. It wasn't for lack of Howard's trying.

He reached to take her arm and she looked down at the strong brown hand against the paleness of her skin. Fuzzy little waves of desire began to creep over her body and she willed them away. How could she be so drawn to him one moment and so annoyed the next. No one had ever affected her like that before.

He stood up to move away and then in one long stride he returned, pulling her up, holding her close, his lips moving over hers, demanding yet tender. Beneath hands that pushed at his chest, she could feel his heart thudding. It was as if he sensed her feelings even as she denied them. Suddenly she ceased the struggle and clung to him, knees weak as she leaned against his lean, hard body.

He stopped kissing her and held her away just far enough to look down at her. She knew her face was flushed and he couldn't help but see the betraying throbbing pulse in her throat.

"Is this how you take care of yourself then?" Before she could come up with a scathing reply, he was gone.

Damn him! So that was what he thought of her. He was afraid she would disgrace his precious King's Ransom by causing a scandal with Raoul.

She sank back onto the bench and a feeling of isolation took her breath away. New York had been a very lonely place, that was one reason she and Howard had fallen into the habit of dating each other. He prided himself on being a sophisticated urbanite, had even referred to himself as a Renaissance man, but he showed himself to be a bore and worse, a liar and a lech. She wouldn't go to bed with him and he apparently satisfied himself everywhere he could. Yet he had wanted to hold on to her.

She became attracted to him in the first place because he admired her work and offered unrestrained praise for her accomplishments. In retrospect, she knew that probably was only because he wanted something more from her.

Danielle spent the remainder of the day in her room, packing her bags and staring out the window. She would leave—to hell with Sebastian and his paperwork. If he had financial problems after she left, it was no concern of hers, was it? She thought of strangers taking over King's Ransom and flinched, but continued to pack.

Toward evening, she wandered into the study and sat curled up in her favorite chair, not reading but trying not to think, either. Hearing Sebastian's familiar step outside the door, she prayed he would go past, but he didn't.

They stared at each other, the silence between them growing.

"Will you dine with me tonight?" he asked politely.

After what had happened, was he joking? She made a little face. "Is this an official command?"

His eyebrows knitted together for a second and then he tilted his head and smiled.

"Ah, I apologize for my rudeness this morning, but it was an important point and I wanted you to remember it."

You flatter yourself, she wanted to say, but she was learning to think before speaking. Soon she would be gone, so why make this last time any more unpleasant than necessary.

"Yes, I suppose I could dine with you," she said formally.

He bowed low and left her alone.

When she came down the stairs that night, she wore her last "new" dress, a pale beige sheath that set off the gold in her eyes. She knew it flattered her small, high bosom and clung to her tiny waist, flowing subtly around her hips with just the merest suggestion of clinging.

She was rewarded by the look in Sebastian's eyes and the low whistle of admiration escaping his lips.

"So, the little pigeon has turned into a magnificent pheasant," he said, taking her arm and leading the way to the dining room.

She didn't know why she'd dressed for dinner, except that he seemed to expect it and he always changed clothes. Maybe it had been her grandmother who insisted on the formality; it would have been like Doña Mercedes. Now that she thought of it, her mother used to make a big deal out of eating the evening meal together. She hadn't thought of that in years. Eating alone in her apartment, dressed any way she pleased, Danielle hadn't realized she missed that, until now.

During the meal, they seemed comfortable enough. Until she began to ask questions about the plantation and the workers. He acted if she were prying into his business.

He answered in monosyllables, and she was about to give up when he laid down his knife and fork and looked at her.

"For a woman, you can ask some damned intelligent questions," he admitted grudgingly.

"What does being a woman have to do with it? You've been to Oxford, you aren't a forest dweller. Maybe you didn't know we vote now?" She said the words lightly, not wanting a full-blown argument, yet wanting to say her piece.

He grinned. "*Touché.* That did sound chauvinistic, didn't it? I didn't mean it that way, but even Teresa who was born and raised on her plantation doesn't show that much interest."

She smiled back at him. Until his next words hit her like stones.

"So, Raoul came to visit you again. That, my dear, is unwise." Suddenly the smooth-as-silk vanilla dessert she had been eating tasted like chalk in her mouth. She should have known this new, enlightened mood of his was too good to last.

She tilted her chin in the air and glared at him. "I know what you said about him, and your responsibilities are discharged, so don't worry about it."

In spite of his seriousness, he had to laugh. "What a combination—an Irish father, a half-French mother. I don't know which one gave you the worst or the best of the deal."

"Don't change the subject."

"You might just get in over your head," he said briefly.

"I don't believe that, but in any case, why should that bother you?"

He shrugged, as if he didn't want to pursue the subject but felt he must. "Raoul's a...he's manipulative, unprincipled, used to having his own way. Both his mother and Teresa and everyone else with a skirt have spoiled him unmercifully."

"Is this a tinge of envy I hear?" She didn't think so, but the conversation was becoming uncomfortable.

"I've seen some of his handiwork. He doesn't take kindly to teasing or rejection."

"Come on, lighten up. You're overreacting, as usual. I probably will never get around to teasing or rejecting him, so why are we having this ridiculous conversation?"

He leaned forward, taking her cheeks between his big hands. "Because I am trying to protect you."

They stared into each other's eyes for a long moment before Peter came in to break the spell.

Both of them retired early and she was left to wonder what Sebastian was really trying to say. She sat for a long time, with just her thoughts to keep her company. Why *did* she stay here? It didn't come as a surprise to admit that for the first time in her life she felt at home. If her grandmother was watching from somewhere up in the heavens, she was making that dry little chuckling sound that served as laughter.

Danielle didn't want to go back. Had she placed herself in the awkward position of not being able to go back and yet not being allowed to move ahead? Her imagination failed as she tried to think of how it would be to live at King's Ransom forever.

And yet that was exactly what her heart told her to do.

CHAPTER SEVEN

The servants had begun to accept Danielle as Sebastian's equal as long as her requests did not countermand any of his. This she was very careful not to do, not wanting to divide their loyalties or challenge his authority. He *was* King's Ransom, without him it wouldn't function. Even with what little she knew about it, she could see the truth in that.

This morning Danielle heard a ruckus in the kitchen, and her curiosity prompted her to investigate—cautiously. Lupe, the heavy-set mestizo cook was very tempermental, even Sebastian treaded lightly in her territory. So far she seemed to be waiting, to see if Danielle would order any radical changes in the status quo of the household. They all knew by now that Danielle owned half of King's Ransom.

As she pushed open the heavy door to the kitchen, she saw a frail-looking girl cringing in abject terror as Lupe railed at her, shaking her frying pan in her direction.

"What's the matter, Lupe? Anything I can do to help?"

The cook whirled around, black eyes flashing. Then she sighed, her large bosom rising and falling in a grand manner. "It's this . . . this chit of a girl. She drives me *loco!* She spills or breaks everything she touches. She trips over a speck on the floor." Lupe stared downward a moment, as if daring a speck to appear on her spotless floor.

The girl had been holding in her tears and any moment she would let go, which would only anger the cook more.

"Do you need her in the kitchen? Are you short of help?" Danielle had a crazy idea.

Both Sebastian and Peter had been pestering her to choose a personal maid during her stay and she had resisted so far with much vehemence. She would feel foolish with some girl trailing her about; as it was, she had little or nothing to do with her time.

"*Por Dios,* no! I am doing her mother and her brother, Manuel, a great favor. Concheta needs to learn a trade so that she won't become a *puta* like her older sister. But I give up." She lifted hands the size of small hams. "I can do nothing more for her."

"I'll take her—if that's all right with you. Sebastian has been after me to choose a maid. She would be perfect." The only problem was, what would the girl do when Danielle decided to go back to New York? Well, perhaps by then she would at least know how to be a maid.

"Ah! *Perfecto!* She will no doubt zip your backbone to your dress or bring ice cubes for your bathwater." She shrugged. "I don't care what you do with her, just get her out of here if you wish dinner tonight."

Outside the kitchen, the girl took Danielle's hand with shy hesitation. "Oh, *señorita,* I have not enough words to thank you."

Danielle patted the small hand on hers. "Never mind. Just go home and get your things. I'm sure there is room in the servants' quarters, if you wish to stay here." She felt overwhelmed by the look of stunned surprise that immediately turned to joy in those wide black eyes. If her home life was so awful, the poor little one shouldn't be there, Danielle thought.

That evening at dinner, she broached the subject with Sebastian.

"I'm delighted," he said. "They are a good family, just very poor. Their father used to work on the plantation. Gossip has it he got into an argument at the village cantina and someone killed him. That was years ago. They lived by their wits, I suppose, until the oldest boy began working. He's my overseer now. Good man."

"But that's cruel! We... ah, someone could have helped them in the beginning, since he did work here." She'd heard of the village that comprised the workers and their families from all the nearby plantations who did not live on the grounds.

"Perhaps you operate that way in the States; however, we do not. Who could take care of all the unfortunates? We would be broke in a second."

She didn't agree, expecially in light of how her grandparents had taken him in as a homeless waif, but she restrained her comeback. It would bear looking into—if she stayed that long. She had heard enough about Sebastian to know he wasn't callous about his workers. There were many stories of how he helped this man or that family. It was just the custom here, she supposed, not to become too involved.

"Anyway, you don't have to clear it with me. I wanted you to have a maid while you are here with us. It is unseemly not to have one."

"I didn't want to interfere with your operations."

"Have you forgotten you own half?" He correctly interpreted her sarcasm.

She flushed, started to speak, but he interrupted.

"I have also noticed that the burden of household management has mysteriously disappeared from my shoulders. I am no longer called upon to settle every little servant dispute or chastise the housekeeper when she begins to let things go so that Peter is upset. Am I to thank you for that? Peter used to be good at managing affairs in the house, but he is too old now."

She looked away from him, and he touched her chin, turning her to face him as he waited to hear the answer.

"I've nothing to do, I feel so useless. You were never around for the servants to ask anything of, so. . ."

"Lord, woman, don't apologize. You're turning out to be a little bundle of surprises. I shall miss you when you leave."

So, he still couldn't wait for her to go. Several times she had packed and unpacked her suitcases, always changing her mind at the last moment. One day she would not, she vowed.

"How are Teresa and Raoul?" she asked sweetly. Not that she cared about them, but it was odd not having Teresa around. For a while after the funeral, she visited every day, causing a lot of gossip and consternation among the workers. Odd the way they seemed to fear her, yet she was never more than coolly civil to any of them.

"All right, I suppose. I haven't seen either of them in days, I've been too busy. I would have thought Raoul might have paid you another call before this."

"You didn't exactly make him welcome the last time," she reminded him.

The sardonically raised eyebrow was her only answer.

Undaunted, she pursued. "I'm surprised that you haven't had her here for dinner yet." Surprised and delighted.

This brought a shamefaced grin. "I have asked, but when I told her you would be dining with us, she declined. Why is it you two don't like each other? You haven't had time to get acquainted."

He had been very polite, very gallant to her since the funeral, most likely because he knew she would eventually leave. What if she decided not to? Danielle looked around the room that she had once thought cold and forbidding. The silver gleamed, the white tablecloth set off the dark polished mahogany of the old table.

She stared at their images in the wall mirror at the end of the room. The soft light from the candles on the table played across her pale skin, imparting an ethereal yet seductive look that was not lost on him—she could see it reflected in his eyes when she turned to face him. He wore a white chambray shirt, collar open even for dinner, which she found refreshing. She'd had enough of men with little suits, vests and ties all cut out of cookie cutters.

His sun-warmed skin, the dark shank of hair that fell across his forehead, his rare, stunning smile, the inner peace and strength that she knew was there—how had she come to love the sight of him?

"What's the matter? You look so *triste*, so sad." He lifted her chin and looked deep into her eyes.

Had he finally realized she was not a gold-digger, down here to inveigle an inheritance out of a relative she hadn't even known?

"I'll miss . . . I'll miss King's Ransom."

"Yes. Everyone will miss you, too."

How formal he sounded, so guarded. He didn't care. Of course he didn't care; he'd welcome her leaving so he could get on with his life. She thought of her grandmother and wondered what in the world the old woman had on her mind to tie them together by joint ownership of the plantation. If it was just to prolong Teresa's taking over, it couldn't work. Sooner or later, Sebastian and Teresa would marry and then Danielle would have to leave.

The next morning, as she dressed for breakfast, the maid bustled around the room as if she had something important to do. Poor girl, what would her life be like when she no longer had work? Could she persuade Sebastian to hire her for something else? She knew women worked in the vanilla grove. Even though she had vowed not to interfere in the running of King's Ransom, surely that wouldn't hurt.

"You like working, don't you, Concheta?" She sat on a wicker love seat and patted it for the maid to sit beside her.

Hesitatingly, with a charming shyness, Concheta sat down.

"Oh yes, *señorita*. My mama sent my brother to the city to school. He came back, taught me English, but I think I'll never have use for what I learned."

Danielle had heard the sad story of when her father died, how the family became instantly poor and her brothers had to stop school to work on the plantation.

"Soon I will leave. Have you heard that?" The plantation was like a small village, everyone knew events before they happened, her grandmother had been fond of saying.

The maid nodded, head lowered. Her single braid was as thick as Danielle's wrist. "*Sí.* None of us likes to think of that day."

"Well, it's not as if you won't have someone else to work for. Señorita Teresa—"

Concheta turned and grabbed hold of Danielle's hand, her eyes round and fearful. "Ah, that one! It will be a sad day for us and for Don Sebastian when *she* comes to King's Ransom. It is whispered that she and her brother beat their servants and keep them on the plantation without allowing them the freedom to see their families in the village.''

''That's just idle chitchat,'' Danielle reprimanded gently.

The maid lowered her narrow shoulders in defeat. ''It started after the fire.''

''What started after the fire?''

''Workers whispered how it is that the brother and sister were unable to save their stepfather. Of course he was old and feeble and in a wheelchair.''

Danielle stood up, turning to face Concheta. ''Is that the gossip? Oh, I hope Sebastian never finds out. What a terrible thing to say. Haven't the Contreras lost enough?''

Concheta's eyes were no longer frightened, she was so certain of what she repeated. ''I have a friend who works there. She says that—that since the fire, those two hate all the workers. It was the union from the city that set the fire, but they blame us.''

Danielle looked out of the window, her eyes feasting on the beauty, trying to reconcile it with the ugly words that this wisp of a girl was saying. ''Let me get this straight. The union set the fire, yet you all believe the son and daughter killed their stepfather? That's crazy!''

''Wait, *señorita,* I did not say they *killed* him. I—we say, why did they not get him out before it was too late? My friend saw the fire and it started slowly, from the top room.''

Danielle didn't want to get mixed up in local politics—she would be gone soon. Yet she wondered if she owed it to Sebastian to repeat some of this gossip. She wouldn't have to say where it came from. But Sebastian was one of them, he would know. Must know. What a dreadful rumor, it almost made her sympathetic toward Teresa.

Later, Concheta came to her in tears. Her brother, Manuel, was being fired because he failed to report one of his men drinking on the job.

''That doesn't sound like such an awful offense, I'll talk to Sebastian if you like.''

That night after dinner, she broached the subject.

"It's not merely a matter of discipline," Sebastian said. "Manuel is a good foreman, but he is young, too easygoing with the men, and they play on that."

"Maybe so. What could be so important about someone taking a nip on the job, anyway?" She knew Sebastian was exacting with his workers but she never thought of him as ironhanded.

"You don't give up, do you? You're like a dog with a bone once you get hold of an idea. Your grandmother was like that, too." Sebastian regarded her with a mock smile.

She didn't like that, but let it pass for a moment, waiting.

"Well, since you and I are enforced partners, for a while, anyway, it's only fair that I explain it to you, I suppose. Manuel's work is with the vanilla plants. The workers in the grove are ninety percent women and children, and the men run huge mowers to keep down the grass between the trees and backhoes to keep the drainage ditches open." He looked somber, obviously not used to explaining. "Two children have been killed and one crippled over the years by men operating the machinery while they are drinking. It clouds their judgment, but they don't think so."

"Oh, that's terrible!"

He nodded. "Children run all over the place, some helping their mothers, others playing in the rows. Not all of the mothers have older ones to watch the children at home so they must take even the babies to work."

"It must take every bit of the men's concentration to run the machinery."

"Of course. As I said, Manuel is young, a good boy and partially educated. But as I've already said, he is too easygoing. I gave him the job because I thought he could handle it but..."

Her heart went out to him as he rubbed his forehead with his thumb and fingers. Her hands itched to smooth it for him. Sometimes Sebastian came in from the fields looking so completely exhausted. Yet she didn't reach out to him, knowing he still had doubts about her motives for being here.

"Well, I suppose that's that," she conceded. "Concheta and her family will probably have to move to the city when I leave and her job is finished.

His dark eyebrows drew into a frown as he watched her. She could feel his eyes, the color of soft fern, boring into her, but she didn't want to look at him. Couldn't look at him.

"Does this mean so much to you then?"

She nodded, not liking to ask favors of him. "I haven't known the girl long, but it seems we owe the family..." The "we" slipped out before she thought—she wondered if that was what made him angry or if it was the subject under discussion.

"We don't owe them anything!" He pounded the table with a fist so that the dishes rattled. She grabbed for her water goblet, just saving it from tipping. "The union tried to divide us, *patrón* against *peón*. It didn't work. We treat our workers better than the union would have us do. However, we do not hold ourselves responsible for all disasters a worker might incur in his lifetime."

That sounded reasonable and she felt certain it was the old line handed down from generations of landowners, but times were different now. A landowner had certain responsibilities that went beyond the laborer's work time. She tried to explain her feelings.

"My mother worked in sweatshops in New York. I didn't have to, because finally she brought work home and we did it together. But she told me all about it. Since then I've worked in the garment industry and I'd like to think I didn't come away without gaining some insight."

He studied her, really listening to her for the first time. It was a heady experience and she made herself talk normally, even though she wanted to rush on with what she was saying before he turned away in impatience.

"The point I'm trying to make is, you must trust your workers, let them know you trust their judgment. If they make a mistake, give them another chance."

"Trust them? Well, I do, up to a certain point. But showing it would make them cocky."

"It might for some, those you probably don't want anyway. The others would feel more a part of King's Ransom, be better workers for your confidence in them."

"Nonsense! That smells like socialism. Our workers are well paid, they get time off when they need it and their hours are not long. That is all that is coming to them."

The silence stretched between them like spun glass, fragile and brittle, ready to snap if either of them spoke. She finally broke it.

"It's true this is not my home and I have no right to interfere in the workings here. Will you give Manuel another chance . . . ?"

He tilted his head back and the high-ceilinged room rang with his delighted laughter. "Ah, Danielle, you are priceless. One moment you are so demure, asking a favor, and the next moment you are determined to right the world. What a pity your grandmother did not know you better. But then, that might have taken two lifetimes."

She smiled in spite of her irritation at his laughter. He was a mess of contradictions, nothing simple about him.

"I think it's time I left—returned to New York. The landlady is taking care of my apartment, but I still have certain unfinished business there."

"Howard? I've heard of him."

So, her grandmother had confided in Sebastian after all. How much had she told him?

"What have you heard?"

Sebastian shrugged his shoulders as if the subject was of no consequence. "I hear he is a very *nice* person."

At her frown, he broke into laughter again, which she soon joined.

Thankfully, Sebastian excused himself before speaking about Howard anymore.

That night Danielle lay in her bed, watching the moon hovering through the sheer curtains in front of her windows. The love she felt for King's Ransom overflowed into the love she was beginning to feel for Sebastian until she couldn't tell where one left off and the other began.

She spoke the words out loud, so that they caught on her whispered breath as she said them. "I am falling in love with Sebastian Beaumont."

Danielle conjured up his dear face and thought of how it would be to tell him. She could never do that. He might frown and turn away or worse, laugh at her. She knew he still mistrusted her motives for coming here. There was Teresa to contend with. Sebastian claimed they were only friends, but her grandmother had not trusted either Contreras.

There were so many things they didn't see eye to eye on. She understood his values concerning the workers and their problems, but it wasn't right. Someday he must change his views. She hoped to be here to help him do that.

No, she couldn't tell him of her feelings, but neither could she give up the guilty pleasure they gave her as she hugged the thoughts of Sebastian to her and fell asleep.

The next morning, Sebastian took the Land Rover, leaving word that he would be gone for two or three days. Her grandmother had once said that he had business to attend to frequently in the city. Danielle could have asked the servants where he went, but pride kept her silent.

The big house felt empty without the clack of his boots across the terrazzo and his rare laughter echoing through the hallways. Instead of relaxing as she supposed they would, the house workers became subdued, quiet in his absence. It was clear that, though he was strict and at times a hard boss, they all loved him.

What a pair he and Teresa would make, both of them so temperamental. The thought was somehow painful and she pushed it away. One thing at a time. She must tell Concheta the good news about her brother.

Later that night, she awoke to a feeling of alarm. She lay still, opening her eyes slowly. The only light came from the pale moon shining through the organdy sheers pulled across the terrace doorway. Was that a shadow beyond the curtains? She struggled to push away the sheet tangled with her legs. Something had awoken her from a sound sleep, some-

thing like a shuffling noise in the hallway, like someone trying to walk with stealth and not succeeding. Was that when
she was still asleep, in a light dream? Or was it real?

The moment she stepped onto the floor, it squeaked beneath her feet. "Damn!" she muttered. Without bothering
to pull on her robe, she hurried to open the glass door to the
terrace. Empty, of course, what had she expected?

Danielle stood close to the edge to peer over. The lawn
and garden, bathed in moonlight, never looked more beautiful and serene.

She went back into her room and sat down on the side of
her bed, wide-awake now. It could have been a night bird,
maybe an owl, but she *had* seen something move on the terrace.

Or was it just her overwrought imagination combined
with the subconscious memory of her grandmother's ap-
prehensions?

Danielle lay back on her pillow, but sleep eluded her the
rest of the night.

CHAPTER EIGHT

The next morning, as soon as she grabbed a bite of toast and a cup of coffee, she began to wander through the house. Occasionally the servants stopped in their work to look at her curiously, but then went about their tasks.

On the wing that housed her own bedroom, there were four doors beside hers. Each opened freely, exposing uninhabited rooms, furnishings draped in white sheets to protect them from dust.

Stepping out on the balcony, she took a deep breath, and headed toward Sebastian's wing of the house. From listening to the servants' talk, she knew it housed his chambers as well as a study and connected library.

Feeling like an intruder, she skirted around the balcony as quietly as she could, looking down on the working servants. The first door opened into Sebastian's room. She stepped inside and closed the door behind her, leaning against it. The faint odor of vanilla lingered, probably coming from his clothing draped across a chair. The room was very masculine as she knew it would be, but neat and orderly.

That was his doing, Concheta said he didn't like the maids poking about, so they only did his room when he asked them to.

Her gaze shifted to the bed and a tremor ran through her body, leaving her weak and breathless. For a brief second she imagined his form lying stretched out, his eyes regarding her in that serious way he had of giving his full attention.

She couldn't help it. Walking closer, against her will, she leaned against the wooden frame, willing herself to back away.

What would it be like to lie there, wrapped in his arms, even for a night?

Shaking herself out of her reverie, she turned and backed out of the room, closing the door behind her.

That left two more doors, both opening to show sparse furnishings, dust motes sifting up from the air of the opened doors.

Only one wing left, her grandmother's, but she hesitated to go there. According to Concheta, the maids superstitiously refused to venture inside her rooms since her death. Later, when her spirit had gone to its final rest, they would accept it as just another suite.

She walked out to the balcony again. So much for an investigation. Why was she investigating, anyway? Just because an owl flew onto her terrace during the night?

If she was going to carry this silliness further, she might well look for the keys to the underground rooms and carry on from there. Instead, she decided to try her grandmother's room.

She turned the knob on Doña Mercedes's door, expecting to push it open as she had the others. It was locked. She went to each of the three rooms in the wing; each was locked.

How strange. Why would that be? Was Sebastian protecting her possessions? That was crazy, he must know the servants wouldn't go near the rooms now. Besides, from what she had seen when she'd visited the old woman, her rooms contained nothing of value and the workers were trusted implicitly. Doña Mercedes had showed Danielle her jewelry, a few fine old pieces, but nothing to get excited about.

Maybe when Sebastian returned, she would just ask him why the doors were locked, even if it was an admission to snooping around the house in his absence.

Just as she was about to turn and go back downstairs, a shaft of light from a dormer window caught her eyes, drawing her gaze upward. Coming closer, she saw a square cut out of the ceiling and a rope dangling just out of reach.

She pulled up a chair outside one of the rooms and stood on it, reaching for all she was worth to grab the cord.

There! She had it. Jumping off the chair, she pulled on the cord, and rickety-looking steps descended almost on top of her. It had to be the attic, although she had never seen one before. Her whole life had been spent in apartments in the city, apartments that seldom varied and held no secrets.

Should she go up? Why not? The servants were within shouting distance if she needed anyone, although that idea was silly. Shakily, she pulled herself up the swaying stairs and pushing up the light board overhead, she shoved her shoulders through the opening.

The room smelled dusty and musty. Crawling forward on her hands and knees, dust motes sifted down past the un-shuttered windows. She stood up under the low, unfinished ceiling, thinking Sebastian would have a rough time of it here; he would have to bend double.

Before she moved, she looked down at the patina of soft brown silt on the floor. There! Tracks! It was hard to make out how large the person was who'd made what appeared to be boot tracks. She followed them, noting that they stopped at every trunk and dresser in the place. Several drawers were pulled out and hanging, some trunks were open, lids like giant mouths waiting to devour.

Staying off the footprints and noticing the ones she left beside them, she looked curiously at the ancient furniture stored here. Back in New York, every piece would bring a fabulous price. Here, they were just excess baggage, left to deteriorate. If nothing else, the villagers could use some of this stuff. Concheta had told her that her family had used a large cardboard box as a dining table when she was a child.

There were many dark corners to the attic, but this didn't bother Danielle; she would have *felt* another person's pres-ence in the room. Brushing away a few cobwebs, she knelt by a large carved chest. Locked. Strange. It appeared that the lock had been jimmied, the metal was scratched, some of the paint missing around the edge of the wood.

She stood up and brushed her hands on her jeans. Peer-ing into the hanging dresser drawers gave her no idea of what someone had been looking for. This would be just above her grandmother's rooms; maybe that was what Doña Mercedes had heard at night.

So perhaps her grandmother hadn't imagined everything after all. But that didn't explain why Sebastian hadn't checked into it for her. If he had, he would most assuredly have seen these footprints; they didn't look so new. And if he had seen them, why hadn't he told Doña Mercedes about them?

So many questions. She could hardly wait for Sebastian to come back again so she could ask him.

Danielle never had a chance to mention what she'd found in the attic. She was reading in the study the day Sebastian returned, bringing Paul LeFarge, the attorney, with him. The older man kissed her lightly on the cheek, glad to see her. Sebastian, who looked broody, refused to meet her eyes.

"Did you have breakfast?" she asked them politely.

"No. Would you join us?" LeFarge asked, taking her arm.

Sebastian's gaze was stony, as if he knew something she did not.

After an uncomfortable hour or so at the dining table, waiting for them to finish eating, Danielle was anxious when they all moved back into the study.

For a long moment, both men regarded her in silence and she felt a stab of impatience. Even the usually exuberant attorney seemed subdued.

"Danielle—" Paul LeFarge cleared his throat, as if making up his mind he must speak "—what I have to propose to you is highly unconventional, but you must not judge us by the rules of your society."

She waited, not interrupting.

Sebastian hunched his wide shoulders and stared down at his boots.

"You must be aware that Mercedes's will has caused a certain amount of upheaval in our patterned lives," Paul began, ignoring Sebastian's rude snort. "And you, my dear, must be anxious to return to New York?"

She felt a flush work up to the roots of her hair. She hadn't thought of New York in days. "Of course. I have my career—and yes, I should be thinking of leaving."

Couldn't Sebastian tell her to get lost himself without having to call in the attorney to do it for him?

"The fact that King's Ransom is now registered in two names, each heir owning equal shares, makes it impossible for Sebastian to conduct business without legal problems cropping up most unexpectedly."

At her questioning look, he continued. "For example, Sebastian wanted to sell some vanilla plants to another grower several plantations away, but they are very valuable plants. For that transaction his signature was necessary on the sales agreement—and now of course, yours. To write a check requires two signatures. To ship merchandise out of the country requires his signature—and yours. So you see, it has become troublesome—vexatious."

What a pity, she thought without remorse. "What does he want from me?"

"Oh, it is not Sebastian who thought of all these inconveniences—and more—it was I. It came to me that he would be virtually powerless to act with dispatch if he needed your signature while you were in New York. Sometimes the market fluctuates and—"

She held up a hand. "I get your point. And I ask again, what do you want me to do? Sign a book of checks in advance? I can do that, no problem. Sign blank papers, whatever it takes. Wouldn't a power of attorney work? I'll sign that."

"My, my, the lady is certainly in haste to leave us, wouldn't you say, Paul?" Sebastian spoke for the first time; his rich voice sent shivers up her spine.

Didn't he recognize sarcasm when he heard it? To tell the truth, she wasn't in a hurry to leave at all. There was nothing back home for her, while here—a different story altogether. The thought of not seeing Sebastian every day made the inside of her mouth dry and she swallowed hard, trying to regain her composure. There were so many things about him, about his daily routine that she didn't know and felt compelled to know. Where did he spend his days? Did he work alongside his men when he didn't have to? She knew he must, to have that incredible tan and muscular build. She couldn't leave now, even if she wanted to.

And she didn't want to.

Even though she had been convinced her grandmother's worries were just the result of an overactive imagination, she knew better now. Then there was that unfinished business with the workers nagging at the back of her mind. She wanted to see where they lived, how they lived, but that would take time and subtlety. And then, there was Sebastian.

"I can't think of what she had in mind, tying my hands like this," Sebastian said.

She meaning Doña Mercedes. "You both knew her as well as anyone—why *did* she do it? She had to know that Sebastian would be nearly powerless, especially when I returned to New York."

No one answered Danielle for a minute; the *tick tocking* of the large grandfather clock in the corner was the only sound in the room.

Paul absentmindedly wiped his half-framed glasses on his immaculate white shirt sleeve. "She was an excellent businesswoman, far ahead of her time. She knew exactly what would happen—but as to why she did it…" He threw up his hands in a gesture of perplexity.

What did they want from her? She tried to hold her impatience in check.

Paul cleared his throat. "I'm afraid a power of attorney would not suffice, but it was clever to think of it, my dear. Sebastian frequently buys, sells or trades parcels of land, plus Doña Mercedes held the deeds to property in other areas of this country. Then there are mortgages and contracts to be considered. No, there are many places a power of attorney would just not be acceptable."

"Then what can we do? Sell King's Ransom? She wants to leave." Sebastian's voice had lost its ringing timbre, sounding weary now.

Paul sucked in his breath at the idea and shook his head. "Lord, no! Mercedes could cause an earthquake by rolling over in her grave, if you'll pardon the indelicacy. You could try giving Danielle a power of attorney if you like, but it's a calculated gamble. If it is ever contested, there is a chance the plantation and all Doña Mercedes's holdings could revert to the orphanage."

The three sat quietly for a while, listening to the clock. Judging from Sebastian's stormy look when he and Paul had come into the house, the attorney had told him something crucial had to be done, but not what. That was coming now, she felt it.

"However, all is not lost. I've given considerable thought to my next proposal, and as far as I'm able to ascertain, it is the only feasible way out for both of you. I warn you, it is very unorthodox, but it is the most expeditious solution." He hesitated only briefly to continue.

"It is my considered opinion that you should marry. Each other," he added unnecessarily. He stopped talking to give them time to assimilate the bomb he'd tossed into the room.

"Marry!" they both erupted at once and the attorney moved back, plainly not expecting such an outburst.

"Impossible!" Sebastian said abruptly.

"My sentiments exactly," she retorted.

Paul didn't say anything for a moment, letting them blow off steam.

When they stopped talking, Sebastian stood over Danielle's chair, looking down at her. "You *do* want to leave, don't you?"

She stared up at him, drowning in the color of an angry sea. Was he asking or telling her? Was it her crazy imagination or had she heard a hint of uncertainty—of vulnerability in his challenge?

How could she admit she didn't want to leave? Or tell about her promise to stay a while longer? She didn't want to have to tell him, he still didn't believe her about the letters and neither of them had believed her grandmother about her concerns.

When she did not answer, Sebastian swung around and began to pace the room, speaking as if to himself. "I've tried not to judge, to point a finger, but it's unjust! I thought I was like a son to her, the only family she had. They even gave me their name. Then this one turns up out of the wild blue sky. It's not the—the cost in economics, it's the destruction of a lifetime of admiration and trust and respect."

As he swerved to face them, her heart went out to him even as the words pelted her like stones. "In the end, she discarded me for someone she didn't even know, because this person was *family*. Can't you see the irony here? I thought *I* was family!"

Sebastian slumped down in a chair, as if drained of emotion. The room sucked up the silence as neither she nor Paul knew how to respond.

Finally Paul spoke, the fragile quiet shattered like fine crystal. "I can see the turmoil this has caused both of you. Can you believe an old man when I say I knew this woman, Doña Mercedes, a long time? Knew her and loved her since the first day I saw her as a new bride, just arriving here. Would you trust me enough to believe it when I say that she did indeed think of you as her son and never meant to bring you a second of pain? Not a second's worth!" He held up a hand in warning, to stop Sebastian's response.

"She had a profound love for you, son. If you search inside yourself, you will have to acknowledge it. But she also had a guilt, a guilt that stretched across most of the years of her life, tainting it. When she found her granddaughter, she saw a way to expunge her guilt before she died, or at least mitigate it somewhat. Surely you cannot blame her for that."

Sebastian, calmer, shook his head. "No, I can't blame her. We had long talks over the years and I know what a terrible burden of remorse she carried. She regretted turning away her daughter, never knowing what happened to her, and she blamed herself for her husband's death. She loved them both so much. I am not begrudging Danielle her share. I just wish she had received a lump sum—wouldn't that have done as well?"

Danielle bristled at the way he spoke of her, as if she weren't present, and the implication that all she was interested in was her share of the property.

Paul understood and shook his head as if to deny the bitter words. "Ah, you know better, Sebastian. This plantation is a valuable asset, but has a cash-flow problem, I don't have to remind you of that."

"Granted. Then she could have provided a stipend, a yearly sum to be paid when we sell the vanilla beans after harvest."

"That wouldn't work, either; you need every cent to pour into next year's expansion. You must modernize your equipment if you intend to compete with the developing Mexican market."

Danielle swallowed past the lump in her throat. "Here's the whole solution. I'll just give Sebastian my half. I don't feel as if it belongs to me, anyway. I never asked for anything from my grandmother nor did I want anything but her recognition."

She felt warmed by the stunned look in Sebastian's eyes. That ought to hold him and his suspicions for a time. She was telling the truth. Although she wanted to stay here a while longer more than anything, she had no designs on King's Ransom.

"Ah, a noble gesture, my dear." Paul said, patting her hand. "However, Doña Mercedes must have thought you would say that. Neither of you may transfer title for a period of two years and then only between you. In other words, she wanted this plantation to keep the Beaumont name, in the memory of her husband, I expect. Otherwise it will revert to the orphanage, who in turn would no doubt sell it. Since Mercedes provided most generously for them with other holdings, I see no reason that they need King's Ransom. Anyway, they would realize very little from the proceeds of this plantation, it would be a dreadful waste. Only the politicians, the probate court, judges and various lawyers would profit from the sale."

"How—how long would we have to be married?" she asked.

Paul leaned back, sighing as if he had won a battle.

"Not for long. It is necessary to maintain the charade long enough to establish credibility. We cannot permit a question of legality."

"What could my grandmother have been thinking of? This isn't fair to either Sebastian or me," she protested.

Paul looked at the two, his expression not the serious one that seemed appropriate as a small smile tugged at the corner of his mouth.

For a moment, she disliked the dapper little man; he was enjoying the drama of the situation at their expense.

"Of course you would have to stay at King's Ransom long enough to prove a marriage took place. Even after the marriage is dissolved in court, I'm sure you would be welcome to stay on. Can you manage it, my dear?"

Danielle stirred restlessly in her chair. She immediately realized why her grandmother had done this—to keep Sebastian from marrying Teresa.

It came to her so suddenly that she felt weak in her knees and was glad she sat instead of stood. She didn't want Sebastian to marry Teresa, either. And yet he'd made it perfectly clear the idea of marrying her, even in a sham wedding, was intolerable.

"Actually, the marriage need only last long enough to establish its legality, that it was not done to defraud or circumvent the intent of the will. Then I can go to court, file your dissolution-of-marriage papers and either of you will be able to transfer title to the other. In fact, that might be unnecessary. Women are not accorded such rights as in your country, Danielle. The property would automatically revert to your husband. *Ex*-husband."

Stung by the grin on Sebastian's face, she retorted, "Suppose I decide to keep my half and buy *you* out?"

Sebastian looked disconcerted briefly and then recovered. "I wasn't aware that you had enough money to buy me out."

It was her turn to look uncomfortable. "Forget it. I was just wondering what you would say to a—well, a partnership."

The sides of his lips twitched in amusement and he raised a black eyebrow questioningly. "At the risk of being rude, what have you to offer a partnership? I've run this place single-handedly since Henry died, almost ten years now. Anyway, the question is academic, isn't it? You don't have the funds to buy me out and even if you did, you couldn't for two years."

"Then do you have the money to buy my interest?" She had been willing to give up her share without a qualm but when he assumed that she should do just that, she balked.

"No, of course I do not. Paul just told you that. Doña Mercedes and I had a gentleman's agreement when it came to money. She knew how I felt about King's Ransom. She knew I only took out enough for my expenses. Any profit we made, we plowed back into the plantation."

"My children, I am certian you do not intend to waste so much time quarreling. There are far more important issues involved here. If you pack up and leave, Danielle, both of you will lose King's Ransom. Could a marriage of convenience for a short period of time be so repugnant to you both to chance that?" His voice was no longer patient, she could hear the sharp edges. "When it is over, you keep King's Ransom, Sebastian, and we can arrange somehow to give Danielle her share in a cash settlement and perhaps a percentage of the yearly profits. We'll work it out any way you want."

"So then we will have a partnership." Sebastian bowed his head to the inevitable. When he lifted his chin, he looked directly at Danielle, his smile so endearing she wanted to cry.

Didn't he see that she wanted him to have King's Ransom? That she didn't want to strap him for a lump sum settlement or anything so dreary. She had made her own way in the world until now, did very well for herself, in fact. She had modest savings and was used to independence. She didn't want to take money she hadn't earned from this place.

"Come on then. Let's give it a try. Look on it as an adventure—it certainly won't be dull."

A heavy weight lifted from her shoulders and she returned Sebastian's smile. "Agreed. But won't Teresa take this pretty hard?"

He shrugged, hands in pockets, looking around the room as if seeing it for the first time.

She thought he might be wondering how it would be to never see this room again, for strangers to live here.

"She'll just have to work it out." He held up a hand to stave off Paul's beginning protest. "I know, I can't very well tell her the truth. You understand, Teresa and my—our future together was an assumption on her part and everyone else's, including her parents', when they were alive. Except for Doña Mercedes, of course."

A small excitement stirred within her bosom at his words. She turned her head in time to catch Paul's look, like that of a cat who had just finished off a saucer of warm milk. It was almost as if her grandmother had reached from beyond her final resting place and joined forces with her old friend—to promote a hidden agenda.

"How soon should we begin our little soap opera, then?"

She didn't like the sound of Sebastian's sarcasm but Paul seemed content to ignore it.

"Maybe it should begin soon. Several weeks from now, perhaps?"

"Oh, I don't know, won't that look insensitive, with my grandmother barely laid to rest?" She felt uncertain, now that the reality of a marriage was upon her. She hadn't realized how much she wanted fulfillment of her dream of an old-fashioned romance and courtship, even if it didn't seem to go with the informality of contemporary relationships.

Her mother and father's wild love affair—clouding judgments and breaking all the rules, wasn't what she wanted from life. That was why she hadn't given in to Howard's demands that they live together first, before they committed to anything more.

Commitment—the mutual rejection of anything or anyone obstructing a conviction that this one person was the most important being in life. Would this marriage preempt her right to this dream?

Sebastian, as if he sensed some of her concerns, took her hand in his and bending in a sweeping bow, kissed her palm lightly. His lithe body seemed to relax for the first time since they'd entered the study and his expression was gentle as he regarded her from behind thick, black lashes.

"Is that all that is bothering you, what people will say, *querida?*"

She loved the way the English equivalent of "my dear" issued from those sensuous lips.

"He is right," Paul interjected. "The provinces are a law unto themselves and do not stand so much on ceremony, as we must in the city. I hear the village does not even have a priest during the summer months—he must move on to another area that has need of one."

"That's true," Sebastian chimed in. "Long ago, before we had a priest, couples were formally married in groups, sometimes on their second or third anniversary, whenever a priest passed through."

Danielle figured he was teasing and suddenly felt lighthearted and happy. "That wouldn't do for us, would it? We must have everything legal and proper." Was she asking for his assurance that he felt more than the obligation? Maybe, but it wasn't forthcoming.

"You're right," Paul said. "The disclosure of Doña Mercedes's will has no doubt spread beyond the confines of these walls—of this plantation—to gradually find its way into the city. There the vultures hover, waiting for us to make a mistake so that they can rip this place apart with their talons."

"I can't believe that grandmother is manipulating us all, even now."

Sebastian laughed, a short burst that showed no mirth. "I can. Part of it was our own fault. Remember when we thought it could do no harm to let her believe we—ah, we enjoyed each other's company? We shouldn't have lied to her. We should have told her we can barely be civil to each other.''

Danielle could see that the mistrust, the differences of opinion were still there, just under the surface, but cropping up less frequently now. He was stubborn and too single-minded at times. She knew herself to be impatient and too emotionally driven. They would just have to learn to live with each other's faults, at least for a while until she satisfied herself that nothing sinister was going on here.

It was a promise made to her grandmother that she intended to keep.

CHAPTER NINE

The news of the upcoming wedding threw the entire household into a frenzy of preparation. Danielle's first thoughts were of guilty shame as everyone seemed genuinely pleased, relieved that Teresa would not be mistress of King's Ransom.

Lupe and some of the older, less shy servants even spoke to her about their joy in the event. She listened with a lump in her throat, smiling gently at them. Peter had a new, bright look in his eyes, as he walked his domain with a jaunty step, supervising everything at once.

What would they all think of her—and worse, of Sebastian—when they split up, as must happen finally? Teresa would come here to exchange places with her, unless of course she was violently angry over this occasion, as well she might be.

"What will you wear, *señorita?*" Concheta had been speaking to her and the maid's voice finally sifted through her worried thoughts.

Danielle shrugged. "I don't know. Perhaps my green dress or the navy. To tell the truth, I didn't bring many dress clothes, my grandmother said in her letters that it was a ranch. Well, you call it a plantation. Same thing, I suppose." Not to mention that she had only intended to stay a few weeks.

"Oh, no! *Señorita,* you cannot do such a...a..." Her smattering of English disappeared in a flurry of excited Spanish.

"Wait! I can't understand a word!" Danielle took hold of the maid's shoulders and shook her gently, laughing as she did so. "Perhaps you could help me with my Spanish."

Concheta nodded happily, then paused. "You can't wear an ordinary dress. We would be the gossip of the countryside. Don Sebastian would never be able to hold up his head again. You must have a grand wedding as befits King's Ransom. One that Doña Mercedes would take pride in. Cook is already planning it."

Oh Lordy, what was she getting into? She had thought a quiet visit paid to the local priest would be all that was necessary. This was getting out of hand. She wanted her wedding to be fine and grand, yes, but she also wanted it to be *real*.

"Concheta, stop carrying on so. A fancy wedding is unnecessary. In the States we do not always have large weddings. Besides, this might not be my only one," she added sadly.

"Oh!" The maid crossed herself. "Never make jokes about such a thing. We do not take marriage lightly. I must talk with the housekeeper and the cook—they have been here the longest and will take offense if I do not ask for their advice about your dress. Do I have your permission to speak to them?"

Danielle sighed, amused by Concheta's earnest little face, so full of concern. "Whatever you wish." She thought of New York and felt sad that there was no one who would care about her nuptials, real or not. She had a few girl friends who went with her to ballets or shopping, but mostly she was a loner. She and her mother had not needed anyone else for so long, especially those last years when her mother was so ill and never left the apartment.

Later in the day, when she went into the kitchen to visit Lupe and the others, they jumped her about the dress.

"You must find where Doña Mercedes put away her own wedding dress," Peter advised. "It should fit perfectly."

"Oh yes, *señorita!* This is what you must do." Lupe stopped the movement of the long-handled spoon she had been using to stir a huge pot of stew. The aroma sifted up into the air and Danielle sniffed appreciatively. The cook and some of the cleaners smiled.

"But I haven't the barest idea of where to look. Can't you look through her closets, Concheta?"

The girl crossed herself hastily. "Oh, no, we cannot go into her rooms until her soul finds peace."

"Well, I'm not afraid of ghosts. Tell me where to look. Anyway, her room is locked. All the rooms on that wing are locked. Do you have the keys, Peter?"

"Ah, no, I don't. Sebastian keeps certain keys that have no duplicates. I would imagine he has those."

"Fine. Then if you insist on the dress, I'll ask Sebastian for the key and look for it. But it seems a lot to do—" She started to say "over nothing," but changed her mind. That wouldn't sound appropriate.

Sebastian, too, seemed to find the hustle-bustle amusing. He had been very attentive the past few days, as if he had begun to immerse himself in the deception.

Somehow that made her feel sad, knowing it was all a sham. Danielle spent a lot of time in the kitchen, talking to Lupe. Once she understood the blustery, excitable woman, they got on fine. According to Concheta, Lupe had turned up at the plantation as a teenager, without a family, sure even then of where she wanted to be and what she wanted to do. Over the years, she and Doña Mercedes had had many heated arguments and Sebastian had always interceded, calming them both. Lupe thought Sebastian was next to God.

"Once we had a terrible drought." Lupe's face puckered with her desire to communicate in a language not her own. "Doña Mercedes was prepared to move into the city, give up King's Ransom. She hated to see the cattle and the horses suffer, and of course the people suffered, too, with no work."

"What happened?" She waited as patiently as she could while Lupe struggled to form her words.

"Don Sebastian refused. He held this place together with a tiny crew of men and women, all of us worked for room and food and not much at that. Finally, it was over and the rains came. Doña Mercedes should have kissed her rosary every day of her life and no doubt did, in thanksgiving for this orphan boy.''

Saint Sebastian! It was admirable how much the servants and workers doted on him, but it was also a little tiresome. He had faults. She sighed. What was she letting herself into? If she and Sebastian had not conspired to make her grandmother think they were getting along just to please her, this wouldn't be happening. If they had shown the old woman the truth, that they didn't care for each other and never would, Doña Mercedes, being a realist, would have done the right thing and not hurt Sebastian like this. She could have at least talked it over with them.

During the ensuing days, it was hard for Danielle to maintain a matter-of-fact attitude about the wedding. Sebastian sometimes came into the room and touched her cheek gently while the servants watched. He looked at her the way she had always dreamed a lover might look at her. Did Paul LeFarge urge him to make it appear so real?

Usually he was up before dawn, into the fields, but this morning she heard his boots coming up the slight incline of the garden toward her. She tried to stop the crazy fluttering in her middle. He must have forgotten something.

''Ah. I thought I'd probably find you in the rose garden. It's your favorite place, isn't it?'' He bent over, kissing the top of her hair. The wicker chair looked flimsy when he sat on it, his long legs stretched out in front of him.

''Want some coffee?'' She looked away from his tawny grace, but the picture of his wide shoulders encased in a light blue shirt, the smooth tan of his upper chest, that hard body tapering down to a narrow waist and those long legs, was imprinted on her memory anyway.

He nodded, watching her pour from the silver coffeepot into the paper-thin cup.

''Uh—I was wondering—are you maybe carrying this a bit too far?'' She darted a glance around to see if any servants worked nearby.

''What do you mean?'' he countered. ''Are we not supposed to reflect a happy couple?''

It was beginning to bother her, she could taste the bitterness in the back of her tongue when he touched her now, knowing it was a sham. But she had agreed to the bargain.

"You are not exactly cooperating, my fiancée." He sipped his coffee, looking at her over the rim of the cup.

"What do you mean?"

"In this country, the servants are a part of a household, like family. They seem to know everything—sometimes, I think, before the *patrón*. Therefore, when we dine together and you do not touch my hand in greeting, when I offer a kiss and you turn your cheek, don't you suppose they notice?"

"Why—I guess so. But how far are we supposed to carry this charade?"

"Paul made it very clear that no one must guess of the arrangement, or the politicians in charge of the orphanage would contest the will. The governing board comprises very influential, powerful men and could bend laws to suit themselves."

"Okay, I understand that. But my question is, how far do we have to take it?"

He straightened, shoving his feet back under the chair to lean closer to her. He reached across the table to take her hand. "Is it not intriguing, this playacting? Do you wish so much to go back to your other life?"

She hedged for time to answer. "I wouldn't be doing it at all if it weren't for my grandmother. She wanted so much to keep King's Ransom for a Beaumont."

He dropped her hand and leaned back, studying her face for a long moment. When he spoke, his words were clipped, his voice cool. "You keep forgetting, I have the Beaumont name also. But then I didn't come by it through blood, did I? You are holding back something. Are you perhaps coveting King's Ransom for yourself?"

Although his words touched a nerve, she sympathized with him. She was the outsider, the one who had come into his settled life and undid everything he had worked so hard for. He had earned the right to King's Ransom. But why did he have to be so thickheaded about it? She'd already told him she would give it up if that would help. Of course it didn't; her grandmother had seen to that.

She couldn't let him know that she had been holding off because of her feelings. She wanted her marriage to be real. Get a grip, she scolded herself. You're acting like a schoolgirl. Your fiancé doesn't even like you.

"Are you afraid of me, perhaps?" Moving swiftly for a man his size, he leaped to his feet and lifted her out of her chair. He pulled her close, his voice sounding soft as velvet with her ear against his chest.

She struggled to pull away so he couldn't feel the tripping of her heart. "Should I be?"

He rested his chin on the top of her head for a long moment. She couldn't bear to move.

Finally he sighed. "No, of course you would not be frightened of me, what am I thinking of? You are a bright, sophisticated woman with a career and a nice man waiting for you—a cosmopolitan woman."

What confidence had her grandmother betrayed to this man? She had told the old woman about Howard, but little else about him, thank goodness. It wouldn't do to have her failure in that department thrown in her face by this overbearing man standing in front of her.

"This is twice I heard about my private life. What else did my grandmother tell you?"

He dropped her arms and moved back to his chair. She felt suddenly bereft without his warm touch.

"The question is, what did she tell *you?* Whisperings of people walking through her rooms at night? Noises down the hall?"

"Well—maybe. I poked around the vacant wings once. It looked very unused and unvisited to me."

He frowned. "For the time being, I would consider it a huge favor if you didn't poke around, as you call it, where you have no business. Some of the railing on the balcony needs repair—you might fall."

"Well, I'm sorry if I infringed on your territory, but Lupe and the others have begged me to find my grandmother's old wedding dress. Unless you know where she put it, I'd like to look for it.''

"It's likely in the attic, in one of the trunks."

Something kept her from admitting she had snooped so far. "Okay, that sounds reasonable. But what if they are locked? What do I do then?"

"I suppose I could help you find it. It's no use asking the servants, they are so superstitious. Henry had his heart attack up there, did you know that?"

"No, of course I didn't. How did that happen?"

"It was so long ago, but none of us can forget it. For some reason, he went up there alone, rummaging around, looking for God-knows-what. Anyway, the whole household searched for him the next day and two maids found him sitting in an old chair. He died with quiet dignity, just as he'd lived.''

"Is that why they stay in their own quarters at night? I've never seen any of them about. How long will they fear a dead person?"

He shrugged. "It's been many years, nothing's changed. You can't really blame them, their world is so narrow, they have no experience to compare with, so they assume what they feel is correct."

"I don't want to put you out, I know you're busy. If you could trust me with the keys, I'll look for my grandmother's dress and never return to the attic again,'' she said, striving to lighten the conversation.

He took it seriously. "Thank you for the courtesy." He loosened one key from the key ring he always wore with his working clothes, attached to a belt loop.

"You didn't answer before. What did my grandmother say about our conversations?" she asked.

"Nothing else. We hardly discussed you. Too many important things about the daily work routine to bother with idle gossip."

Idle gossip. More important things. Who did he think he was? Besides, she sensed he was not telling all the truth. Her lips narrowed in anger. It was plain she had to guard against showing her feelings. He would only seek to take temporary advantage of her and then drop her when it was time to pick up Teresa again.

She had no place here.

"By the way—a marriage of convenience does not grant you conjugal rights. I want to be sure you are aware of that."

He tilted his head back and roared with laughter.

When he wiped the tears from his eyes, his look turned serious. "But of course, we have a business deal, do we not? When this is over, we each go our own way, you give me what is mine—full title to King's Ransom and receive a sum and part of the yearly profits for the rest of your life. It is very simple, really."

Perhaps to him, but she wasn't so sure.

Hours later, when the house closed down for the usual lazy afternoon rest, she took a flashlight and climbed upstairs to the attic again. Kneeling in front of the big trunk and fitting the key into the lock, her heart leaped into her throat when it opened. As she riffled through the contents, she felt disappointment at finding only clothing and a few old books. She pulled out half of the clothes until she felt the lace beneath her fingers. Cautiously, she removed everything and held up the beautiful wedding dress that had been her grandmother's.

Holding it against her body, she pirouetted in front of a mirror so old that it was like seeing one's image reflected in a rippling brook. Oh, it was lovely, lovely! She hugged the garment to her and felt something push into her hip bone.

Just then she heard a noise, it wasn't much, just a soft scraping sound. Mice? Probably, but she wasn't afraid of mice. In New York she had stepped over giant rats in garment district warehouses.

Draping the dress across her arm, she ran her hand lightly over the front of the garment, feeling something hard in a pocket. When she tried to see what it was, she felt the pocket sewn closed. How odd.

She closed the cover of the trunk and locked it again. Another oddity—why would this particular trunk be locked when none of the others were? Carefully she folded the long dress over her arm, and kneeling, she backed into the opening of the attic and stepped off, her foot feeling for the first rung of the—

The flashlight clattered to the floor below as she lashed her legs out frantically, trying to reach stairs that weren't there. Her arms grew tired and heavy as she struggled to pull herself up. For a moment she thought she was losing the battle and wondered how best to land with the least damage. Giving one last urgent push up on her arms, she fell up over the side of the square opening, lying on the dusty attic floor, gasping for breath.

There the steps lay, below on the floor of the hall, crumpled like useless bits of wood and chain links. *Where she should have been, lying beside it.* She yelled down, but doubted if anyone could hear her. The servants were probably all in their quarters now, reading or sleeping or whatever they did to relax.

How did the stairs come apart? They seemed to be secure, if wobbly, when she'd climbed them. That would have been a long and nasty fall. She could have broken her legs if not her neck.

As soon as her breath trickled back into her body, she leaned over the opening, looking at the start of the chain where it fastened into the wood at the top. Hard to see anything without the flashlight, but she felt the ends of the chain link, open on both sides. Tomorrow she would return to check it out, if she could get someone to fix the stairs.

Still shaky, Danielle searched for a cloth to wrap around the wedding dress. She remembered looking into a quaint iron staircase that wound around the back of the house, ending on one side of the roof that appeared to be an unused little balcony. If she could get down, she could reach the stairs.

She panicked when the dormer window proved stuck. What if no one ever looked up here for her? She ridiculed her fears out loud, trying not to look in the direction of the big chair covered with a dust cloth, the chair where Henry died. Hearing her own voice gave a little comfort, even while her heart fluttered high in her throat.

She might have to wait until the servants came in to work again, hours from now. Even then, would they hear her scream?

Sebastian sometimes didn't show up for dinner; often he came in very late. Concheta only worked in the mornings, since there wasn't that much for her to do. Besides, she and her brother lived away from the house, in the workers' compound.

In the faint light from the windows, she rummaged around and found an old rusty screwdriver. With her greatest surge of strength, she pried at the dried paint on the sill and she felt the window give, then open.

Gulping in great breaths of fresh air, she sat on the ledge, her feet touching the iron stairway. Funny that the stairway led past the attic. Apparently her grandfather had planned another room up here. But, why?—there were so many rooms unused. Could it be that her grandparents had started out hoping for a large family? This house would have been perfect for a half-dozen children running around, laughing and playing.

But her woolgathering wasn't getting her out of this predicament, and she jolted rudely back to the present.

Taking a deep breath, she climbed out onto the narrow stairs, clutching the wedding dress in the crook of one arm. It was a narrow, winding way, but the steps were strong and sturdy and finally, with a sigh of relief, she touched her feet on the ground behind the house.

She sat on the lawn for a moment, pondering the situation. So many things didn't make sense.

Tomorrow would be soon enough to try to find some answers, but for now, she was happy to be alive and in one piece.

CHAPTER TEN

The next day, Sebastian, along with half the household servants, walked up to inspect the damage done to the attic stairs.

"Are you certain you are not hurt? I can drive you into the city to see a doctor." He sounded genuinely distressed about her near accident, which comforted her.

Until they reached the wing where the stair had fallen.

"I—I don't understand. The stairs were in a pile on the floor. Look—there's the flashlight." She ran to pick it up. As she bent, Danielle searched for telltale marks on the wood where the stairs might have hit. Nothing. Only the glass was cracked on the flashlight and it didn't work.

Sebastian turned to the crew who followed them. "Did anyone come up here yesterday or this morning early?"

They all shook their heads. Concheta crossed herself, for emphasis.

Danielle felt her breath pull out of her body as if something sucked it out, leaving her hollow. Sebastian pulled on the looped rope and the steps came down, good as before.

Shooting her a sardonic look, he climbed the stairs and heaved himself up through the opening. She followed close behind, noting that the servants all stayed back, their brown eyes wide with fear.

He helped her through and then flashed his light at the top. "I don't see any problem here."

"Neither do I, now. But these two links were opened. Look, they're marked up, both of them."

He bent his head close to look, his hair brushing against her bare arm. That felt too good for comfort, so she moved back a little, out of his way.

Sebastian's tone was guardedly polite. It bothered her more than if he had sounded skeptical. In fact, his answers sounded too pat. Was he involved somehow? When her grandmother had cautioned her not to trust anyone, surely she hadn't been referring to her beloved Sebastian.

"I don't know what's happening, but those steps *did* fall to the floor below, as did the flashlight. I just barely managed to pull back before I landed down there, too."

"Oh, I have no doubt you almost fell, if you say so," he said. "Maybe it was a question of being scared by this dimly lit place. It *is* a little spooky, and—"

"Please. Don't patronize me. I don't scare easy. There was nothing in this room to frighten me, unless you count those extra footsteps all over the floor. Did you come up here to check on the noises Doña Mercedes heard? I'd be very surprised if you hadn't noticed the prints. Unless you made them." She looked down at his boots, but it was hard to tell.

He shook his head. "No, never thought of coming to the attic. No one has been up here in years, maybe since Henry died."

"Well the prints were all over the floor in the dust. Come on, let me show you." They stood up from their kneeling positions and he bent low, following her. She peered around, and suddenly felt a tremor of alarm.

There was only her set of footprints leading to the old trunk. The side where the other prints had been was as if untouched, a patina of fine dust covered them.

"Can I—can I use your flashlight a minute?"

"Of course." He sounded as if he was trying to be patient.

She didn't have much hope as she shone the light on the floor. "They were here—I tell you—a set of bootprints. I was careful not to walk on top of them."

"Can we go? My back is going to snap in two with all this bending," he said.

What the devil was going on here? Was it Sebastian playing with her mind? Did he hate the thought of marrying her that much? Or were Teresa and her brother involved somehow? Was it so important to the Contreras to have King's Ransom? If that was true, then Sebastian wasn't safe, either.

During the next week, Danielle decided she had to take the offensive and not wait for something to happen.

"I'd like you to unlock my grandmother's bedroom," she asked Peter one morning. "Sebastian said you had the keys now."

His bushy white eyebrows shot up into his permanently wrinkled forehead and he waited a moment to answer. "May I ask why?"

"Of course. Everyone wants me to wear Doña Mercedes's wedding gown. I'd like to find it first, see if it fits. The logical place would be her room, wouldn't it?" For some reason, she hadn't told anyone about finding the bridal gown in the attic.

"I suppose we could ask Concheta..."

Danielle smiled, and Peter, knowing the reason, mirrored her grin. "Of course. We both know not one of them would go into your grandmother's room," Peter said.

"Why, I wonder, are they afraid of my grandparents' ghosts or spirits or whatever, when they must know neither would have ever harmed them when alive?"

"It isn't the same, not the same at all to them. Once dead, spirits are no longer friendly, but jealous and resentful of live ones left behind."

"No one could believe that!"

"They do." Peter nodded his head vigorously. "I'm not certain Sebastian is immune to these concepts, either."

"But that's ridiculous. He was raised by my grandparents, went to the university—"

"Nevertheless, it is an inbred element in their culture, I do believe."

Sebastian hadn't been too keen on going up to the attic, she belatedly thought, and she scolded herself for not being more sensitive. Poor Henry died all alone up there; no wonder no one wanted any part of it. She wasn't superstitious in the least and yet...

In her own room, with the door locked, she gently cut the basting in the pocket of the old gown and pulled out the keys. Four keys. To what? She laid them on top of her dresser and decided to forget about them for the moment. There was her grandmother's room to dwell upon now.

That night she grabbed the keys and tiptoed up to Doña Mercedes's room, unlocked the door and crept inside. Someone must have shut off the generator to the wing. When she tried the light switch, it didn't work. No matter, she didn't want anyone to see a light from the window anyway. She placed the keys on the bureau, knowing they'd be safe here; no one ever came into this room.

The rose garden was beautiful in the pale radiance of the half-moon. A different perspective was granted from this side of the house than the view from her window. Within the room, it was as if her grandmother, that feisty old lady who probably couldn't have said "I love you" if her life depended upon it, wrapped her skinny arms around Danielle and hugged her. She could feel her grandmother so close.

Danielle stripped off the dust cover from the bed and arranged herself comfortably on top of the spread. Now all she had to do was wait.

She awoke suddenly out of a light sleep, her heart beating wildly in her chest. Above, in the attic, the sound of footsteps came loud, as if someone had no fear, nothing to hide. Why should they? Who would suspect her of lying awake beneath them, listening?

Danielle swung her feet off the bed and stepped on the floor, only to have the narrow boards squeak loud enough to be heard in the city. With a sinking feeling, she heard a door slam somewhere and knew anyone up there had gone.

The next evening, she drank a lot of coffee, not wanting to take a chance on sleeping through anything. She pulled the narrow mattress off the nurse's cot and lay close to the closed door.

Nothing happened that night, but on the third night, as she listened to the sounds of the creaky old house settling in the damp night air, someone walked across the floor in the attic. Then she heard whispers! It had to be more than one person. She tried to gauge the weight or size by the tread above her, but couldn't.

Crawling on her hands and knees, barefoot, she opened the door carefully and, once out in the hallway, stood up clutching the flashlight. Clinging against the smooth hallway walls as a point of reference, she didn't dare use the flashlight to relieve the sudden darkness surrounding her like a shroud.

Moving slowly, so that the floor didn't creak beneath her feet, she flashed the light into her cupped fingers to locate the stairs. They were up, the attic entrance shut and no way to reach the chain hanging just out of reach.

She turned the flashlight downward and knelt to study the floor below the attic entrance. Two different sets of footprints were visible in the powder she had sprinkled on the floor earlier. The idea had come to her when she saw how someone had erased one set of footprints in the attic. If footprints in the dust could be erased, they could be revealed, too.

She squatted back against the wall and the floor, wondering what to do now. It didn't seem wise to confront whoever it was up there, even if she could have. What were they doing? Looking for something, from the sound of chests being moved around, furniture sliding across the floor.

Maybe they were after the keys that had been hidden in the pocket of the wedding dress. She tiptoed back into her grandmother's room, locking the door firmly behind her. In the morning she would try to find out what the keys opened. She quietly opened the door again, tiptoed out and locked the door, then went back to her own room.

Danielle awoke to Concheta coming up the stairs, humming to herself as she always did. After she dressed and grabbed a cup of coffee from the sideboard downstairs, she went outside to greet the early-morning splendor of the countryside.

She walked along the far fence, near the stables, loving the sounds of the strange birds in the nearby trees, the rush of moving water somewhere close, possibly a river. She made a mental note to ask about that.

Some flash of color caught her eye near the edge of the pathway to the Contreras plantation. She dropped to a crouch and waited. Her wait was rewarded by two figures emerging partially between the sunshine and shade of the huge trees in the background.

At first she tasted the bile in her throat, when she recognized Teresa, thinking the other figure was too tall for Raoul and had to be Sebastian.

But she caught her breath when she saw it was the foreman, Manuel. What were they doing together? Their body language spoke of a familiar relationship as the man bent his head to listen to Teresa. She'd figured Teresa for a snob, one who would never stoop to mingle with a worker, even a handsome one like the foreman.

Oh, she'd given anything to be close enough to hear that conversation!

Their demeanor was hurried, nervous as if they argued. Teresa had her hand on the man's arm as if to keep him still, but he pulled away abruptly and stalked toward the stables, leaving Teresa alone at the edge of the jungle.

That put Danielle in an awkward position. If Teresa came in her direction for any reason, she would see her crouched in the grass like an idiot. Gradually Danielle crawled behind a tree trunk and then slowly rose to her feet. She turned in another direction as if she had been walking along, unnoticing anything in particular.

"Ah, Señorita Beaumont. Wait, I must talk with you." Teresa's voice carried across the open grounds in an imperious way that reminded her of Sebastian. She couldn't have suspected that Danielle had seen her.

Danielle turned and waited. As she watched, the graceful approach was marred by the tight-lipped anger, plain to see even from a distance. It gave her a small satisfaction to know that Sebastian must have told Teresa the news about their coming marriage.

"You have accomplished a great deal in the short time you have been here, no?" Teresa spoke softly.

Danielle felt uncomfortable standing so close to the woman; Teresa was at least five inches taller. Rejecting the need to step back a pace, Danielle stood her ground and the two women continued to look at each other. In spite of her dislike for Teresa, Danielle felt a twinge of pity. What if she had really loved Sebastian and had not merely wished to acquire King's Ransom as her grandmother and most of the workers believed?

Before she died, her grandmother had condemned the brother and sister as evil schemers who wanted to combine both plantations to make it the largest in the country. At the time, Danielle had dismissed the talk as sour grapes from a disapointed old lady who wanted her own way.

Sebastian said Doña Mercedes had never liked the Contreras', even when he and they were growing up together. Not liking was one thing, but ascribing sinister plots to the two was quite another. Yet she had to believe Teresa and her brother had something to do with the stairs, the footprints and the noise in the attic—who else could it be?

Whoever it was, the incident with the stairs had been more than a prank; she could have been killed in the fall. But who knew *she* would go upstairs for the wedding dress? Common sense answered that question. Everyone probably knew where Doña Mercedes stored the dress and everyone also knew the servants would never go up there to get it.

Pity Teresa didn't know she might still have everything she wanted—including Sebastian—after the mock marriage was over.

Teresa misinterpreted the tiny smile that etched the corners of Danielle's lips. Her eyes slitted and her full mouth twisted in an unattractive grimace.

"Don't laugh at me, *puta!* I know you came here to get King's Ransom from Doña Mercedes. Fool that she was, she wasn't that foolish. Sebastian said she tied it up so you couldn't get at it."

"He said that?"

"*Por supuesto!* Of course he did, I would not lie about such a matter. He said that was why you had to marry, so you could not steal the plantation from under his feet."

Danielle felt a shock wave through her body and her legs trembled, but she held herself firm, not wanting to show the effect those words had on her.

Just as she had hoped she and Sebastian had buried most of their mutual animosity. Was he so reluctant to face Teresa's jealousy head-on? It put her in a very awkward position. Still, she did not really believe Sebastian had said any of those things.

A sly look took the place of the anger on Teresa's face. "You are taking leftovers. *My* leftovers. Does that not bother you?"

Danielle swallowed, hating the picture that formed in her mind of Sebastian and the exotic beauty together.

"I'm sorry you feel that way, but it's done and you can't change it. You'd be very foolish to try."

"*You* are the foolish one! You have no idea what your interference might cost you. It could prove dangerous—it *will* be dangerous—if you persist. There are events that are unstoppable."

What was she rambling about? Teresa was almost incoherent with frustrated anger. Danielle started to open her mouth to confront Teresa with Doña Mercedes's suspicions, but at the last moment, looked into the narrowed dark eyes, felt the anger and hesitated. Suppose, for a crazy moment, suppose the old woman had not been hallucinating about seeing Teresa while Sebastian was gone. The charge was too implausible to make up.

Teresa saw the hesitation and took another tack. "You cannot love him! That old viper is reaching out from her grave to torment me. She knew we would be married one day."

Danielle understood the hurt in her voice, but the ugly words Teresa had spoken in rage still rankled.

Suddenly Teresa laughed, a very unpleasant sound. "Sebastian is a man—like all the others. In my country, a marriage is not as significant as a man's sex life."

With that said, Teresa turned and stalked away, past the stable workers and gardeners as if they didn't exist. So, that was a ground rule here. Marriages of convenience were common and then the silken mistress entered the scene. A feeling of sorrow crept through Danielle's being as she argued with herself that she didn't care. It meant nothing to her. But she knew she was just blowing smoke, she did care. Very much.

As soon as she entered the house, Danielle thought of the keys and ran up the stairs into her grandmother's wing. The door was ajar. She knew she locked it behind her last night!

Slowly she moved toward the door until she was close enough to push it open. No one inside. She went straight to the dresser and heaved a sigh of relief when she saw the keys lying on top where she had left them.

But there had been four keys, now there were only three. She sat on the edge of the bed, cursing her stupidity. That meant someone had to be watching her, or at least snooping behind her. What did the missing key mean? Did it mean the other keys were worthless as far as her finding out anything, or did the person just need the one key for some reason? It was getting harder and harder to follow.

Later that afternoon, Danielle decided to ride out into the meadow on Princessa. Sebastian had forbidden her to ride alone but she prevailed upon the stableboy to saddle the fidgety horse anyway. Why should she give Sebastian the impression that he could boss her at every turn? She was only going to go once around the field and then come back.

As she rode far from the stables, she heard galloping hooves nearby, and a rush of blood came to her face. Sebastian! She stopped her horse and turned in the saddle to confront— Raoul. A tingle of disappointment crept into her throat, turning her mouth dry. What nonsense.

If he sensed her disappointment, he didn't acknowledge it. Why didn't she like him? She could imagine what a stir he would make back in New York, handsome, gallant, typical dream-of-a-hero type.

She tried to imagine Sebastian in the same setting and almost giggled out loud. He, too, would be admired greatly by both men and women, but he would never sit still for it, not for a moment.

"Something gives you pleasure, *señorita?*" His honeyed words crashed her daydream to little bits.

"Oh, no, just a passing thought. Beautiful afternoon, isn't it?"

Raoul nodded, never taking his gaze from her face. "Ah, yes, beautiful. Would you care to dismount and walk with me?"

She shook her head. Somehow she preferred to be on horseback; they were so far from the stables now.

His look was one of amusement as he swung his horse closer and lightly touched her hand that held the rein to stay her.

"Why are you marrying Sebastian?"

"Why not?" His bluntness shocked her.

"For a start, my sister must be quite hurt. Also, I have become quite taken with you. I had hoped that if you stayed long enough..."

Not in a million years. She strained to keep her smile polite. There was no need to cause animosity between Sebastian and his only neighbors for miles around.

"I have more to offer. I could maintain you in a very elegant style. He and the foolish old lady poured back every *lempira* into their place, while I have not committed such an idiocy."

"I'm sorry. Sorry if you had expectations." She almost said *designs.* It was Sebastian's dire warnings that were causing her to dislike Raoul. "I am not concerned about comfort or money. In the States we don't marry for those reasons." Most of us, anyway.

"I do not give up so easily, *cara mia.* I must warn you, neither does my sister. The men of my country do not consider their marriage vows unbreakable. When the time comes and Sebastian turns to Teresa, perhaps you will find my company a great solace." His smile was tender, but his eyes cold.

"That is not my intention, to violate my—my marriage vows," she said stiffly.

"This marriage, it is a very grave mistake. You do not love Sebastian."

Teresa had spat out similar words, and it was quite a co-incidence they had both caught up with her on the same day. Had they gone over together what they would say to her? Sounded like it.

She pushed back the cloud of curls from her face and looked at him steadily, not flinching. "What Sebastian and I think of each other is our business and no one else's. I would like to return to the house now." She looked down at his lean brown hand, which still lightly held her horse's rein.

With a courtly gesture, he removed his hand and nudged their horses forward. "May I see you to the stables?"

She shook her head. "That won't be necessary. It's only a short distance."

He smiled, like a cat that swallowed a parrot. "Ah, Sebastian is already jealous of his new possession."

Danielle started to retort that she was no man's possession but thought better of it. He wanted a spirited argument, that was clear, and she would not oblige. She waved to him and trotted the horse toward the stables, relieved to be away from his piercing dark eyes, but felt those eyes burning into her back.

When the stableboy had taken Princessa away, she climbed the terraced steps toward the garden. Sebastian waited at the top, his expression grim.

"The boy told me you asked him to saddle Princessa. I requested that you not ride the horse alone. You know she is very unpredictable—look what happened with Doña Mercedes—an experienced horsewoman."

Did he know she'd met Raoul? Oh, what did it matter. Sebastian didn't own her. Her sense of guilt made his reproach harder to take and she became defensive and angry, remembering Teresa's words.

She looked away, feeling a warm flush rising from the hollow of her throat and creeping up into her cheeks. "You don't own me. Not yet. Not ever." She didn't want him to know how Teresa's words had hurt. She could imagine the two of them having a good laugh over that one.

He towered over her, and as he reached out a hand, she tilted her chin up, unafraid. He touched her gently on the cheek, brushing a curl away. "Such lovely hair, I have never seen the like." He turned away, as if torn by his feelings. "Come, sit with me a moment."

They sat on a bench and in the damp morning air, the scent of a thousand roses and other flowers permeated the air. It was pleasant, light, not cloying as she might have expected.

Silent for a moment, they then both spoke at the same time.

"You first," he said graciously.

She wanted to tell him about seeing Manuel and Teresa speaking so intimately, of her own conversation with the brother and sister. She wanted also to tell him of the noises upstairs at night. But that would be foolhardy, she had no reason to trust him any more than anyone else around here.

"You mean well, but I don't like to be bossed. I'm capable of riding that horse—if I didn't think so, I wouldn't do it. By the way, I met Raoul out there, he sends his regards."

She was unprepared for the anger in his face. His eyes narrowed and the muscles in his jaws worked spasmodically. He obviously struggled for control.

"*That* is the problem, not the damn horse. I warned you about him but you persist in going, like a moth to flame. Now I must insist, for the appearance of our marriage. Reputations are never recovered, once lost."

"What about yours? As soon as the ink is dry on our marriage certificate, you'll be in the sack with Teresa."

He looked shocked for a moment, for once speechless, but then his rich laughter rang out over the garden.

At first it made her angry, but his laugh was infectious, hearty and natural as it was. His throat down to the middle of his chest was exposed, the warm butternut tan of his skin so... She wrenched her eyes from there and concentrated on their previous anger, trying to hold the fire.

When he stopped, he wiped his eyes and shook his head. "Is that what you think of us? We are not all alike, surely you do not assume that every man in my country is..."

She felt like a child being scolded by an adult. "I've heard—Teresa and her brother—"

"But of course! They would have revealed this aspect of themselves. That is how they think."

"But you and Teresa . . ."

"Teresa and I have not—how did you put it so sweetly?—crawled into the sack."

Her heart began doing crazy things in her chest as she took a deep breath, trying to slow it down.

"It was her *assumption* from the time I returned from England, that we would eventually marry and combine the two plantations. It was her mother's dream, too, although Doña Mercedes hated the idea."

"Well, it just seems as if you two would have—I mean that you're the only single people for miles around. Except Raoul, of course."

"That's not the only reason to marry or to make love. Is that how you do it in the States? There are plenty of wealthy men nearby, single and otherwise. A woman who looks like Teresa does not have to go begging. She has had many dalliances, waiting for me. I admire her honesty, she is a passionate woman and never tried to hide her flirtations. Still, I am old-fashioned. I expect fidelity in my marriage. I am not so sure she can be faithful."

So that was what had kept him from marriage more than anything else. Did he operate on the familiar double standard, though, expecting total allegiance and offering none in return? She started to ask him, thinking of how to put it, when the mood was broken by his standing abruptly.

She swallowed, blurting out the hurtful words Teresa had said earlier in that day.

He stared away for a moment; she thought he might not answer her.

"I simply told Teresa that I had chosen to marry you. I reminded her, as gently as I could, that I had never made any promises to her. I didn't want to hurt Teresa, but apparently I have. Teresa can be very vindictive. If she even imagined that we were marrying to save King's Ransom, she would go to the city at once and stir up trouble."

"But that would only hurt you. If she loves you so much, she wouldn't do such a thing."

He shrugged. "I am not naive. Besides, I know how Teresa thinks. You don't. Her pride has been damaged, you can see that, surely. She would fight back without reasoning the consequences. The Contreras have many powerful friends in the city. The father played in politics until the day he died, using his money for influence."

They didn't speak for a long moment.

"Well, enough, I must go back to work. But be warned, Danielle, that even though we will only be married on paper, I do not wish to be laughed at or made an object of disgrace. We must abide by our vows."

Danielle watched his broad shoulders, the graceful vitality of the man recede down the pathway and with him went the sunshine.

Had he meant what he said about keeping his marriage vows? In spite of Teresa's harsh words, deep inside Danielle knew that Sebastian would be a faithful husband, it was the sort of man he was. But he didn't owe that loyalty in a sham marriage, did he?

Surely he must sense the physical attraction that existed between them. She had caught him watching her, surprising her at times with a look of need, a provocative urgency in his eyes that disappeared as quickly as it came. Didn't he feel anything special when he touched her hair so gently or the time they kissed? Maybe these feelings made him uncomfortable, as the feelings she had for him troubled her.

Danielle wanted to believe what her heart told her, that he was attracted to her and fought against it.

She shivered and went indoors, determined to find out what was going on in King's Ransom. She had the feeling that unless she left right away and never looked back, marriage to Sebastian might provide her only measure of safety.

But she had been wrong before.

CHAPTER ELEVEN

The day of the wedding arrived, warm and sunny with the lightest of breezes. Danielle felt grateful; she had hoped to have the ceremony performed in the garden under the profuse shade of the jacaranda tree. It shouldn't matter, one way or another, but it did.

For the past week, the cook, housekeeper, Peter and Concheta had fairly smothered Danielle with attentive consideration. She remembered several days ago, when Concheta insisted she preview the wearing of the wedding gown. The girl had been fluttering around like a butterfly, while Danielle, laughing, slipped out of her skirt and blouse and into the delicate old gown.

"Ah! I knew it would fit *perfectamente!* Come, let us show the others!" Concheta was so excited, she fairly jumped up and down and ignoring Danielle's embarrassed protests, coaxed her downstairs and into the kitchen.

"Oh!" Everyone stood staring. Lupe recovered first, crossing her ample bosom with a hasty blessing. "It is a miracle. You look just like La Chaparrita."

Her grandparent's wedding picture, a warm, unfaded sepia, still hung in the hallway, where Danielle had stared at it many times.

Peter walked forward and took her hand with a natural familiarity of a trusted and valued friend of the family. "Oh my, yes. With your hair hidden beneath your veil, you are the image of her when she married." He turned her toward the large antique mirror at the end of the room.

She cleared her throat nervously, not wanting to put a damper on their excitement. "I—I don't think I should wear this." Lordy, she couldn't wear it. It was gorgeous, the material so fine, like air against her skin when she moved. It made her feel, well, it made her feel beautiful, for the first time in her life.

The gown was the color of eggshells with tiers of lace cascading from the waistline. The entire bodice was encrusted with tiny hand-sewn white beads. It floated around her feet, molding to her trim figure as if it had been made only for her.

Her grandmother would have surely given it to her or maybe to Sebastian, but Danielle didn't think it should be used for this sham of a ceremony.

Abruptly, her thoughts came back to the present with a jolt as she watched servants carry out the old grand piano from the living room and someone began to play. Thinking so strongly about her grandmother led her to the unpleasant reminder of the attic, the footprints and the keys. She touched the pocket of her wedding dress, feeling the small bulge in the material. From now on, the remaining keys would never be out of her sight. But was it too late? The stolen key might have been the only useful one in the bunch. Would she ever discover where it fit and why someone wanted it so desperately? Butterflies fluttered in her middle as she wondered where Sebastian was.

Maybe he wouldn't go through with it. Lately, perhaps to make a show for the servants, he had spent every evening dining in with her. He had a very droll sense of humor and made her laugh when he wanted to amuse her. Otherwise, he was withdrawn and moody.

The music started—nothing she recognized—and as she and the maid proceeded out of the house, down the wide stairs toward the garden, she could see Sebastian's head above all those dark heads around him. Paul LeFarge waited at the bottom to take her hand and escort her to the priest in the middle of the garden.

When she reached Sebastian, she was rewarded for all her trouble by his look of stunned surprise and sharp, indrawn breath.

He bent low over her hand, his hair black like a crow's wing. "Exquisite!" he murmured as if the word was drawn from somewhere deep inside him.

Concheta had forced Danielle's usually curly, undisciplined hair into soft waves that framed her face like a cameo. Even under the lacy mantilla, the fiery auburn strands were sought out by the sun.

Danielle's chest rose and fell with alternate feelings of guilt for tricking these people, wondering what Sebastian was thinking and the excitement of the marrriage, real or not.

The ceremony did not take long. Danielle had been so nervous that she couldn't remember a word the priest spoke—or the brief kiss she'd received from her new husband. When it was over and so many guests commented on how happy Doña Mercedes would have been, she felt a little calmer. She would never know what her grandmother had in mind, tying up King's Ransom so that Sebastian could not operate it alone.

Perhaps Danielle's suspicion had been on target, that it was all an elaborate plot to discourage Teresa. If so, it worked...temporarily, at least. Neither the brother nor sister had come to the wedding. Sebastian had to be relieved. Teresa wouldn't be above creating a scene to ruin the ceremony.

"Where will you go for your honeymoon?" A woman's high voice cut through her thoughts. *Luna de miel.* Spanish made ordinary words sound so pretty. She had never spared a moment for the idea of a honeymoon, but looking up at Sebastian, she knew he was far ahead of her.

"Ah, we are going to the city—to the beach. Danielle has never been off of the plantation since she arrived and I confess, a rest would be good for me."

"He's looking for a rest! Some honeymoon that will be!" Someone clapped Sebastian on the back and the crowd around them broke into good-natured laughter.

The cook had outdone herself providing the food. The long table displayed baked pigs, cooked whole by wrapping them in banana leaves and roasting in a pit in smoldering coals for several nights. Roast pheasant and duck with crispy, crackly golden skin, stacks and stacks of tortillas, native breads, little baked meat pies. The Latin cuisine happily blended with European, to please everyone's palate.

"Surprised at the menu?" Paul asked her. The attorney had presented her to Sebastian during the ceremony and never strayed far from their sides. Did he fear they would make a mistake? They sat down to the sumptuous meal.

She nodded. "Amazed."

"Mercedes didn't believe in relinquishing her old heritage just because she assumed a new one. Her kitchen help knew how to cook and serve both kinds of cuisine, or they didn't stay here long. She ran through quite a succession of cooks until she trained Lupe to her satisfaction."

"Lupe's been here a long time."

Paul nodded. "From the beginning, she has always been just as stubborn and opinionated as Mercedes. It was something to see them together for the first year or two. Sparks lit up every time they entered the same room, but Mercedes was too intelligent to let Lupe go just because they rubbed each other the wrong way. Gradually it worked out. They learned to respect each other."

She listened to Paul with part of her attention, the other part fixed on Sebastian. What a quaint custom, putting the bride and groom at each end of the long table, probably so all the guests would be able to sit near one of them. Once or twice when their eyes met, he raised that sardonic eyebrow and lifted his glass to her.

As the day wore on, Danielle began to feel light-headed from the champagne and weary of keeping up the smiling pretense. Once she wandered off to a remote corner of the garden where Paul found her.

"Ah, here you are, my dear. I was looking for you." He handed her a multicolored rosebud.

"Ramon will have your head for that. Even the housekeeper has to ask him which roses she may pick for the house."

Paul laughed. "You are right, of course. The servants consider themselves family—a part of King's Ransom. The only one they never dared trifle with was Mercedes."

"I think Sebastian holds his own pretty well, too."

"Nonsense. Lupe has him around her finger and he wouldn't know what to do without Peter."

"Why did you want to find me? To give me some last-minute instructions?"

"What a pity this is all for business. You and Sebastian look perfect together."

"Yes, well, this is a marriage of convenience and I hope everyone connected with it remembers."

"Do you regret your decision?"

She looked down at the flower in her hand. Did she? "No. In spite of Sebastian's high-handed manner, for his sake and my grandmother's, I'd hate it if he lost King's Ransom. It's his whole life."

"So true. Just be patient, my dear. Things have a way of working out."

"I'm sure my grandmother confided everything to you. What did she tell you about—about noises in the house late at night, when everyone was supposed to be asleep?"

He turned and gave her a searching look from under his bristly eyebrows. "What have you heard?" he countered.

"Well...in the beginning, I thought it was just a weary old person's imaginative meanderings. But my grandmother was scared. Something that even an outsider like myself would recognize as uncharacteristic."

Paul looked uncomfortable, and then he sighed.

"Mercedes told me of her suspicions, of course. She also told Peter and Sebastian and anyone else who would listen. I believe the servants gave more credence to her apprehension than either Sebastian or I did."

"Did anyone ever check it out?"

"How? I'm sure Sebastian had a look around, if for nothing else but to set her mind at ease. Since one of the maids found Henry dead in the attic, and that was ten years ago, none of them will come into the main hall at night unless summoned."

"Did Sebastian find anything odd?"

"No, of course not. We are in agreement that it was the natural anxiety of a bedridden woman who couldn't stand her own helplessness. Poor Mercedes, you came a little too late, but you did give her comfort, child, I'm sure you did."

"She had Sebastian."

"She did, certainly. But you must know sons are not the same as daughters. She missed her daughter more with every passing year. Guilt played a big part in it, too."

"I think she was right." Danielle took a gulp of fresh air and continued before she could chicken out. "Too many things have happened lately. I just don't know..."

She told him about the stairs falling and then no trace of the accident afterward, the erased bootprints and the noises and whispers in the attic.

Could she trust him? She had to trust someone. Danielle pulled the keys out of the pocket she had first found them in. "I think someone was looking for these. Whoever it was, took one. There were four to begin with."

Paul took them from her and looked at each one carefully. She watched him but detected no outward appearance of him hiding anything.

He shrugged and handed them back to her. "You've shown these to Sebastian and told him about the disappearance of the fourth key, of course."

She shook her head. "No, not exactly. He didn't believe my grandmother, laughed at her. Why would he believe me? Doña Mercedes said not to trust *anyone.*"

"You are trusting me," he reminded her.

"Yes. I have to. I need you to do some checking in the city, if you can. Find out if there should be any reason for this area to be more valuable than we think. Someone wants something on King's Ransom—my grandmother thought so and so do I."

"Very well. In the meantime, you be careful. If I thought you were in any real danger..."

So, he was being polite and would do as she asked but he didn't really believe her, either. She would have to settle for that.

As they walked out of the shadowy bower into the sunlight, she looked up at the house, suddenly feeling some of the emotions that Sebastian and her grandmother felt about

King's Ransom. What a good feeling it must be to know you were home.

Danielle felt a strong need to protect King's Ramsom, something she couldn't do while away on a honeymoon. She would be doing everyone a disservice if she left now. Things could happen while she and Sebastian were away. Or maybe things would stop happening until he returned. Ah, Lordy, it was very confusing.

She was unprepared for Sebastian's quick step to her side and the hug he bestowed upon her, lifting her feet off the ground.

Before she could protest, he set her down carefully and turned to his guests, who had shifted their full attention on them.

"Danni looks tired. I think it is time to begin our journey. Paul LeFarge and Peter will see to your comfort. For those who wish to spend the night, rooms have been provided."

He'd called her Danni. An endearment coming from him that was totally unexpected. They all waited expectantly, as if they wanted her to say something.

"Thank you for honoring us with your company. We hope you will feel free to return as guests to King's Ramsom anytime." It was all she could come up with, but she meant it, and the simple words seemed to satisfy everyone, for they all applauded and gave one more toast.

Amidst a flurry of goodbyes, Danielle pulled away from Sebastian's firm grasp on her arm. "Wait. I can't just run off like this. I need certain things from my room..."

"Your maid has packed some things. You can buy anything in the city that you lack."

"Can I see you alone for a moment, before we leave?" She smiled as sweetly at the onlookers as she could while indignation rose up to choke her.

When she drew Sebastian off to the side, near the hedge, she pushed his hand from her arm. "What's going on? I don't like this—we never agreed to go away together."

"I just assumed that was a given. Everyone goes for a honeymoon, even men like me who can't afford to take the time. You shouldn't be put out about it. I'm the one who is inconvenienced—it's nearly time for propagating the new vanilla plants.''

"You are inconvenienced! Why I never heard—''

"Shh. Lower your voice, please. Heads are turning. Want them to think we are having our first lover's quarrel?'' He bent down and bestowed feathery little kisses on her lips that made her knees weak.

She pulled away. He couldn't turn her on and off like a faucet, she wouldn't permit him to do that. "I don't care what they think, this is going too far. I don't want to leave King's Ransom.'' *Alone with you,* she wanted to add. She didn't know much about him. He was practically a stranger, and one who would be best served as a widower. Then King's Ransom would be his without any problems. She hadn't thought of that before, and the idea made her decidedly uncomfortable.

"I should have told you, but I thought you would like a surprise.''

"Well, just count me out. I'm not going.''

"Be reasonable, Danielle. I've reserved a suite of rooms for us. If you think I wish to take advantage of the situation—nothing could be further from my mind. This is a business agreement, no more, no less.''

She calmed down, not sure if she should feel relieved or mortified.

"Is Concheta going with us?''

"No, of course not.'' His words dashed her last hope for space between them. "She'll be needed here to help put the place back in order again. Look, we won't stay long. There are a few business meetings I've been meaning to take care of and this is an excellent time. You can shop or whatever women do. We'll be back here before you know it.''

"Where are the lovebirds? Come out, Sebastian, come out, Danielle!'' The guests were beginning to grow restless and a few called out to them.

"Well, we carried it off this far, we might as well continue. But I refuse to leave without going to my room and changing my clothes.''

In her room, she found new clothing laid out on her bed. What presumption! He must have guessed she would insist on going upstairs one more time. This was too much—there was even new underwear for her. She picked up the flimsy, soft material and held it to her cheek for a moment. She wouldn't wear it. Where was Concheta, anyway?

When she came down the stairs, Sebastian waited at the foot. She felt elegant in the gossamer batiste overblouse and slim skirt. It was a medley of burnt orange, soft browns and greens that went perfectly with her coppery hair and pale skin. How had he guessed?

"Thank you for the clothes, but it wasn't necessary," she said. "Were you afraid I would disgrace you with my own?"

"Not in the least. I do not waste energy worrying what others think. I was in the city and saw the outfit in a window and..."

Don't be churlish, she scolded herself. The look of admiration in his eyes made her uneasy and, as usual, she reacted defensively.

She smiled, taking his arm to face the guests waiting to see them off. "Thank you again. They are lovely."

In a flurry of leave-taking, she had little time to think of the coming days. Days and nights spent alone with a stranger and only a promise between them as a boundary. She was in his country, and according to their rules, she belonged to him.

CHAPTER TWELVE

As they drove away in the washed and polished Land Rover, she tried to keep her wayward thoughts on the passing scenery. There were times when he looked deep in thought, positively formidable. For years she had prided herself for being in control of most any situation, of taking care of herself. But this situation was out of hand and made her uneasy.

"Not cold, are you?"

"What makes you ask?"

"I saw you shiver. The wind can get a little brisk in the shade. There's a lap robe in the back seat."

He looked distant and unapproachable, in spite of his pleasantries. Perhaps he'd had a big argument with Teresa before the wedding. In her anger and jealousy, Teresa was capable of anything, Sebastian had admitted that.

At first Danielle was self-conscious and restrained, but soon the magic of the countryside claimed her. Strange noises emanated from the lush green jungle, carrying even above the steady drone of the heavy car. Birds, monkeys, wild animals of every description probably filled that dark area on both sides of them. Suddenly uneasy, she thought of what might happen if the car broke down. She knew nothing about cars or wild animals, city life had not prepared her for this.

Danielle turned to look at Sebastian and took comfort in his chiseled profile, the set of his wide shoulders, the strong brown hands on the wheel. He would not *permit* anything to happen to them—or her. Would he?

After breaking the silence occasionally to offer comments about their surroundings, he lost that guarded look and began to relax.

Soon she wriggled down comfortably in the seat, ignoring the jarring potholes and the dust. She must have only closed her eyes a moment when she sat up, wide-awake.

"What is that smell? It's delightful, makes me hungry."

He laughed. "Vanilla. The lifeblood of King's Ransom."

"I heard talk of vanilla, but I didn't know it was our—your major source of revenue. Somehow I thought it was bananas."

"I'm surprised Doña Mercedes didn't discuss it with you. She was probably too ill. I never thought I'd see the day when she lost interest in King's Ransom."

"Oh, I don't think she lost interest. Helplessness would have eaten up a lesser person than her. From what I've observed, she remained deeply involved in its workings."

He still wasn't able to talk about Doña Mercedes freely.

"To answer your question, we do have bananas and cattle but we couldn't compete with the big banana companies so we diversified. Growing vanilla beans is tricky. Everyone told Doña Mercedes I was crazy, going to put her in the poorhouse. But we've managed to come out with a profit for the past several years."

"Whose idea was that—to diversify, I mean?"

"Mine," he admitted. "Doña Mercedes trusted my judgment enough to take the chance. It could have lost us the plantation, turned into a very costly mistake. No one had ever tried it in this area."

"But it turned out fine, looks like." He was willing to take chances and she liked that.

"This verdant paradise can be lethal at times," he said, changing the subject abruptly.

She searched his face for the joke and then looked back at the myriad colors of green and the brilliant blue sky above. "I don't understand. It looks very serene and peaceful."

"The rainy season will be on us soon. Monsoon weather." He waved an arm toward the jungle growth on both sides of the narrow dirt road. "Most of the time, this road is passable. Just barely. But when we get severe storms, the dams to the north of us overflow. Then—watch out!''

"Has the road ever flooded while you were driving?"

He nodded. "Once or twice. That was enough excitement for a lifetime. Especially when the bridges go out, which they do in the occasional bad year.''

"You mean we can be confined to King's Ransom for days—weeks at a time? What about emergencies?''

"We usually manage to take care of everything ourselves. We have a priest in the village nearby, a midwife who also pulls teeth and knows a little of medicine, even if part of it is kind of like voodoo.''

He grinned at her shocked expression. "I'm teasing. We're not that isolated. Teresa's brother owns a light plane and usually flies us wherever we need to go during monsoon. I've been meaning to take lessons and get my own plane but I'm so damned wrapped up in the plantation— and now this . . .''

She assumed he referred to their marriage. That seemed like dangerous territory; now that he was in a cheerful mood, she didn't want it to change.

"You went to England, to school. Did you like it there?''

"Not at the time. Later I could appreciate it. It did open a whole new world to me. I couldn't wait to get back home though, and I've never wanted to get far away since.''

She leaned back and closed her eyes, trying to visualize a young Sebastian, appearing a bit wild and exotic compared to his British schoolmates, trying to fit in with the unfamiliar culture. He probably spoke with a Spanish accent then. He must have been so lost and alone. No wonder the plantation meant so much to him.

"Tired? It's been a long day, hasn't it?" He touched her hands that lay in her lap and then concentrated on the road again before she opened her eyes.

"No. I'm not really tired. Well, maybe I am, it's a lot to absorb. I could really get to like this country—''

"You probably won't be here that long," he interrupted brusquely.

She sat up, the mood broken into little pieces. So, he was still suspicious of her motives and wanted her gone.

They didn't speak for the rest of the journey.

"Wake up, Danielle, we're here," were the next words she heard.

Sebastian had parked the car in front of a three-story, rambling old hotel. It had a shabby gentility about it, like an elderly woman of imposing appearance, dignified without ostentation, poised without arrogance.

She was charmed at first sight.

"I hope you don't mind—it isn't one of the fancy hotels downtown, but Doña Mercedes should have shares in it, we've spent so much time here over the years."

"No, I love it."

Two men rushed out to greet Sebastian by name. The younger took the baggage while Sebastian introduced the older one as the owner of the hotel. As they were ushered ceremoniously into the lobby, the maître d' hurried through the dining-room doors and everyone shook hands.

It happened so swiftly, she barely had time to notice that she was now *Mrs.* Beaumont. How strange that sounded. She always assumed that her last name would change when she married. Wouldn't her grandmother be surprised at the turn of events?

Or would she? Danielle suspected that Doña Mercedes had orchestrated this entire scenario.

Danielle felt Sebastian watching her and knew he wore that amused expression that just curved the hard lines of his lips and put crinkles around his eyes. She tilted her chin and tried to maintain her decorum. It was plain these people were not merely being polite to a good customer, they liked him. Had he ever brought Teresa here? She pushed away the intrusive thought before it could dim her pleasure of their entrance.

The small parade of people surrounded them until they climbed the stairs to the special suite reserved for the honeymoon couple.

When they were finally alone, she dropped all pretense of staying calm, spinning around to look at everything at once, dazzled by the elegant old furniture, the paintings hanging on the wall, the exotic plants around the room.

She moved to the terrance. "Oh! I wondered what that sound was. We are right over the ocean." She looked down into the crashing waves that leaped against the breakfront. The white shimmering sand glowed under the full moon, turning the water behind to a dark mystery.

"It's the Gulf of Honduras." As he stood behind her, she could feel his breath stirring the hair on the top of her head. "Know what I admire most about you?"

She turned to face him, the moonlight playing tricks with his eyes so that the color looked identical to that of the water below.

"No, what?"

"It's your childlike enjoyment. I noticed that the first evening we dined together. You tried everything first, reserving your judgment. Even during our wedding ceremony, you let yourself enjoy the day, knowing you'd never have another first wedding day. For that I am heartily sorry. And now this. I was afraid you would be disappointed and prefer to stay at the Hilton, in the center of town."

She felt a thrill of pleasure that he had noticed so much about her, tempered with a concern that he was too close for comfort. Danielle moved away, back into the room.

The queen-size bed looked gigantic. Before she could voice the question, he spoke with laughter close to the surface. "Do not worry. I could hardly request twin beds in the bridal suite—at least not in this country." He pointed toward a sofa. "That will be more than adequate for me."

Not knowing how to respond, Danielle looked away.

"How about sitting for a minute?" he said, sinking down on the bed and patting a place next to him. "I want to know what would please you to do tomorrow—or tonight for that matter. Want to go out now? There are a lot of nightclubs, piano bars, that sort of thing."

"No. Thanks for asking, but it's late. I'd like nothing better than to crawl into a nice warm . . ."

Afraid of what she'd been about to say, she sat next to him on the edge of the bed. As she looked at him, perfect from the white chambray shirt down to his polished boots, she realized she wanted him to hold her, to touch her.

As if he read her thoughts, he turned and swept her backward on the bed with his hands pressing against her shoulders. He leaned above, looking down. Danielle's heart thudded so hard in her chest she knew he could hear it.

"Ah, how beautiful you are to me."

She could feel his warm breath caress her skin, smell the faint vanilla scent of him that she had come to cherish. She reached her arms up and encircled his neck with her hands, moving her fingers in his hair.

He leaned across her body and kissed her softly at first, tentatively, teasing her lips gently with his teeth. When his kisses became ardent, demanding, she was ready to be consumed by the fire that began deep in her middle and swept through her body.

Danielle felt the length of him pressing against her, felt the passion in him rising.

His mouth released hers and he began making fiery trails of kisses down her neck and shoulders as he pushed the material away. She felt his fingers working at the buttonholes of her blouse, her heart beating faster and she wanted to help him.

When his hand, so big and warm, reached inside her blouse to touch her breast, she gasped in surprise at the overpowering feeling of pleasure and bent her head back with eyes closed, to fully savor the moment.

"Sweetheart, your heart is beating like a caged bird," he whispered hoarsely as he kissed the pulse at the bottom of her throat.

Danielle put her hands under his jaw and pulled him gently upward until she again felt his lips moving on hers. She couldn't get enough of the sweetness of him, the kisses that melted something inside her body she had been holding back for so many years.

"Sebastian," she spoke softly, not wanting to break the mood. "Let's pretend—for one night—we have a real marriage." What she wanted to say was, I love you so much, my beloved Sebastian, I want this to be a real marriage, but she dared not risk rejection, he would have to say the words first, and he didn't.

After a long moment, he pulled away from her and sat up, raking his fingers through his thick hair that she had mussed.

"Ah, yes. I almost forgot. This is a business arrangement, is it not? You keep reminding me and I keep forgetting like the idiot I appear to be."

She turned her head away so he wouldn't see the tears in her eyes.

The next morning she awoke to a tray of hot coffee in a silver thermos carafe, an assortment of delicious-looking hot rolls and a single red rose in a cut-glass vase. No sign of Sebastian. She found a note, taped to the bathroom mirror.

Have to meet with bankers today. Amuse yourself and I'll be back as soon as I can.

She was disappointed that he had gone. Perhaps last night hadn't meant anything to him. Danielle bit into the soft, sweet roll and drank the fragrant brew, tired of wondering what was going on in her new husband's mind.

What to do today? Walk on the beach? Read? Swim? Suddenly life felt good, so unique, so different, as if she didn't have a care in the world. It was the first time in her life she had been pampered and indulged, the first time she had felt desired. The feeling was seductive, but no need to get used to it. As soon as the terms of the will were fulfilled, she was history.

All day she enjoyed walking along the surf and then lying on a lounge in the shade of a tree at the edge of the sand, reading a light novel and dozing. When the sun went behind a cloud, she realized that it was almost evening. Better get back for her shower; Sebastian would return soon. The

hought suffused her with warmth and she brushed the idea
away.

He had been in the room while she was out, leaving behind the lingering smell of vanilla that was so much a part
of him. He left something else, too. She looked at the gauzy,
many-layered dress spread out on her bed. She would have
never chosen the soft rose color. Just to show him how
wrong he had guessed, she showered and slipped the dress
over her head.

A perfect fit, from the low-scooped neckline to the tiny
waistline, the skirt flaring out gracefully at the hem. She
stared at her image in the mirror. It went beautifully with her
hair and pale coloring. How had he known?

She was beginning to think there was more to Sebastian
han his macho exterior.

That night, when he escorted her to the dining room, he
held her arm possessively. They did make a striking couple.
Only the ruggedness of his profile and the taut planes of his
high cheekbones kept him from being Hollywood-
handsome.

She saw admiration and delight reflected in his eyes as
hey sat across from each other, with the snowy tablecloth
and candles between them. If only he trusted her not to be
a manipulative conniver, just after the property. If she had
brought the letters with her, if she had not made that ill-
advised promise to her grandmother— A whole lot of ifs.
Too many ifs to suit her.

"Penny for your thoughts?"

She smiled. "They aren't worth a penny. Just woolgathering. How did your meeting go today?"

He frowned. "Come, surely you have no wish to bother
your pretty head about such mundane matters. Every man
here is staring at you. You must have noticed."

She hadn't, but in looking around now, she could see dark
eyes frankly studying her. "Why would they be looking at
me?"

He laughed. "You are a rarity in this land of dusky
beauty. And of course, since we wear matching wedding

bands, they have no idea how long we've been married and
assume there may be a chance for them.''

''Are you saying that if we were lovers—that if I did not
wear this wedding ring—they would expect we were content and leave me alone?''

''Exactly! Married people soon grow bored with each
other, but lovers . . .'' He grinned.

She tried to join with his playful manner, but her usual
sense of humor deserted her as she recalled the night before. Danielle was suddenly no longer hungry. There was no
way Sebastian could know that his bantering hit too close to
home, reminding her of her father's treachery and her
mother's unhappiness because of it. ''I don't believe that for
a minute,'' she finally managed to say. ''Not even here.''

He leaned closer to put his hand on hers. ''Ah, lovely one,
can you not see I am only teasing? Of course we probably
have different traditions here than in your country, but we
are not uncivilized.''

''I have heard—'' She wanted to say Teresa told her but
didn't want that name to intrude on their evening. ''I have
heard the men in your country do not find their wedding
vows so . . . ah . . . sacrosanct.''

He raised an eyebrow, his greenish eyes twinkling. ''I assure you, and have already told you, that mine will be.'' He
leaned forward and took her hand, kissing the palm, slow
and lingering.

She pulled it back, as if she had held it over the candle.
Darn him, she could never tell when he was teasing or serious.

''Your parents—did they set a good example of married
life?'' he asked.

It was as if he read her thoughts. ''My father ran off before I was born. My mother never remarried, so I wouldn'
know about examples.''

''Your beau back home? How would he feel about your
marriage here? Did you write and tell him, perhaps?''

''Of course not! And he isn't—what I mean is—we
aren't— I've broken it off, if you must know. That was one

of the reasons I wanted to come here, to get away for a while. When my grandmother wrote to me—''

"Ah, the mysterious correspondence." He shook his head, sipping the wine slowly as if deep in thought. "I can't believe she would have hired a detective to find you, wrote you letters inviting you here—all without telling me."

"Why don't you ask Paul? I heard it was his idea to hire a private detective." She still hated to involve Peter without his consent and obviously he wasn't about to confess to having helped her grandmother.

"Oh, I have, my dear, I have asked him. It was an idea of his to be sure, but Doña Mercedes shot it down. Said it was impractical after all the years that had passed. Now I would have to believe that she went behind all of our backs to do this. Why?''

"Why?" It was suddenly so important that he believe her, believe that she'd received the letters. "Because she didn't want to hurt you, I think. If she had told you, you might have felt as though you weren't family enough for her, that she wanted or needed her own flesh and blood. I believe that she didn't want you to misunderstand her need to find me. Perhaps she also assumed that you would understand, given time.''

They looked at each other for a long moment. She felt her heart in her throat, smothering her. A strange sensation came over her as she remembered the feeling of those hard lips against hers, softening just so, his muscular body pressed to hers—

"You're a paradox, that's what you are. Sometimes you remind me of a little girl, full of wonder and enthusiasm. Then at times, you become thoughtful and preoccupied, as if the weight of the world lay across your shoulders. Which person are you, Danni?" He looked at her over the rim of the wineglass.

Confused by his attention, she fidgeted with her silverware, relieved when the waiter brought their meal. They ate in silence for a while.

"Like to walk on the beach after dinner?" His voice had turned a little cool; he probably thought he had gone too far, gotten too personal.

Outside, the night air was warm, the breeze off the water refreshing. From far away, the faint sounds of the city sifted toward them, muffled by the smattering of white clouds hanging just over the water like soft cotton balls.

They walked a while in companionable silence. She had taken off her high-heeled sandals to feel the moist sand. He walked with his jacket thrown over his shoulder, held by a finger. Reflecting the moonlight, the waves curled ripples of silver up on the beach as if reaching for them.

"What a charming place." She didn't feel like talking but the silence had begun to feel uncomfortable. Alone out here with him, she couldn't help but remember last night—and think what tonight would bring.

"Are you cold? You can use my jacket or we can go back to the hotel."

"Oh, no. It's perfect. I've never seen a large body of water without smelling it first."

They both laughed.

"You must tell me about New York sometime. I've never had the desire to visit, until recently. Someday I will go. When I get King's Ransom the way it should be again. Back when Henry was alive, it was quite the plantation. Grew everything. He used to say, stick a banana in the earth and next month you'd have a banana tree."

Her grandfather sounded like someone worth knowing. "Sounds like you've no need to go anywhere else. This is a beautiful country and you've made a lot of King's Ransom on your own." Somehow the shallow, frenetic day-to-day workaholics she had seen in New York City paled beside the grandness of what he was doing so quietly without fanfare.

"Well, it's not exciting all of the time," he said, echoing her thoughts. "But it is rewarding."

"Can you spare the time away? Did you have your meeting earlier as you planned?"

For once he wasn't put off by her questions. He motioned toward a bench and spread his jacket beneath her before she sat. "Yes and yes. Manuel is getting to be a top-notch manager. I'm glad I didn't fire him after all. That was your influence," he added.

His spare praise warmed her. "Well, I like Concheta very much and..."

"Concheta?"

"Why, yes, you know her—Manuel's sister. Lupe had her working in the kitchen a while but it wasn't the best arrangement. I would have thought you'd know all about Manuel's family, since the father used to work here and..."

"There you go again. Are you trying to be my social conscience? It won't work. We do not conduct our business that way here. I have no reason to know Manuel's entire family."

"Then you're missing a point." She didn't want to argue, but she'd worked since she was a child and knew how things were supposed to be. But the night was too breathtaking to spend arguing social issues. She would be here for a while, perhaps she could make some changes of her own. It would be interesting trying.

Danielle looked at his rugged profile in the moonlight and all other thoughts fled into the mist.

CHAPTER THIRTEEN

Later, after escorting her to their room, he left but re
turned early. She feigned sleep while he climbed out of hi
clothes, but he didn't try to wake her. When she could no
sleep, she raised up on her elbow to look in the direction o
the couch. The moonlight streamed through the thin cur
tains, touching him where he lay faced toward her. She fel
an almost irresistible urge to brush that swoop of dark hai
from his forehead. He looked so vulnerable lying there, hi
eyelashes making dark smudges against his tanned cheeks.

In the morning, the sound of the shower woke her. Sh
swung out of bed to answer the discreet knock of roon
service just as Sebastian emerged, wrapped in a towel.

They stood in the middle of the room staring at eacl
other, while the waiter laid out the tray for them. When th
man left, she turned her back on Sebastian and sat down o
the bed. She felt it sag with his weight as he sat, too. S
close. She tried not to squirm.

"Do you always sleep in your robe? I watched you las
night. It was warm."

"Do you always sit on a person's bed with only a towe
around you?" she countered.

"Are you afraid of me?"

"Should I be?"

"You looked so lovely last night. It torments me to be s
close to you—and not touch you." He leaned over an
touched his lips against her neck. She could feel his warr
breath against her skin, as he worked his mouth gently alon
her shoulders, pushing away the fabric. Her heart starte
racing and a strange quiver began somewhere in her mid
dle.

"It feels terribly wrong to make love, to consummate a marriage that is only a sham. We had an agreement—one we almost broke the other night."

He looked at her, taking her hand. "Yes. You are right." He stood up and dropped the towel, moving toward the bathroom.

She turned her eyes away but not before she saw the wide tanned shoulders, narrow waist and... Danielle tried to wipe out the vision as she poured her coffee. He must work in the fields without a shirt—his torso to his waist was tanned, but the other half of him— She shook her head and smiled in spite of trying to be indignant.

When he came out, dressed casually in a T-shirt that hugged his muscled chest and a pair of chinos, she turned to face him as if nothing had happened.

"Come, sit and eat. Are you going to a meeting today?"

He laughed. "You sound like a wife." He pulled up a chair to sit across from her and after a long drink of steaming coffee, he leaned back with a sigh of pleasure.

She wished she wasn't sitting on the edge of an unmade bed, looking like the inside of one herself in her robe and tousled hair. She would have liked to have brushed her teeth before she drank the coffee but he'd hogged the bathroom. Danielle told him as much.

He grinned. She liked the way his full, sensuous lips curled up gradually, his eyes crinkling in the corners.

"Sorry, that was not very courteous of me, was it? To-morrow I will let you have it first. It's just that you looked like a child sleeping with your hands beneath your cheek like that. I didn't want to disturb you."

It made her uncomfortable to think of him watching her while she slept, but it was only fair; she'd watched him last night.

"Getting back to your question, no, I'm devoting the day to my beautiful wife. Let's go swimming, I'll have them pack us a lunch. There's something down the beach I want to show you."

"Great! Sounds like fun. I brought a bathing suit."

He stood up and stretched. "I'll go downstairs and leave instructions—meet you out on the veranda. Oh, and the hotels have strange customs here, strange by your standards I'd imagine. We wear our street clothes down to the beach. I'll rent a cabana so we can change there."

"It won't take me long to get ready."

Once alone, she unpacked the skimpy bikini, wondering if she would feel odd wearing it here. When she'd packed it, Danielle remembered imagining long, boring afternoons at the plantation, tanning herself so that when she returned to New York, the models would be envious and imagine her spending long days on the beach. She left her room thinking how trivial that seemed now. Who cared what any of them thought?

On the veranda, he took her arm, the solicitous husband, and they walked down to the beach. Now she could see little canvas rooms dotting the sand, puffing out in the breeze. What a charming custom.

She changed first and as she emerged into the sunlight, she heard his gasp. In two strides he was at her side, grinning down at her. "Such a lot packed into a neat little package," he said.

She caught her breath at the naked desire in his eyes and then tried to match the lightness of his words. "Go on with you, it's your turn." She moved away from the doorway, flopping down on the sand to wait.

The sun felt good on her body. The air was cooled by a breeze off the water so that the temperature was perfect. When he emerged from the little room, she tried not to stare but it was difficult. His upper torso was rich bronze, his hips slender and legs untanned and just slightly bowed, probably from riding horseback. She let him pull her to her feet and they set off walking.

The late-morning air sparkled, with the sun catching little motes in front of her. They stopped once; he surprised her when he dropped to the sand and beckoned for her to help him make a sand castle. Then they continued to walk down the beach.

"Aren't we getting a little far from civilization?"

He gave her a searching look and then turned his gaze toward the water without speaking.

Danielle cursed her outspokenness, hoping she hadn't spoiled the mood of childlike enjoyment he had surprisingly revealed for the past hour.

"I'd like to show you something, a very special place," he said, his voice tentative for the first time. He waited politely for her answer, his expression composed as if it were no matter to him one way or another.

Suddenly she knew it must be important.

"Of course. I'd like to see it."

They walked almost a quarter of a mile farther and then rounded a bend. She could no longer see the tallest city buildings over the treetops; not even the hotel was visible. The closest people playing on the beach looked like dots on the horizon.

As she turned back, she almost bumped into him, for he had stopped. There, tucked against the side of a large sand dune, as if carved by human hands, stood a huge hollowed-out tree trunk. She could see it was well back from even the highest tide.

He took her hand and began to pull her through the opening.

"Wait! Maybe there are snakes or spiders or..."

He turned back and smiled, such an endearing smile her berath caught in her throat. "Not so close to the sea. You'll be fine."

The air inside was shadowy and smelled faintly of damp seaweed. The wind had ceased and the waves sounded miles away; it was like listening to a seashell against your ear. He pulled her gently to the sand and sat beside her. It was like a little room, with a canopy of jungle behind them, a panorama of the sea in front of them.

"This used to be my home, before I found the Beaumonts and King's Ransom. I've never shown it to anyone before except to your grandmother."

Her throat tightened as she realized how inadequate words really were. How could she tell him how much his trust meant to her?

"Were you born in this port city?" Suddenly she needed to know about him, where he came from, how he had felt living here alone as a young boy.

He shrugged and lay back to look at the canopy of leaves overhead. "Truthfully? I don't know. My father was English, a captain with his own ship, or so people who knew told me. He was lost at sea before I was born. I can't remember my mother, they say she was beautiful. *Mestizos,* we call them, half Spanish, half Indian. She dropped me off at a monastery, and disappeared forever."

"Oh, no!" Her exclamation of dismay slipped out.

He turned to regard her, his expression soft. "I've long since forgiven her. Why should I judge her, she had no way to earn a living. Women here have a rough time of it without husbands or a provider."

"Yes, I'm learning about forgiving. All my life I carried around a hatred for my grandparents. It's finally gone. Completely. But don't tell me these things if it's too painful for you."

He turned his face away toward the tree trunk. "Oh God, I don't know why I'm telling you anything. I haven't been here in ages. No one but Doña Mercedes knows about this place."

The silence filled the void of words for a while, but this time it wasn't uncomfortable. "Please," she said, touching his shoulder. "I'd like to know more. How did you come to live here? Weren't you afraid to be so alone? Didn't anyone try to help you?"

He rolled over on his side and propped his head on his hand, elbow digging into the soft, white sand. Even though he was on his side, his stomach looked hard and flat as a board. Amazing, he was in such great shape as if he worked out in a gym all day long. She thought of the pasty-white skins and soft bodies of most of the men she had seen at the gym she belonged to and turned away, embarrassed at her wild thoughts.

"I guess I was just too much of a handful for the good fathers. They tried, Lord knows they tried, but I had a chip on my shoulder as big as this tree. When I was nearly ten, I left there and began wandering. I found the beach and lived here for a while, scrounging my meals from the hotels' garbage bins."

She pictured this lost little boy, too tough to ask for help, too proud to accept it if someone offered. But who would offer? Orphan boys were like fleas on a dog here.

"And then?" Gently, so as not to break the spell.

"Miguel from King's Ransom caught me scrounging one day, while he waited for Henry and Mercedes. He was the foreman at the time—long since died. He was as old as Moses then, or so it seemed to me. Anyway, he caught me and dragged me in to see the Beaumonts. For some reason, they took me to their bosoms, accepted me without question. I'd never had anyone do that before."

Danielle didn't know what to say. All along she'd felt sorry for herself, thinking *she'd* had it tough.

"And did it feel like home?"

He nodded. "Right from the first I felt I *belonged*. You have no idea how that felt to me. I still wonder at it, after all these years."

She did know how he felt. From the moment those big iron gates of King's Ransom opened, she felt a homecoming, a peace within herself. It would never do to admit it to him, though; he would surely think it part of her scheme to wrest a share of the plantation from him. Oh, there were so many things she longed to tell him but didn't dare.

"Did you and my grandparents hit it off right from the beginning then?"

He laughed; it sounded a little rueful. "No, afraid not. You don't lose a chip on your shoulder the size of a rainforest that quickly. It took time to wear off my rough edges, but Doña Mercedes and Henry were so patient with me." He tilted her chin and looked deeply into her eyes. "At the risk of offending you, I think they poured all the love on me that they wanted to give to your mother and couldn't."

"It doesn't offend me," she assured him. The touch of his fingers made her skin tingle, but she held still, hoping he wouldn't take them away.

"When they sent me away to school the first time, I was shattered. They thought they had done me a great favor, and they did, except I couldn't see it that way. I only saw that they, like my mother, didn't want me."

Her hand itched to touch his jaw line, smooth the rigidness away, but she held herself taut, afraid of breaking his mood.

"Peter managed to get it through my thick head just how good they had been to me, how they did everything for my benefit and how much they cared for me. It was even harder for Doña Mercedes to send me away to Oxford. Henry had died and I was all she had, yet she did it. I've tried to repay her for everything, but I'll be in their debt forever."

"I'm sure that's not what they wanted from you."

"Danni, come here to me." His hoarse whisper filled the silence, and shivers played involuntarily up and down her spine. He reached for her and bent to kiss her. In the semi-darkness, the sand dune and jungle background echoed the soft shush of the waves outside their hideaway. She looked at him, feeling as if she might drown in the sea-green of his eyes.

He had confided in her, told her things he had never told anyone before. He must love her! Blood raced through her veins, and a warm feeling of longing spread across her midsection in waves—feelings she had never known before.

She flicked her tongue nervously over her dry lips and before she could move back, he had captured it with his lips on hers. When the kiss was over, he began kissing her throat, working downward slowly. Every touch of his lips left a trail of fire. "I want you so much, Danielle." He groaned and pulled her closer to his hard body. For a long moment, she lay still, nestled against his chest, listening to his heart thudding in her ear. He put his leg over her hips and now she felt the heat in her thigh, and couldn't feel where one body began and another ended.

"I've wanted to possess you since the first time I saw you," he murmured into her neck.

She wanted to return his ardor, more than anything she had ever wanted in the world, but something held her in spite of her demanding body. She waited for words of love, but they never came.

Danielle pushed him away gently but firmly, tears edging through her closed eyelids. His words, "I want to possess you" sobered her, as if he had thrown a glass of ice water in her face. He would make her his mistress, and as soon as their marriage could be terminated, Teresa would step into King's Ransom. The thought was intolerable.

"We have an agreement," she whispered, her voice hoarse with unexpressed desire.

He pulled away from her and sat up, raking his hair back from his forehead. She could see his struggle for control over his emotions and when it finally came, she knew she had won—and lost.

"Yes. How could I have forgotten?" he said, sarcasm lacing his voice. "It won't happen again." He stood up gracefully as she looked away from the sand entwined in the dark hairs of his legs.

"Let's start heading back, it's a long hike." He held out his hand to help her, the hand of a polite stranger.

Danielle felt a perverse stab of disappointment. At least he might have disputed her decision, as if he cared.

They walked back in silence, both subdued, thinking their own thoughts. She closed her eyes and again felt his lean, hard body against hers and nearly stumbled. She felt his strong fingers beneath her elbow and he asked her politely, coolly, if she wanted to stop and rest.

Danielle shook her head, unable to speak. Soon they were back in the center of the beach, among a crowd of laughing children and adults. They took turns dressing in the canvas room and silently went back to the hotel.

She felt they had come to a turn in their relationship, but where was it going?

Danielle pleaded a headache, saying she wanted a nap, would probably skip dinner.

Pulling the sheet up over her body, she closed her eyes and waited for sleep to come. How terrible to love someone the way she loved Sebastian and not know if he would ever care deeply for her—ever need anything from her but sexual pleasure. She cursed herself for being unable to gamble, to take a chance that, if she surrendered her body and soul as she longed to do, he would in time return her love.

Hadn't her mother taken that gamble? And lost? Did her mother feel this same agonizing, glorious awareness, this need to be so much a part of someone that nothing else mattered?

Suddenly she wished her grandmother had known this about her mother, knew she wasn't weak, but very, very strong. Stronger than Danielle would ever be, for she could not do it.

She loved Sebastian—she knew she always would, but she couldn't diminish that love by offering it to someone who could never return it.

Danielle rolled out of bed and walked across the room to the closet where his working clothes hung. She buried her face in them, inhaling the smell of sweat and vanilla. Tears streamed down her face and she wept, wept for her mother, for her grandmother and for herself.

CHAPTER FOURTEEN

He woke her early in the morning by tickling her nose with a long-stemmed rose. She sat up and sneezed.

"You look just like that Raggedy Ann doll Doña Mercedes used to keep on her bed."

She wanted to retain her usual grumpy command over the morning but couldn't, with him standing over her laughing.

"Thanks for the rose." She wondered when he'd come in, but didn't ask. It wasn't her business.

"I have appointments at several banks and insurance companies—to change the names on deeds and— You wouldn't be interested in the details, very boring."

How did he know what interested her?

"I'll bring the papers for you to sign tonight. Meanwhile, here's some money." He began to peel off a pile of paper money and laid it on the nightstand.

"What for?" *I didn't earn it,* she wanted to add and then for a change, thought better of it. It wasn't an area either of them wanted to get into again, probably.

"I'd like you to go shopping. You'll need more clothing. Paul said you must remain here for at least three or four months—otherwise the marriage dissolution would be filed under annulment, not divorce, and becomes a useless gesture."

Is that all he worried about? Damn King's Ransom, anyway. She wished with all her heart there was some way she could have started over again with him. He never looked more handsome, sitting on the bed across from her, with a little-boy slickness to his damp hair. It would soon dry and become curly at the nape of his neck, the top fluffing up in near waves. Despite how familiar the sight of him was to her, he seemed a stranger with a polite, faraway look, as if he'd rather be any place else.

"Thank you. Like all giddy females, I love to shop." She might as well play his game. He typecast women; not all men did that, but Howard had, also. You were supposed to fit neatly into their preconceived notion of who you were and what you wanted from them.

"Any further instructions for the day?" she asked innocently.

He grinned, not taken in by her pretense of submission. "Get dressed—I'll meet you in the lobby and we'll walk into the city, if that's all right with you. It's a nice day for a walk."

When she arrived downstairs, he was looking out the window toward the ocean. As he took her arm, she felt an upsurge of happiness. The day was beautiful, the moist breeze off the gulf freshened the air, giving it at least a momentary sensation of coolness. She wore one of the new dresses he had brought her, a lime green cotton, airy and light as a butterfly wing. The primly scooped neckline was very flattering and she felt alive and happy.

They walked for a while in silence and then he stopped as they entered a busy intersection. "Here's where I leave you. You won't get lost, the city isn't that big, especially for someone used to New York. Just don't flirt with anyone, the men here don't take teasing lightly."

"What do you think I am?" She began to bluster until she saw his mischievous grin. "Okay, you got me. I'll try to behave. Anything else?"

"Only that I'd like you to meet me for lunch at Freddie's—Alfredo's Place. You can't miss it. It's on the main avenue, but ask if you need to." He looked down at her head and pushed away a curl scraping her cheek. "Your hair shines like a copper penny in the sun, did you know that?"

Before she could think of an answer, he was gone. She watched him for a moment. He was taller than most of the people on the sidewalk, and his long stride took him around a corner before she was ready to let him go.

As the morning progressed, she began to enjoy walking through the streets. People looked at her curiously, then answered her smile with one of theirs. The place had a style all its own—a makeshift little taco stand nestled against the side of an elegantly expensive department store. The bus station, full of black smoke, the noise and smell of powerful diesels, perched next to a seafood restaurant with tables and chairs outdoors in a lovely patio.

She shopped a while and then decided to look for a place to sit. Green parks dotted the city; she usually heard the rushing fountains before the parks came into view. Just as her packages began to grow heavy, she found a bench in one of the parks and sat down, hugging her purchases close.

If this was anything like New York, one couldn't be too careful. No one approached her, only the occasional curious stare and polite smile that always followed.

She was pleased with her purchases, a little something for everyone back at the house. Just then she thought to look at her watch. Lordy, it was late! She should have asked someone earlier how to locate Freddie's. She turned away from the park and took a diagonal street, thinking it would get her back to the town center sooner. The more she walked, the narrower the streets became and the quieter.

Worried, she stopped passersby to ask directions, but they just shrugged, smiled politely and moved on. Danielle began to panic; she'd always had a fear of being lost in large places.

Finally she stopped in the middle of the sidewalk, took a deep breath and tried to get a grip. She looked down at the box with the department store name emblazoned on the front. She stopped a woman and pointed to the box with a helpless smile. The woman in turn pointed, and Danielle got the drift of the instructions.

Groups of men leaned indolently against buildings here and there. She could smell beer and worse coming through doorways left ajar. The men stopped their talk abruptly when she passed; she could feel their stares follow her like flies on a side of beef. She hurried on, shoving down the panic.

Beginning to think the woman had deliberately given her wrong directions, she saw the spread of open light beyond the last building on the street and relief flooded her through her.

"Sebastian!" she called out, recognizing that silhouette and distinctive stride. He hurried toward her, taking long steps that ate up the sidewalk. She threw herself into his arms, packages flying on the sidewalk, some squashing between them.

"Are you all right?" He held her away a moment before pulling her back close. "I've been searching for you, thought you might have gotten lost."

He looked at her as if he truly cared what happened to her and the panic of being lost disappeared. Flustered, she moved away to pick up the dropped packages.

"Let's sit in that park a minute. Tell me about your adventures."

He helped gather the packages from the street then took her arm in his, and led the way toward a wrought-iron bench underneath a huge banyan tree.

She sank down gratefully in the shade, leaning her head back and closing her eyes to get her breath.

"Are you sure you're okay?" he asked again, a sound of worry beneath the lightness of his voice.

She opened her eyes to look into his. "I am now," she said, remembering the concern in his expression when he first saw her. "I've had a lovely day! Then, like Cinderella, I saw the time and must have thought I'd turn into a pumpkin if I didn't make it to Freddie's before you grew tired of waiting and left. I got lost." She said it all in one breathless sentence and they both laughed.

"Well, let's have a look at your treasures and then we'll go to lunch."

"Open them here—now?" She looked at the surrounding park benches, just now noticing the people watching them with open interest.

"Of course. Unless you prefer to keep them to yourself. That's probably the first thing an 'old married' couple does when they meet after a wife's shopping spree."

"Oh, okay, Mr. Know-it-all. I can't see why you'd want to look at my packages though."

He probably wanted to give her time to calm down before they ate lunch. He could be surprisingly intuitive. She liked that.

Danielle opened Concheta's gift first, spreading out the lovely shawl across their laps.

"Enchanting, although I'd never have bought that color for you."

He was very sure of himself and his preferences. He did have an excellent fashion sense, though.

"It isn't for me, it's for Concheta."

She opened the next package, placing the delicate tortoiseshell comb on top of the shawl.

"Before you make another comment—" she brushed her fingers through her short, curly hair "—this is for Lupe. I've discovered her one vanity is that head of glossy black hair."

"Enough, woman. I'm waiting to see what you bought for yourself."

She ignored him, opening Ramon's and Peter's gifts for him to look at. "I didn't get anything for me, the time was going so quickly. Next time, maybe. Actually, I didn't need anything. You've spent quite enough on my wardrobe."

Trembling at the strange look he gave her, she was surprised when he pulled her close, tilted her chin with a finger and looked deep into her eyes, as if searching out the bottom of her soul. He kissed the tip of her nose and stood up abruptly, as if the moment was too emotional. "Let's go find something to eat."

He called one of the street urchins to him. They seemed to know each other and after Sebastian gave him some coins, he handed over the packages with instructions to deliver them to the hotel.

As they entered the cool, semidarkness of the restaurant, Danielle couldn't help but notice the cessation of conversation at the tables when they passed. Sebastian seemed amused at everyone's interest and stopped from time to time to introduce her to people he knew, graciously accepting their condolences on the death of Doña Mercedes and congratulations on his marriage. The maître d' hovered around them, gently maneuvering them toward the table he had chosen.

She felt certain the excitement of the day would prevent a desire to eat, but when the lunch Sebastian ordered arrived, she couldn't resist. The waiter served a tureen of shrimp bisque with just the hint of lemon flavor, to begin their meal. Then he brought golden broiled flounder fillets with side dishes of brown rice and sautéed mushrooms, fresh, crisp vegetables marinated in a piquant dressing. For dessert, they had a colorful fruit compote lightly coated with the unmistakable flavor of vermouth.

"Aren't you drinking your wine?" he asked.

She shook her head. "Thanks, but I don't like the taste. Never got the hang of social drinking," she admitted. "That was a lovely meal. I could sleep the rest of the afternoon," she added.

"It *was* good, wasn't it? Freddie's never disappoints. Doña Mercedes loved this place."

She noticed he'd managed to return to every place he and her grandmother had shared together. It was as if he wanted to draw on the old memories even though it must be very painful for him. She hadn't given that a thought. He was becoming more and more complex, refusing to be contained in the simple, domineering macho category she had stuck him into.

They left Freddie's, walking for a while until he stopped at a storefront and ushered her into a thickly carpeted jewelry shop. A heavy, older man with steel-gray hair rushed to greet them.

"Ah, Don Sebastian. So this is the lovely bride the whole city is buzzing about." He smiled at Danielle and bowed low over her hand. "Charming, charming. Doña Mercedes, your sainted grandmother, has long been a valued client of this humble establishment. We offer our condolences on your loss. How may we help you?"

Danielle could see nothing remotely humble about him or his shop, but she returned his smile with a sense of relief.

Somehow it was comforting to know it was her grand-mother and not Sebastian who was such a valued client.

Sebastian bent over a display case. "I'd like to see that tray, Señor Mendoza."

He turned to Danielle. "You wouldn't buy anything for yourself today so this is your punishment, young lady. Turn around," he commanded in a tone that brooked no argument. She could sense that rare playfulness lurking just under the mock severity of his voice, so she decided not to spoil it. She turned and felt the slim, cold chain around her neck as he fastened it with suddenly clumsy fingers.

"Now give me your hand—the right one."

He slipped a beautiful marquis-cut gold and topaz ring on her finger. She held her hand out, staring, at a loss for words. When she looked down at the white swelling curve of her breasts, the smaller version lay in an exquisite filigreed gold setting.

"But Sebastian—I don't want this. It's lovely and I thank you, but it's far too expensive and extravagant—" She broke off in sudden confusion.

"Don't shame me about costs, sweetheart," he whispered in her ear. "You don't have to worry your pretty head about such things."

The mild reproof momentarily dulled her moment of joy. Was he just "doing his duty as a husband" for the world to see? But he told her one time that he didn't worry about what others thought of him, and somehow she believed that.

"Look at yourself," he turned her toward the mirrored wall.

She stared, first seeing his face. For a moment his eyes reflected a faraway sadness, then quickly the look was gone.

"It was made for you. The topaz matches your eyes perfectly, I remember thinking that the first time I saw you. Topaz eyes." Their gaze met in the reflection and held for a long moment.

Later, back in their suite, she enjoyed a leisurely bath while he rested on the bed. When she opened the door, she stood for a moment, looking at him sprawled across the bed, feet dangling over the side touching the floor, fast-asleep.

This was probably the first vacation he had allowed himself in years.

She knelt at the side of the bed and removed his boots carefully and tried to pull his long legs up on the bed. His dead weight was too much for her, so she covered him lightly with a spare blanket and then she laid down on the couch.

When she awoke some time later, she felt warm and soft, as if he had been caressing her with his gaze. She sat up, looking at his silhouette against the backlight of the terrace.

"Have a good sleep?"

She nodded, stretching.

"Don't you ever wear anything but that frumpy little robe?"

"Why? Does it annoy you?"

"Not necessarily, but considering the clothing Concheta packed for you, it seems you might permit yourself a little luxury."

She flushed, suddenly uncomfortable. "All those things you bought me— They're lovely and I'll get around to wearing them. But not yet. My mother gave me this robe. It's kind of like—it's kind of like family to me." She rubbed the worn material between her fingers, remembering their last Christmas together.

His tone gentled, the sarcasm fled. "I understand. I've got a pair of boots like that. I've had to guard them for years from the merciless clutches of Doña Mercedes and the housekeeper."

They laughed. "By the way, how did you know so much about sizes, colors and styles? You must have had a lot of experience in buying women's clothes." Her voice stayed lightly bantering, as if his answer was unimportant.

"Well, perhaps someone helped me," he baited.

A flicker of angry jealousy touched her eyes for a moment until she realized he was teasing. She knew the sultry Teresa would never have chosen such a becoming wardrobe for a hated rival.

"Oh, you!" She tossed a pillow toward his smirking face before she jumped up and ran into the dressing room. When she had dressed, she opened the door.

"Does this suit Your Highness?" She had put on the caftan he bought her. Very feminine, with yards and yards of material several varying shades of browns and greens in an abstract leaf design.

He smiled his approval.

They sat down to the croissants and coffee the room-service waiter had delivered. "When do you expect to return to King's Ransom?" She hadn't, for even one moment, forgotten about the attic and the missing key.

"Are you making polite conversation or are you serious?"

"I seldom make polite conversation," she said.

"Then you are bored here?"

She shook her head emphatically. "Of course not. It's lovely and I'm sure you could use the rest. But I get the feeling you are really impatient to get back—ah—get back." She'd almost said *home*, but thought better of it. King's Ransom wasn't her home, she had to remember that. "I can tell something's worrying you, even if you won't talk about it."

"Where have I failed? I never saw a bride so anxious to end her honeymoon."

She smiled, hugging the thought to her that he was learning to unbend in her presence. His dry humor showed that.

They spent the day apart and the evening walking along the beach. There seemed to be no need for talk between them. How would it be when they went back to King's Ransom? It was like a dream sequence, her near accident with the stairs, almost as if she'd imagined it. Yet she knew she hadn't imagined it. Someone hadn't wanted her to marry Sebastian, she felt that very strongly. Now, after the deed was done, would she be safe or made even more vulnerable?

Later, he excused himself to attend to some business and when she awoke sometime during the night, he lay there, sleeping on top of the covers, at her side.

When had he laid down next to her? She reached out her hand to touch him and then pulled back, afraid of wakening him. Those eyes were closed, those eyes that could hold such tenderness and yet reflect so much distrust. What she longed to see in them and never would was love, pure and simple.

Her wedding day had passed in a blur, her honeymoon was nearly over—where had she lost her dream? If she could stay forever at King's Ransom with Sebastian, would it be enough?

It might have to be.

She was getting used to having him near. That could be dangerous. Almost as dangerous as returning to King's Ransom. Someone didn't want her there.

CHAPTER FIFTEEN

When they entered the big iron gates of King's Ransom, the servants ran out to greet them. Even Lupe emerged from the kitchen, wiping chapped hands on an immaculate white apron. Concheta stood by shyly, waiting for the others to finish their greetings.

Danielle handed out presents and there were exclamations of joy as each recipient tore off the wrappings. She had chosen an ivory-headed cane for Peter and when she handed it to him, his eyes lit up like a Christmas tree. He just shook his head, unable to speak.

Sebastian smiled, watching the scene as he leaned against the Land Rover. "She used to do that, bring them back presents," he remarked.

Danielle knew he meant Doña Mercedes. He had to miss her so much, she had been a part of his life for so long.

When the thanks had been dispensed with, Sebastian stopped Concheta and Ramon from taking the luggage upstairs. "Wait until I call you. I want my wife to come up first."

My wife, the first time he'd said the words. The sound of it turned a knife in her breast and she took a deep breath, striving for calm.

What was going on? She climbed the wide stairs beside him. When they got to the long hallway, he stopped. "Not that way. Remember when I asked you not to go into this wing, where my rooms are?" He beckoned, his eyes lit mischievously like a little boy's with a secret he could barely contain.

How could she not remember? She had thought it suspicious in light of what happened to her with the falling stairs and the stealthy sounds.

"Shall I carry you over the threshold? I've heard that is a quaint American custom."

She smiled. "No, thanks. The servants aren't here to see, anyway." Now why did she have to say that? His eyes darkened for a moment before he regained his humor and led the way.

Danielle pushed into the room and gasped in surprise. She could smell the faint odor of new paint and wallpaper. He had redone the suite of rooms in cool shades of avocado green combined with the warmth of a copper rust shade, her favorite colors.

"Oh! It's beautiful! When did you...?"

He smiled at her obvious pleasure. "I started even before the wedding. This part of the house is so far away from your room, I didn't think you'd be suspicious, even though I've never seen anyone so curious about everything. There is a back staircase for the workers to come and go."

She felt odd, with relief and guilt fighting for supremacy. She hadn't trusted him, thinking he might hurt her, wondering why some rooms were locked and some not.

On one side of the room, two chaste twin beds were divided by an antique nightstand. On top of the stand stood a huge green fern that dropped almost down to the rug.

She walked into the next room. "It's like a sultan's harem!" she exclaimed. The bathroom had an exotic sunken tub, tiles of hand-painted mosaics with delicate flowers and butterflies circled the tub and wash basin. A huge dresser faced her, with mirrors in a semicircle. On top of the dresser stood an arsenal of expensive-looking perfumes and potions. She picked up a delicate tortoiseshell comb and brush set and looked at him.

"You did this for me? I can't believe you did this." Her first thought was of practicality, he had spent a lot of money. Right away, she knew not to voice that idea.

He looked at her, his eyes unreadable in the soft, indirect light around the perimeter of the bathroom.

"There's more." He nodded his head toward the double doors of the closet. Hesitatingly, she opened them and stepped back in shock.

A row of dresses, skirts and blouses—all colors she instinctively knew would be flattering, colors and styles she would have never had the audacity to buy for herself. She always considered her taste leaned toward the practical, the classic look that one could wear many seasons.

"Oh, I can't accept all this. It's...it's overwhelming." Tears rolled from her eyes and she rubbed furiously at them with the back of her hand.

Her tears must have moved him, for he turned away but not before she caught the look of tenderness in his expression.

She reached out and touched one of the dresses, shimmering and gauzy but ladylike and demure at the same time.

He looked wistful for a moment, an expression seldom seen on his strong face. In the mirror she saw this small, delicate-appearing young woman and the tall, dark man in the background, almost in the shadows.

His eyes turned brooding, but he continued to stare at her. Was he still wondering why she was here? Did he still mistrust her motives? He couldn't have done all this just for appearances. The color left her cheeks, but she was determined not to let anything spoil this moment.

"Why do you look at me like that?" she asked.

He looked down at his boots and absentmindedly rubbed the toes on the back of his pants leg. Before she realized he had moved, in two long strides he was at her side, his big hand resting on her shoulder. He turned her to face him.

They stared deeply into each other's eyes for a moment, her lips parted with an effort to catch a normal breath. He released her as suddenly as he touched her, sighing. Whatever he had been searching for in her eyes, he had failed to find.

"You like it then?" His voice leveled out into a courteous politeness.

"It's a lovely surprise, must have cost a small fortune, though."

He shrugged his wide shoulders. "Maybe we'll just have to deduct it from your share of the partnership."

So, the idea of their business arrangement *had* intruded. She had been right, he wasn't convinced that her coming here was the result of an appeal by Doña Mercedes and entirely coincidental with her death and the subsequent will.

"We will stay here at night, for the sake of the servants. Your old room is still intact, you may use it anytime during the day. I plan to use mine as a study."

Sometimes he could sound so pompous and stuffy. Why couldn't he let well enough alone—it was as if he feared she might find a chink in his armor.

Later, she rested in a big chair facing the wide dormer windows as Concheta unpacked the suitcases. "You knew all about his fixing up the rooms, didn't you?" she accused.

"*Sí.* We—all of us knew. We couldn't wait for you to return. Was it not a grand gesture from Don Sebastian? A fitting tribute to his beautiful wife, the new Chaparrita? Of course, we do not understand about the beds," she added, pointing to the twin beds.

Danielle smiled at the wide-eyed enthusiasm. "A wonderful surprise. The beds are an American custom." She only wished his "grand gesture" had been real. He wouldn't trust her, couldn't trust her. He was probably deeply regretting his make-believe marriage.

She slammed a drawer in a sudden temper, looking for the clothing she had brought with her from New York. She would wear her own, and leave his in the closets.

That night, she begged off eating dinner in the big dining room to retire early. He had been outdoors all day, in the vanilla grove, she supposed. Tonight he could be with Teresa. She brushed the painful thought away hurriedly. He wouldn't dare; it was too soon.

She picked up the shirt he had tossed toward the hamper and held the fabric to her cheek. As she closed her eyes, the odor of clean earth and vanilla smoothed away the resentment she had felt against him since their return to King's Ransom.

Locking the bedroom door and going into the sumptuous bathroom, she kicked off her clothing and drew a bath,

putting in a generous dose of bath salts. As she stood waiting, her gaze was drawn to the full wall of mirror facing her,
delicately webbed with gold. How would she compare with
Teresa? She looked at her small, high breasts, the rosy nipples hardening under her scrutiny. Her waist was tiny, her
hips round. Not too shabby, she thought—only a compact,
small version of what Sebastian craved, apparently.

Danielle had to face up to the physical attraction between them, and the knowledge that he wasn't hers to touch.
She desperately wanted him, and she was sure that he would
be more than willing to make love to her if she allowed. But
her mother's marriage came back to haunt her. Danielle
wouldn't let Sebastian make her feel vulnerable and in the
end, used and discarded.

You had to keep emotions in a compartment, doling them
out cautiously only to those who would reciprocate in kind,
didn't you? That was the only sensible thing to do.

That night, she awoke to go to the bathroom. The light
played softly over the walls as her gaze turned to the other
twin bed. He had slipped in sometime during the night. His
bronze shoulders and chest lay bare, a contrast against the
white sheets. He looked so vulnerable, his eyes closed, the
dark swath of eyelashes against the hard, brown planes of
his cheek. His long, sensuous mouth relaxed, looking so
kissable.

She turned away and closed the door behind her.

The next morning, Concheta woke her by pulling back the
drapes and opening the windows.

That morning, Danielle became anxious to try the remaining keys on the underground chambers. Instinct told
her the fewer people who knew about her explorations, the
better, so she didn't ask Peter or Lupe how to get to the
rooms. She would have to locate them on her own. Problem was, it sounded as if there might be two sets of underground chambers, one that housed the generators or those
closer, underneath the house itself.

To clear her mind she rode Princessa, alone, with no comment from Sebastian. She walked the perimeter of the cleared meadow, hesitant to venture into the thick jungle.

Sebastian's relaxed, playful mood at the seashore had vanished on their returning to King's Ransom. It was as if he was reminded of their business agreement and wanted to keep it that way. He was polite and attentive this morning, and if the servants thought the cool behavior of the newly-weds was odd, they kept their own counsel.

Back at the house she had no problem locating the underground passage to the generators. There was no use for keys down there because there were no locks on the doors. The rooms were filled with noise and the smell of diesel fuel, but no side rooms that looked promising. She couldn't wait to get out.

Pocketing the keys, she wandered outside again, walking nonchalantly around the perimeter of the house. It took a while to make the circuit. She became dusty and scratched from pushing back bushes and roses near the house, crawling behind, but there were no doors from outside, she could vouch for that.

That meant the hidden rooms had to be accessed from inside the house. It would have been so much simpler to ask Sebastian, Peter or even Lupe where the rooms were, but then everyone would know about the keys. Apparently someone already knew. The feeling that she was being watched was so strong as to make goose bumps rise along her arms.

She waited impatiently for the household to settle down for the afternoon siesta.

Since the logical place to start would be the study, she began there, feeling the walls, moving paintings aside. Just about to give up and move into another area, she touched the side of the desk and felt a whiff of stale air.

The hairs on the back of her neck stirred as she turned and saw the small door behind a bookcase that she had thought permanently attached to the wall. The door had a lock, which was probably opened only by the stolen key. Before she had a chance to try her set of keys, the grandfather clock dolefully tolled out the time—siesta was almost over. Everyone would be underfoot and Sebastian was due back for his shower and appearance at the dinner table.

Her explorations would have to wait.

To pass the time, she went out to the gardens, offering to help Ramon, but it seemed to make him nervous, as if he thought she did not approve of his work. He obviously did not want anyone to intrude in his domain.

Danielle couldn't remember when she hadn't worked, after school to help her mother make ends meet and, then learning her trade in the garment industry. She wasn't used to a life of indolent luxury and even though at first it felt extravagantly grand, she was becoming bored with the uselessness of her existence.

She wandered back into the study, unable to stay away from the forbidden room. Patting the keys in her pocket, her fingers itched to try them on the secret door. Patience was not one of her virtues and she knew it.

A set of books lay scattered across the big rolltop desk, and she opened one, recognizing the delicate, lacy handwriting of her grandmother. After that, someone else's handwriting took over—Sebastian's maybe? The pages were smeared, half-filled, the entries sporadic, some days entirely missing.

Great! She had learned something about bookkeeping in one of her jobs. It couldn't be that hard to transcribe bills and receipts. At least it was a way to keep busy for a while.

She picked up a sheaf of papers and the afternoon sped by. Before it was time for dinner, she hastily stashed everything away again and pulled down the roll top exactly as it was before. She would bring it all up to date and surprise him.

"Who in the hell has been messing with my books?" She heard the bellow all through the house that evening as she prepared to descend the stairs for dinner.

She rushed into the study and stood at the door, watching Sebastian for a moment before she answered, chin in the air.

"It took me hours, I thought you'd be pleased to have it in order."

"Well, I am. But you might have asked first. These are private papers and..."

There he was again, thinking she was trying to gain some control of this place. As he flipped through the neat pages, she could tell his anger was fizzling out.

"You did a good job." His tone was grudging. "I forget that you have as much right to do what you want here as I do."

She saw no need to take any guff from him, especially for trying to do a favor. "You're missing the point. It isn't that I have a right to be here. The simple matter is, I've nothing to do with my time. I saw a need to help—or I thought it was helping—so I did it. I guess I should have asked."

"Me and my big mouth. I hate those damn books, you can see that. I'm sorry if I came on so strong. I apologize. Feel free to pitch in anytime."

It was the first time he had made a concession when he was angry. She considered it a good omen.

That evening after dinner, Sebastian retired to his old room early, said he wanted to read. She lay awake for hours, waiting for the noises of the house to settle so she could begin exploring. Tiptoeing downstairs, she crept toward the study. Sebastian was the only one she had to worry about awakening; the servants had their own quarters and would stay there until morning.

She opened the study door carefully, her heart beating wildly in her chest. Then it almost stopped still as she shone her flashlight toward the desk. A figure sat behind it!

Making a sudden decision, she flipped on the light.

Sebastian sat in the chair, sound-asleep. Even the sudden intrusion of the light did not waken him.

Danielle looked at him for a long time, feeling guilty at seeing the vulnerable, unguarded Sebastian. He had been looking so tired today. Something to do with the vanilla was worrying him, but he refused to talk about it. She wouldn't have known that much if Concheta had not passed along gossip she'd heard from the others.

Disappointed in having to wait until tomorrow, Danielle retreated to their bedroom to an uneasy sleep.

The next morning, as she stood on her terrace to look out over the garden, she saw Sebastian and Teresa walking together. They didn't come close to touching, but the aura surrounding them bespoke familiarity.

Why should I care? She turned away from the sight and flopped down on her bed.

Raoul came to pay a polite call in the late morning, and even though she did not like or trust the handsome, suave man, she desperately needed the boost of ego he gave her by his compliments and the way his eyes devoured her.

Even though Sebastian had warned her countless times not to be alone with their neighbor, she felt certain it was only childish possessiveness on his part. He could not bear to have the servants spread rumors that she might prefer another's company to his, and yet he had Teresa's friendship.

"Will you ride with me today?" Raoul asked.

She moved a little away...he always wanted to sit so close. "Ah...I don't think so."

He laughed, the amusement not touching his dark eyes. "I see. The new husband—he is guarding his property. Sebastian has warned you not to be alone with me, yes?"

Even before we were married, she wanted to say, but didn't. "I'm not anyone's property. Of course I can ride with anyone I choose."

"Come then, let's give the horses a good run."

As they trotted off together, he gallantly ignored her inexperience and held his mount back to stay close to her.

"You know what I can't understand?" Danielle spoke after a small silence when they'd started back toward the house.

"What is that?" he answered.

"How Doña Mercedes could have been thrown by Princessa. She was a much better horsewoman than I'll probably ever be. Yet this horse has never tried to throw me. Except that once when you..."

"When I stopped so suddenly and you rammed into me?" He said it so suavely, giving her part of the blame.

"Yes. Well, I just can't understand it, is all."

He shrugged. "*Quien sabe?* Who knows how things happen? Fate perhaps? I hear you had a little accident yourself...with the attic stairs...before you ah—before you went on your honeymoon."

She started to tell him about it, explain that she didn't think it was an accident but stopped in midbreath. How silly to confide in him; she hadn't changed her mind about its not being an accident. The logical ones wanting to prevent her marriage to Sebastian were the brother and sister. They feigned nonchalance about their mother's obsession to combine the two plantations, but Danielle hadn't missed the stark avarice in Teresa's expression when the woman had visited.

"Yes, well, it was nothing, really. A stair broke underfoot, clumsy me."

"You could have been hurt. That is a long fall."

So, he knew the details. That didn't prove much, servants were so talkative.

"One wonders what you would be doing in a dusty old attic."

She started to retort that it was none of his business, and then changed her mind. Maybe she could draw him out. She had to take a chance; he was easier to talk to than his sister.

"I went upstairs to look for Doña Mercedes's wedding gown. There's something fishy about the attic," she said in a confiding tone she hoped he would swallow.

"What do you mean?" She watched for a flicker of interest in his dark eyes, but saw nothing unusual. Maybe he was just a good poker player.

"I think someone is snooping around up there. I have no idea why they'd be doing that."

He didn't comment, only waited for her to continue.

"I don't have anything specific, I guess. My grandmother imagined she heard strange noises at night and I thought I heard something one night."

"I do not think you heard anything, *cariña,* but I do wish you would be careful. You are too lovely to be..."

"To be what?"

He shrugged, with his shoulders and his hands. "It is just an observation. However, I can tell prudence is not your nature. Neither was it Doña Mercedes's."

Was that a threat?

"It is only gossip you have listened to. I have heard none of your silly servants will go near the room since Don Henry died there. For myself, I would never tolerate such insubordination from the hired help. They do as *I* say, not as *they* wish."

Disgusted by his attitude, Danielle was more than able to hide her disappointment that he didn't seem the least interested in her bait.

When he brought her back, he leapt from his horse to help her dismount before the stableboy could do it. Bowing low, he held her hand and kissed her palm lingeringly.

Nothing prepared her for the anger Sebastian turned on her when he stepped up on the veranda that evening. She had been sitting, listening to the birds in the nearby jungle getting ready for night... it was a comforting, cozy sound. She wore her new lime green dress, hoping he would notice. He did.

He reached down, and placing his big hand behind her head, lifted her to her feet, pulling her against his dusty, work-stained body. Then he lifted her chin and kissed her brutally, his tongue reaching inside her mouth, searching, probing. She could feel her pulse quicken and knew he must feel it through the thin fabric of her dress. No! He wouldn't humiliate her again as he did once before to make a point. She struggled against the iron bonds of his arms.

He released her abruptly. Shaken, neither of them spoke for a long moment. When she regained her composure, she looked up at him angrily.

"You said you would respect our arrangement," she whispered. "You promised." Her voice trembled, making her even more angry.

He smoothed back her hair, his hand suddenly gentle, but his eyes were hard, his mouth a cruel line. "I think you enjoyed it as much as I, Danielle. At any rate, I will not permit you to share the charms you deny me."

"This is about Raoul, isn't it? I..." She started to say she only went riding with him, but changed her mind. Why should she defend herself, she'd done nothing unseemly. They were neighbors, after all, and what about Sebastian's walking with Teresa?

"If I didn't know better, I'd think you were jealous," she taunted. "But no, nothing so human, it's just that arrogant, macho pride." She still couldn't bear to confront him with his walking with Teresa. If she did, she would appear no better than he with his silly possessiveness.

After they shared an uncomfortable dinner, she went upstairs to their rooms. He was not long in joining her, which was a surprise—last night he came in after she fell asleep. At least now she knew he spent most of last night in the study *alone*.

He made no move to dress privately, but sat on his bed, taking off his shirt and unzipping his trousers as he had done once before at the beach. He completely ignored her presence as if she weren't there. Already in bed, she refused to allow him to know he infuriated her, so she pretended to sleep, turning toward the window with her back to him.

He apparently wasn't buying it.

"Did you enjoy your little ride today, then?" His quiet voice raked aside the barrier of silence she had erected between them.

She sat up in bed, looking at him, oblivious to his state of dress or undress. "Of course I did. A harmless ride with a neighbor, I might add. And did you enjoy your walk in the garden with Teresa?" There, she'd finally said it.

His face suffused with anger and she hastened to add, "How long do we have to continue this pathetic farce of a marriage? I could fly back to New York tomorrow."

"You are joking!" he bellowed. "It is too soon."

"No, I'm completely serious." She refused to let him intimidate her with his scowl and raised voice. "Doña

Mercedes did not want King's Ransom merged with the Contreras plantation, you know that better than I." He had prodded her to speaking with her anger and not her heart.

His mouth dropped in astonishment. "You must have guessed it had been my intention to buy out your interest, but I needed time to get in this season's crop. I told Paul from the beginning that was the only reason I could agree to the marriage. I bargained for time."

She felt the stab to her heart but she yawned and stretched, a nonchalance that was only pretense. "I'm growing fond of this old place. You might never get rid of me. Maybe we'll have to build two separate houses."

He groaned and turned his body away from her. She could see the wide, tanned shoulders, the muscles in his arms working spasmodically as he clenched his fist.

"This place wouldn't last a month without my supervision. I'm the only thing that has held it together since Doña Mercedes became ill."

"Maybe Raoul would help me," she offered. Once she had spoken, she knew she had gone too far.

"Damn it, woman!" He lunged out of bed and stood facing her, shaken with anger. He had put on pajama bottoms; she confirmed that once she dared look at him.

At last he was goaded out of his smug self-control and now she wasn't sure she could handle him.

With a visible effort, he gained his composure and went back to sit on his bed. "What you need is a little sterner discipline, my sweet wife. Women here do not possess the equality that you take so much for granted." His voice sounded gentle, but she was not deceived.

"What do you mean? What could you possibly do to me?"

"Oh, nothing so crude as you may be thinking, *mi vida*. King's Ransom needs a proper hostess, and in spite of your flirtation with Raoul, I perceive you as every inch a lady. Until such time as you leave of your own free will, if you step out of bounds with Raoul, I will be forced to divorce you on the grounds of adultery. I can take everything from you."

Her golden eyes glinted with unexpressed tears. She had once made herself believe that the only reason she'd stayed was her promise to a grandmother she barely knew. But that wasn't true. She wanted to be near Sebastian. She had made the mistake of falling in love with her husband. And now he was saying things that hurt to the quick. She put her hands over her ears in an effort to shut him out.

When she saw that he was not speaking, she took her hands down and regarded him, the room crackling with expended intensity. "What about Teresa? Am I not to be accorded the same respect you demand for yourself? Somehow I thought you'd be different."

"Teresa is a childhood friend. You and Raoul are barely acquaintances. Further, there is no reason for you to be jealous of my relationship with her. If I had ever wanted to marry her, I would have done so long ago. Your grandmother knew what her interference in your mother's marriage cost her—had I chosen Teresa as my bride, Doña Mercedes would not have disowned me."

He took in a deep breath, then continued. "However, Beaumont is a respected name, and whether I came by it rightly in your eyes or not, your grandparents were willing to share it with me. I would not care to see it diminished by scandal."

"You sound so pompous!" she retorted. "You make all the rules, pass out all the stipulations as if I were of no consequence. Like I'm a boarder here. I suppose you are ready to mete out more terms for me to follow? And what am I to receive from you in return?"

He looked pained. "And what in hell do you expect from me, Danielle? We've been together—how many months? If I don't make some rules— I'm not made of steel, only flesh and blood."

This admission, wrung from him against his will, gave her a surge of joy mixed with sadness for the ugly words that lay between them. Yet she had to stay on guard.

He would use her love, toss her aside when the marriage was finished, and she could go back to New York with her tail between her legs like her mother had. No thanks.

"Look," he said, "it'll work out in time. You once told me that, remember?"

She remembered. It seemed like a year ago, so much had happened so quickly.

"Maybe you've just got too much time on your hands. Tomorrow, I'll take you out to the vanilla grove. You can see the workers' quarters and look around to your heart's content."

Her ruffled feelings quieted at his reasonable words. "I'd like that."

As she lay in the dark, so close to him and yet so far away, she knew what she really wanted. She wanted him to love her. Really love her as a husband loved a wife.

She would hold on fiercely until the last. Her way was a gamble, but it was the only way she knew.

CHAPTER SIXTEEN

Early the next morning, after a hearty breakfast together, Sebastian walked with her in the direction of the stables. She was surprised, expecting to use one of the trucks or the Land Rover.

"We could drive, but I wanted you to see something of the countryside," he explained as he patted his black horse. He wouldn't let any of the stable workers saddle the huge stallion, and Danielle surmised that was just as well with them.

Neither of them spoke for a while. She inhaled the heady scent of the jungle on both sides of the road, actually little more than a trail wide enough for a vehicle or two horses side by side.

Finally she broke the silence, feeling she should say something. "Is this where you spend most of your time? In the vanilla grove?"

He shook his head. "Not usually. Manuel is damn good as an overseer, even if he is young. The women and children do most of the work this time of year. I spend a great deal of my time on the west side of the plantation, with the banana crop. We had a blight last year and lost a big share of the plants. I had to bring in new ones."

"It's odd to think of women and children doing most of the work," she began, trying to avoid the intrusion of the picture of Teresa and Manuel together so close. What would Sebastian think about it? she wondered.

He laughed, an easy laugh, the kind she liked to hear. "Don't go getting your Yankee dander up about women and children working. This time of year the flowers on the vanilla plant must be pollinated. It requires a delicate hand; letting Mother Nature take her course would be too haphazard. It's not hard...a good worker can pollinate two thousand flowers a day."

"How?"

"You'll have to watch. That's what you came out to do, isn't it? Another half hour and we'll be there. Tired?"

Her back ached and she knew the muscles in her thighs would be on fire by tomorrow, but it was worth it. Huge orchids hung on the sides of the big-leaved trees, amazing colors she would have loved to capture in some of her clothing designs. "I'm okay. Even Princessa is enjoying the day."

"Of course. She needs a good run. Mercedes used to do it often before her accident."

"Speaking of my grandmother, she mentioned strangers in the village. Strangers asking questions about King's Ransom. We never did get to finish that conversation."

"Doña Mercedes had full control of her mind even to the end, but her emotions—that was something else again. She always felt someone wanted to take King's Ransom away from us. From her."

"But did you check it out?"

"My, you're persistent, but then so was Doña Mercedes. Yes, of course I checked it out. Strangers, that's all, curious strangers. Probably land speculators. They left and never came back as far as I know. And I would know if they had."

"Well, how about the union sympathizers that came here years ago? Couldn't they have caused the big plantations to split up? You must own thousands of acres, the Contreras also. Didn't those men have other axes to grind besides stirring up the workers?"

"You're right, they did. Some of them were Communists, rebels imported from Cuba. They wanted an uprising, almost got it at the Contreras's place, but we managed to thoroughly discourage them; I doubt they'll ever come back. Our people are treated well, and they know it."

"Maybe so, but there is always room for improvement."

A grunt was his only reply and she let it go.

When they arrived at the vanilla grove, she didn't have to be told. The smell wafted through the air as if on a pleasant fog. "Are those vanilla trees?" she asked, amazed at the huge, towering trees planted in rows.

He grinned. "An easy mistake to make. No, the trees are planted to support the vanilla plants which are vines. Actually, the vanilla is an orchid. We have some older vines over three-hundred-feet long."

They passed through a narrow opening and into the fragrant grove. Shy smiles greeted them as women and children stopped their work for a moment to look at Sebastian and Danielle. He helped her dismount and said something in rapid Spanish to the nearest workers. They giggled and rolled their eyes heavenward.

"What did you tell them?"

"Only that you are the new Señora Beaumont."

"Only? It sounded more than that to me."

He grinned and brushed the hair from the side of her cheek in a familiar gesture that quickened her heartbeat. She turned away before he could see what the nonchalant action meant to her.

He took her arm to draw her closer to an older woman who was ignoring their presence and was busy pollinating.

"The flowers only stay open one day, so it is a continual process. After that, it takes nine months for the pod to ripen."

"Nine months!"

"Exactly. The same gestation period of a human. Odd isn't it?"

The sun filtered down into the dappled grove. Far away she heard a voice singing one of those doleful Spanish ballads. It was like being in another world, a strange feeling. Danielle turned to watch a woman as she skillfully lifted a little tongue of a flower with a small stick and pressed the stamen and pistil together in one motion of her deft fingers.

"Amazing. I had no idea what went into making vanilla."

"Most people don't. That's why the real stuff is so expensive. And you wouldn't believe the amount of red tape involved in importing and exporting the beans. We don't have any decent processing plants here in this country. Not yet."

As they walked along leading their horses, here and there she could see a mother with a baby strapped to her back or front, working among the greenish-yellow flowers.

Sebastian grinned down at her. "They are all talking about your hair."

"My hair? Why?"

"They think it is beautiful, but they also think you are too skinny." He laughed.

She smiled back, unperturbed. "Well, I guess one out of two isn't bad. If I'm here long enough, they'll be calling me La Chaparrita like they did my grandmother."

"Don't laugh. Most of the household servants do now. At first they thought I might object, but if the shoe fits...well, you know what I mean."

"Did my grandmother know?"

"Of course, but no one ever dared use that name to Doña Mercedes's face—she would have cremated them with a glance. She didn't go in much for pleasantries . . . she was from the old school, the European way, I guess. Sometimes I think a lot of that rubbed off on me."

There it was again, the vision of an orphan boy growing up with plenty to eat, a sumptuous place to live, an education to be proud of, but did he feel loved? Had her grandmother been too old and too hardened by what had happened to her to give him the love he'd needed? On the other hand, who ever got enough love?

She did, for one thing. She had been very close to her mother right up to the day she died, neither having anyone else to cling to.

"Sure you don't mind?" she asked. "Them calling me that, I mean."

"I'm sure. The sound of it brings her back a little. Funny how they have accepted you so early. People here reserve little names only for those they most admire and respect."

Just then, Manuel rode up to greet them, mounted on a trim, dark gelding. There was no mistaking the relationship between Concheta and her brother, although Manuel had none of Concheta's sweet shyness.

"Ah, Don Sebastian, welcome Señora Beaumont." His smile behind the black mustache was wide, as if he had just invited her into his living room to meet his family.

His meeting with Teresa could have been very innocent. She wanted to believe that.

"Don Sebastian does not lately offer us the favor of his visit. I fear the bananas have claimed his attention." Manuel spoke with a teasing banter, an easy smile on his lips. He dismounted and walked beside them.

Sebastian put a hand on Manuel's slim shoulder. "It is because you are the best overseer I have, that is the only reason I can turn my back on this place and attend to something that needs me more."

As the young man swelled with pride, Sebastian slanted a look of gratitude toward Danielle that made her smile. So, he had taken her advice and showed Manuel that he trusted him. Maybe he shouldn't have.

"I'm going to show the *señora* the workers' quarters next," Sebastian was saying.

"*Por supuesto.* But of course, we have very good homes for our people," Manuel said proudly.

"He's right, they're not fancy, but more than adequate."

"Workers from all the plantations around here want to quit their *patrónes* and come here. Sometimes I think the women make their men come just for the houses," Manuel said.

"Here it is." Sebastian pushed back an outcropping brush for her and they walked inside a large clearing with huge trees left here and there for shade. Children played all around the compound. The loud, happy shouts stopped when some of the older ones saw the visitors and stood watching their approach.

Danielle looked at the small, compact houses, with shaggy, thatched roofs. Open doorways and glassless windows looked out at them, as if open to their invasion of privacy without complaint. She could see no signs of curtains or anything to cover the gaping doorways. The area was clean and litter-free in spite of all the children.

"This is—ah—nice. Nice, Sebastian. But it almost looks too clean. No curtains, no flowerpots in the yards, nothing personal, looks like a row of motel rooms. And shouldn't these kids be in school?"

Sebastian grimaced. "You cannot judge our country by your standards, my love. These people have come from laborers, generations ago, as long as anyone has had a plantation here. The small ones do not work, of course. The next in size must stay home to watch them, and the next size up works in the fields, or if they are females, in the vanilla. It is all they know. They are not unhappy."

Manuel flashed a smile, white against his dark face. "Oh, they are very happy, *señora.*"

"It looks fine." She didn't want to hurt anyone's feelings. It did seem as if a lot of planning and workmanship went into the little settlement.

"You think about curtains, about flowers, about covered doorways, I understand that a woman..."

He sounded patronizing. She didn't mean him to take it "from a woman's point of view."

"It's just that it looks sort of... bleak. Cheerless, I don't know..." She threw up her hands in frustration of trying not to hurt his feelings and trying to express her own. How odd, she had never before given a thought to what she said before she said it.

To her surprise, he seemed to appreciate her interest. "You're right. There are no frills here; the women probably don't see the need. In the village a few miles away, there are cantinas. The men go at night to gamble, and drink, and often there is nothing left for anything but food."

"I'm sure women have the need. It's not much different in parts of New York—"

"We are not a slum!" he interrupted her, his frown crashing together over his eyes.

"No, I didn't mean that." She didn't mean it—the houses were clean, high and dry, the landscape grassy and perfect for children.

"We set up a supply wagon twice a month, bringing back food from the city. They pay only what the food cost us. That way, I know the families are getting a fair share of the food."

They continued the inspection and Danielle felt impressed by what she saw. The women working in the vanilla grove looked contented. It was shady, they shouted, sang and gossiped back and forth as they worked. She thought it a very pleasant place to be on a hot afternoon.

On the way back to the house, they rode side by side, content to listen to the jungle sounds around them. Danielle had ideas that thrummed around in her head, but had no concept of how to implement them. As if he knew her thoughts, Sebastian spoke into the stillness.

"I've been thinking. You should have some funds of your own to spend on personal things. I'll see to it when we get back."

"You don't have to do that," she protested. "I have a small trust fund at home that my mother left me." How could he have known what she was thinking?

"Nonsense. It would be difficult to draw from money in the States, and why should you? Half of this plantation is yours, are you forgetting?"

"I don't have anywhere to go to spend money." She made one more weak attempt at a protest.

"Someone goes into the city as often as twice a month, more often when necessary. Manuel is going tomorrow, I think. I imagine they get bored bringing back the same old supplies. Tell me what you need, I'll explain it to them if they don't understand. Or you can ride up with them any time you feel the urge to get away for a while. This must be pretty confining to you."

Was he asking a question or making one of his irrefutable statements? She looked at him, but his head was turned, watching two parrots together in a tree. A flash of color and they were gone as the horses passed.

Gone as quickly as the moment when she could have told him how much she was coming to feel at home here and how much she worried about what could be happening behind the scenes at King's Ransom.

The next morning, Sebastian kept his word. Lying on the dresser between them was a long envelope with a generous amount of currency in it.

Danielle sat on the edge of her bed and formed a plan. Only it surely wasn't necessary that Sebastian knew of her plans; he would either think it a typical woman's thing or mistrust her interference. Either way, she didn't want to bring that out of him. If what she wanted to do worked, she could tell him later.

She didn't want to tell Manuel, for some reason, but telling Concheta was a must, so she had to trust Manuel for now, at least with this little secret.

Peter was the unknown quality. Fiercely loyal to Doña Mercedes, and now Sebastian, all the household servants never let him hear any of their idle gossip. Ah well, he was inside most of the time.

Manuel was making one of his city trips today, and Danielle gave him her long list and cautioned him to store the supplies away from Peter or Sebastian's sight.

"Are you certain this will not anger El Jefe?" Manuel looked worried. Since the last time he was nearly fired, he had lost some of his cocky self-assurance.

"No. You see by the list, it is nothing to concern Don Sebastian." She felt a little shame, knowing she was calling on his indebtedness to her for having spoken up on his behalf to Sebastian and having helped save his job. The gossip had made its rounds about that long ago.

That night, she crept down the stairs, flashlight in hand, heading straight for the study. Once there, she closed the door firmly behind her and flipped on the lights, as if she expected to see Sebastian sitting in the chair again. She pushed against the desk corner. Nothing happened!

Panicky, she pushed on another corner, and with a loud squeak, the bookcase swung away, showing the low doorway. She rushed forward, to try the bunch of keys in the rusty old lock. She didn't expect any of them to work, the missing key was probably the one she needed. But no, finally one clicked and she pushed the door open, bent her head and walked in before she could change her mind.

Once inside the chamber or tunnel, she had no recourse but to close the door behind her, otherwise she couldn't get past it on the narrow stairs. Before it shut, she went back to the study for a book, sticking it inside the door so it wouldn't close all the way.

The stairs were on a gradual slope, as if they were carved out of the earth beneath the house and petrified with time and protection from the elements. The dank mustiness clogged her nostrils, causing her to sneeze. She didn't feel nervous about making noise, certain that no one was here. She had the only set of keys, didn't she?

Unless that stolen key had been a duplicate of the one that had opened the door.

She shone her light ahead and saw the leveling off as the tunnel continued. Danielle tried not to think of bugs and snakes, maybe it was too dark and closed for them, anyway.

The tunnel suddenly divided. Which way? She kneeled down to inspect the earth closely. The right side seemed more worn, more used. She turned in that direction. She hadn't walked long before the air smelled fresher, as if a breath of outside air mixed with the stale, earthy smell.

She hurried toward it.

Suddenly, the tunnel ended in a wide room. Her gaze was drawn to a grill up high with pale, shaded light coming through. An outside door! And she had looked so thoroughly for one.

Walking the circumference of the room, shining her light against the walls, disappointment took the edge off her unease when she saw the piles and stacks of burlap bags along the edge. Then a terrible thought came in a flash.

Oh Lordy, was it cocaine? Was someone on the plantation mixed up with drugs? She hurriedly bent to open a bag

Pods! Vanilla pods. So preoccupied with sinister visions of dope smuggling, she allowed the rich, strong smell of vanilla to penetrate her senses.

Why would someone go to such lengths to stash away vanilla beans? Perhaps Sebastian was just hiding the vanilla here to protect it. But then the conversation with Sebastian came back to her; he had said the beans were very valuable and the paperwork with officials was an even greater deterrent to free trade. Then did Sebastian himself conspire to sell these, maybe on some kind of black market?

She shook her head, not believing it. Not quite. From what she had seen, he had poured his whole life into King's Ransom; he wouldn't do anything to harm it. The set of books on the desk in the study, the outrage he first revealed when he knew someone had worked with them, his belief that she was out to wrest her share from him, all those doubts assailed her now and she broke out in a cold sweat.

Who could she turn to for answers? Should she let it alone? If it was Sebastian, it was his business, wasn't it? She had asked nothing from King's Ransom.

It was something she would have to think about, long and hard.

CHAPTER SEVENTEEN

To take her mind off what was happening below the house, she concentrated on her plans for the workers' compound. The purchases had been stashed away in a corner of the stables, so that Sebastian wouldn't find them.

"This afternoon I must go to the coast for a few days," Sebastian told her this morning as she sat in the rose garden watching Ramon. "I could take you, but it will be so dull. No honeymoon this time." His mouth curled around a grin.

She looked away, disappointed that he was leaving, until she realized it would give her the perfect opportunity to work on the compound. "I don't care to leave, really. I'm perfectly satisfied here, thanks."

He looked skeptical, but said no more.

"I hope you have a good journey," she managed to say. "What vehicle are you taking?" Already she was thinking of her plans, having trouble holding in her excitement. No one worked on Sundays, the women and children would be in the compound.

"The Land Rover, I think. I was going to drive the pickup, but I don't trust the automatic transmission on those roads."

Sebastian looked at her strangely as he kissed her on the cheek and left.

Perfect. She had to wait until late afternoon, when the pickup was free. Now if she only remembered her driving lessons. One year she'd had the remarkably silly idea of buying a car and had taken lessons. A car in New York City was the dumbest idea she had ever had, but with an automatic, there shouldn't be much of a problem remembering.

She and the stableboy loaded her purchases in the trunk. "If anyone asks, I am visiting the Contreras plantation," she told the boy. No one had ever invited her there, but she needed some excuse to take out the truck. The gossip would begin immediately, this might put a stop to it.

Concheta was supposed to wait beyond the bend in the trail; Danielle wanted to protect her if Sebastian found out about this before she told him and didn't approve. Concheta wanted her brother to help but Danielle still felt odd about Manuel, somehow not trusting him since his meeting with Teresa. If only she knew whether she could trust Sebastian!

After she picked up Concheta, waiting by the side of the road as promised, she pointed the truck down the rutty road. They didn't talk much on the trip. Danielle could tell the young woman was worried, probably about Sebastian's reaction if he learned of this.

When they arrived at the workers' compound, Concheta leaped out of the cab after her, rapid Spanish rolling off her tongue. It was mealtime, the smell of cooking beans and scorched tortillas filled the air. The women cooked outdoors in front of their houses, each with a fireplace built from a discarded rectangular gas tank. It looked as if they used hubcaps for a wok to fry in.

Concheta called everyone, introducing the new Señora Beaumont. Soon children, dogs and women crowded around the truck. The women and older children wore expressions subdued and reserved, while the little ones and the pile of dogs set up such a noise that Danielle had to cover her ears, laughing.

"Ask them to bring a blanket and lay it in front of each house," Danielle instructed Concheta.

When the women hurried to comply, Danielle and Concheta divided the contents of the packages.

A collective gasp broke from the throats of the watching women as they looked in round-eyed awe at the assortment at their feet. Danielle reached down and lifted one bolt of brightly colored material; in the other hand, she showed them thread, needles and scissors.

"I thought you may like curtains on your windows."

Concheta translated and the women looked back in stunned disbelief.

"I hope there are enough flowerpots and seeds for every one of you, I just guessed." Next trip she would bring pots and pans to cook with.

Concheta told them they could each have several of the brightly painted clay pots for their little patios.

"Also here is some netting, to hang on your windows and doorways to deter mosquitoes and flies," she told them.

They all nodded, not needing Concheta's translation to understand what the netting was for.

The women looked at the treasures and then back at Danielle. No one spoke, even the children were silent, sensing their mothers' moods. Finally, an older woman broke out in rapid Spanish, shook her head sadly and turned away, the others beginning to follow.

"Wait! Don't go!" She turned to Concheta. "Why are they leaving?"

The girl smiled. "They say it is all very beautiful, but they cannot buy any of it."

"But it isn't for sale."

"I know. You tell them," Concheta said, smiling.

"Ah, I can't . . ."

"Yes, you can. Your Spanish is as good as my pitiful English and you understand me. They must hear it from *la Patróna*."

Haltingly at first, prompted a time or two with a whisper from Concheta, Danielle explained that King's Ransom was giving them the gifts, no strings attached. They did not have to pay anything. She explained that all must share equally, that the material was for curtains and doorways and anything left over could be used to make clothes for their children.

Danielle watched with tears in her eyes as the women cried out in gratitude and began thanking her over and over. Some of them picked up a piece of material, holding it to their cheeks as if inhaling the odor of newness.

Several men stood in the background, not speaking, looking with masculine disdain at this woman-thing taking place. When Danielle looked toward them, they were clearing their throats, suspicion in their eyes, while Concheta cried and hugged the women.

Danielle had to visit each little house, sit for a sip of cocoa or coffee, whatever the woman had to offer, listen to the older ones talk of *La Chaparrita Vieja,* her grandmother. She didn't understand a lot, but it was coming in more and more, with Concheta's help.

It was dark by the time they headed home.

She and Concheta didn't speak for a while. Danielle had to concentrate on holding the pickup steady on the road with only the headlights to guide her.

"Now, if only there was some way to bring schooling to the children," Danielle mused aloud.

"Señora Rodriguez has a daughter—she wanted her to become a nun and gave Marta to the church."

"What happened? What does that have to do with us?" Concheta rarely finished one story before starting another.

Concheta looked sad for a moment. "Her mother became ill, Marta had to come back, there was no one to care for her. She never finished her training but decided not to go back. She never married. Works in vanilla now."

"Are you saying maybe Marta could teach the children? Would she?"

Concheta nodded. "Could be. She is very bossy, like a teacher and hates working in the vanilla grove."

"Wonderful! I don't have much money left but I'll have enough to buy some books, tablets and pencils." For the first time since she'd arrived at King's Ransom, Danielle began to feel useful again. For a while, she had to admit, pampering felt good, but that old Yankee enthusiasm for work, that inability to sit around doing nothing, made her feel like one of those captured finches that each household in the compound seemed to own.

She wondered what Sebastian would have to say about all these new developments—and how much could she tell him?

* * *

When Sebastian returned, he remained shut in the study with Peter for a while, which disappointed Danielle. She had hoped he might search out her company after being gone so long. She missed him during the day, but the nights were intolerably long—nights she spent staring at his empty bed. Sometimes she lay on his bed and fell asleep, just to feel close to him.

Her next thought was, had he found out about her project before she was ready for him to know? Secrets were hard to keep around the plantation, yet everyone loved surprises. That might keep a lid on things until she decided when to tell him.

She probably should have confided in him from the beginning except that he could have refused permission for her to "meddle." She didn't want to take that chance. Later it wouldn't matter so much, he couldn't undo it, could he?

Danielle didn't see him until dinner. It was as if he was staying out of her way deliberately.

"Well, how was your trip?" She had been sitting at the long dining-room table, fiddling with her silver, thinking maybe he wasn't coming down.

"Fine." His eyes, with their smoky fringe of lashes, searched her face for a long moment and then he sat in his usual place. "Fine, thank you." His voice was exceedingly polite, as before her grandmother died. Since then, he had acted warmer, less formidable. Until now.

"Anything wrong?" She spoke and then they had to wait until the salad was served and they were alone again.

He shrugged. "What could be wrong? It was a difficult trip. Aggravating."

"I'm sorry to hear that. Perhaps you will tell me about it." She felt uneasy, wanting now to tell him about her project, but feeling it wasn't the time, not when he was so troubled.

"How did you amuse yourself while I was gone?" His voice was calm, but the muscles in his jaw were tight. Did he know something? Something more than about her project—something about the underground vanilla?

"Ah, well, I just meandered around the plantation a bit, you know, poking into things here and there." There was a new, watchful mistrust in his eyes. No, it wasn't the time to tell him anything.

For the next several days, Danielle thought Sebastian acted very strangely. He rarely spoke to her, the camaraderie displaced by something akin to the early mistrust he'd shown her. She asked Concheta one morning.

"Did you tell Don Sebastian about our trip?" she asked. "Wait, it's okay if you did, I'm not going to hit the roof about it, I just want to know."

She shook her head vigorously. "No, *señora,* I said nothing about where we went. You ask me not to. *El Jefe* did ask Manuel if you took the truck out and of course he had to say yes."

"Oh, so that's it . . ." Danielle began.

"But *gracias de Dios,* Don Sebastian did not ask if we knew where you took it. We cannot lie to Don Sebastian, not for anyone."

"Of course not, I wouldn't want you to. I just don't want you to volunteer any information until I tell him."

"You will tell him then—soon? Lupe said that if Peter finds out first, he will surely tell and it will look bad for you."

Danielle had other things on her mind now than "looking bad," the underground tunnel with its stash of vanilla, for example. She heard no more searching in the attic at night, obviously someone had been searching for the key up there—and found it on Doña Mercedes's dresser. Danielle was glad for the new distraction she'd created for herself.

Marta volunteered to teach the children, according to Concheta, so she had to get that project going immediately before they all lost heart and abandoned the idea.

Rummaging through the garage this afternoon, looking for extra garden tools for the compound, she found a stack of old *National Geographic* magazines, some dating back from the forties. Perfect. They could practice English while they learned geography and history. Maybe even the adults would become interested.

"The children will start their school tomorrow," Concheta told her later while they were in her bedroom. Danielle followed the girl's troubled glance toward Sebastian's bed, understanding her fear of keeping such a secret from him.

This evening, if she even saw Mr. High-and-Mighty, she determined to get it out into the open. As if on command, he appeared in the hall.

"Sebastian, we have to talk." On his way in from the fields—dressed in his well-fitting cords, tall boots and open-at-the-throat shirt—he looked as if he might have posed for one of those cigarette company billboards back in the States.

She more than realized how much she had missed him.

"Very well, let's go into the study."

When they faced each other, she began, since he obviously wasn't going to open his mouth first.

"What's the matter with you? Is something wrong with the plantation? I've never seen you so grumpy."

"Grumpy?" The word came out like an explosion before he got control and calmed himself. "What reason would I have for being—ah—grumpy?"

"That's my point! I haven't a clue." She could think of a handful of reasons, for one, that he was stuck in a marriage to a woman he did not love.

He took her arm and stared down into her eyes. She felt mesmerized by the intense green. She longed to reach up and touch the scowl away from his dear face, touch the corners of his lips to turn them up just so, in that endearing grin.

Though he might not love her, Danielle knew that he was drawn to *her,* wanted *her.*

If she could just hold on to this thought and not let her temper become involved . . .

"Did you have a good shipment of bananas?" She changed the subject abruptly, moving away from him, wanting to prolong their time together.

He was silent a moment until she thought he wouldn't answer, but then he nodded. "Yes. It was a good one, but we're having trouble with that shipping line. They're a hard lot and their men are threatening strikes. I'll be working in the study through the night. I've got to go back tomorrow and look for another ship to use if I can't get it sorted out."

The vulnerable look in his eyes while he discussed mundane business surprised her; it was as if he wanted to tell her something and couldn't.

"I hope you don't roam too far from the house when you do your 'poking around,' as you put it." He held up his hand to stop her protest. "Oh, I know you're a grown woman, but we are on the fringes of the jungle. I'd prefer that you stay closer to home while I'm away," he said, before leaving the room and her bewildered.

It was as close to a request and not a demand as he'd ever allowed himself to make and she knew it. Though she hadn't had the chance to mention the compound, the time had come to ask him about the vanilla she'd found underground. But what if it involved more than she could even imagine—insurance, fraud—or what if it was such a serious matter that she could be in danger?

But if he wasn't involved, the very existence of King's Ransom might be in jeopardy. She made the decision then to investigate more before she told him. Time enough when he returned.

The next day, she grew restless and followed the sound of laughter into the kitchen. Several of the servants were there, and for a moment, the talk stopped until Concheta gestured toward a chair.

"Come, sit down, *señora*. Please."

"I don't want to interrupt," Danielle said. The kitchen was filled with delicious smells and she gratefully sat on the stool, propping her elbows on the bar and cupping her chin in her palms.

They smiled at her uncertainly, then Lupe, being the older and more respected, spoke.

"It is a good thing that you do for the people. School started this morning. The women and children are grateful—the men will be one day."

"Oh, it's my pleasure," Danielle answered.

Lupe cleared her throat importantly and continued. "We feel bad that you and Don Sebastian quarrel. Concheta thinks he loves you very much, but then what does *she* know, she's never even had a lover."

Danielle laughed at Concheta's outraged expression, but of course the girl dared not talk back. "We do not quarrel," she said firmly.

"No, perhaps that is the problem," Lupe countered. "I, too, think he loves you very much, but like most men, he has an inability to speak of it."

"No." It was time to speak freely to these loyal people, they deserved more than a brush-off. "No, I think he regrets our marriage. I don't think he loves me." There, she'd said it. She stood up and looked at them in turn. "But do not worry, I will not give up and just walk away!"

The women giggled and talked all at the same time in their excitement. Only Lupe remained unimpressed. Danielle could see herself, a fragile-looking young woman mirrored in Lupe's liquid chocolate eyes.

"You are a beauty. A honeybee is not drawn to a cactus. You wear *pantalones* like *hombre*. Concheta says you refuse to wear the beautiful clothing Don Sebastian bought for you. She said you even wear *pantalones* to bed!"

Danielle looked at Concheta, who flushed and refused to meet her stare. That was probably what the laughter had been about when she'd entered the kitchen and they all stopped. Curiously, it didn't bother her—maybe they had a point.

"Peter is the one who told Sebastian about me taking the truck, right?" She knew that for a certainty. He had to be the one spying and telling Sebastian she left the grounds.

Concheta nodded, her dark eyes filled with pity. "But, *señora,* he is not against you. I heard him tell Don Sebastian that you took the truck. It is his duty to tell Don Sebastian. That is all he said. You should have confided in Peter about the compound."

Danielle shook her head. "I couldn't. Peter would have told Sebastian and he might have stopped everything."

"But why would he do that? Sebastian is one of us, he loves the people." One of the maids spoke up.

"Maybe so, but it wasn't *his* idea. That could make the difference between what he considers meddling and what he thinks of as acceptable improvements."

As the women talked, Danielle stopped listening. All Sebastian's anger, all his sullen moods—only because he thought she had visited Raoul. For a mere second, the idea of Sebastian's being jealous sent a wild thrill through her body and then she stopped to think about it. No, he was only being protective, obsessive about his macho image.

She stood up and brushed her hands against her thighs with a gesture of finality. "None of you are to say a word until I tell him." If Sebastian could not trust her on his own accord, their relationship was doomed before it started.

The women looked at one another with uneasy concern on their faces, but nodded agreement.

Later that evening, Danielle dressed carefully for dinner. Maybe Lupe was right. It wouldn't hurt to try a little sex appeal. As much as she avoided the memory, the feel of his strong arms around her and his hard lips pressing against hers became more vivid with each passing day.

But what if he was the one who had tampered with the stairs in the attic? It wasn't such a foolish idea—here she was, somewhere in the jungle with no one at home in New York to care. If she didn't return and payments on the apartment stopped, the landlady would just bundle up her possessions, store them in the giant locker in the basement and get a new tenant.

It would be easy enough for Danielle to have an "accident" when she and Sebastian rode out on horseback. But no, that didn't make sense. He could have done anything with her on the way to their honeymoon and on the way back and anywhere in between.

There were good times, when he was so gentle and approachable, like the trouble, time and expense he'd taken to remodel their wing of the house. No, she couldn't believe he would ever harm her.

But someone else could.

That didn't rule out Teresa or Raoul or even Manuel. Did it start with her grandmother? She hated to think so, but how did Doña Mercedes have that accident with Princessa? It didn't make sense. It would have been the easiest thing in the world for someone who knew her grandmother's routine to kill a snake and leave it on the trail to spook the horse.

Sebastian would never be a party to harming Doña Mercedes, not for a dozen King's Ransoms, but Teresa was another story.

When Sebastian joined her for dinner, his eyebrow shot up at her appearance, and his smile showed admiration that he didn't express in words. He pulled out her chair and she felt the touch of his chin on the top of her hair, as if by accident.

"So. You decided my taste in clothing was not so horrible," he said mildly.

"I guess I was just being stubborn. This is lovely." She smoothed down the softly pleated wool skirt that stopped at the tops of her small, elegant boots. Topped with the cream-colored long-sleeved blouse that showed her slim waist to perfection, she was pleased with her image mirrored in his eyes.

After dinner and the small talk was dispensed with, she made up her mind to tell him about her project. Tonight he seemed not to be so distracted as usual.

"Sebastian, there's something I want to talk about. You know, when I left King's Ransom the other day—"

He held up a big hand to silence her. "You don't owe me an explanation," he said abruptly. "It's not as if we are really..."

She picked up her goblet of water and drank to cool her temper. Every time she tried to open up to him, he put her down. How could this man be reached? Was sex the only thing he understood? If she had succumbed to him back there on the beach, maybe by now they would be real lovers.

But that was too much of a chance to take. That old saying of "why pay for the cow when you get the milk free" had been drummed into her head since she was little.

"I have to go away again on business, to see to the banana shipments." He scraped back his chair and made a low bow. She couldn't tell if he was mocking or not, his eyes were unreadable. "Thank you for your fine company, I have something to do now and will see you when I return."

He had come to bed long after she'd fallen asleep and the next day he was gone without another word. She thought of looking for that outside door to the underground rooms, but she'd have to wait until the servants retired for the night. Then it might be too dark to see. Frustrated at every turn, she moped around the house for a while, until she decided to clear away her doldrums with a visit to the vanilla compound.

The truck was not in the garage; she saw it parked near the stables.

"*Lo siento,* I am sorry, *señora,* but Don Sebastian says no one must drive the truck." The man, a worker she didn't recognize, moved his hands nervously around the brim of the straw hat he held in front of him, as if in protection.

"Nonsense, I'm sure my husband didn't mean me. Please go ask Ramon to come here right away." Why would Sebastian forbid anyone to use his truck? They were the only two who ever used it; the workers had full use of the vehicles with regular gearshifts.

She thought of going by horseback but knew she wouldn't make it back before dark. Concheta's godmother was ill, and the girl was off today, to visit her in another village farther away. She didn't want to involve Manuel or any of the other workers.

The gardener appeared, his forehead wrinkled in worry. "Ramon. What is going on here?"

"*Señora,* Carlos says no one is to use the big truck. I cannot understand, no word was said to me on that subject."

"Well, then, it must be a mistake. Tell Carlos that I take full responsibility and will tell my husband so." Carlos spoke only a few words of English, maybe he hadn't understood her completely.

"Of course. You are right. *El Jefe* would not have forbid *you* to use anything on King's Ransom. Go bring out the truck." He gestured to Carlos and after a rapid-fire argument in Spanish, the younger man went to do his bidding.

"Will the *señora* be long? We will worry about you on the road. Maybe you should wait until tomorrow for Concheta's return." He couldn't ask directly where she was going, that would have been a terrible rudeness. This was as far as he dared go and for a moment she felt sorry for his dilemma.

"No, I won't be late. I just want to go for a ride, clear my head." Ramon couldn't know about the compound or he wouldn't have asked so many questions.

When she backed the vehicle out into the driveway and headed out the wide gates, she caught a glimpse of furtive movement on the walkway to the house. Someone was watching her departure, but she couldn't see who it was.

By the time she arrived at the workers' compound, the shadows had crept in under the giant trees of the jungle. Candles and lamps were lit all over the area, creating a sea of fireflies. Behind in the jungle, the light was sucked up into the darkness.

She felt a thrill of delight to see curtains hanging on each window and netting covering the doorways. It was a small beginning, but a woman should be able to take pride in her home.

The women and children poured out of every doorway, rushing to stand around the truck. They all smiled and tried to speak at one time, no longer shy and reserved. A young woman walked closer and put up her hand with a quiet dignity. All the hubbub subsided miraculously. This could only be Marta, Danielle thought, smiling. Concheta said she was too bossy for her own good, but everyone loved and respected her.

For a nervous moment, Danielle wished she would have waited for Concheta who could have translated. Too late for that.

No need to worry, Marta spoke slowly, carefully, part English, part Spanish. To her surprise, Danielle understood everything.

"The women wish to thank you so much for the curtains, they are beautiful. They also wish to apologize for not having the door coverings finished." She took Danielle's hand and they made a tour of the compound with every creature including all the dogs, following.

Danielle saw with satisfaction that all of Ramon's discarded rose cuttings had been planted, divided equally in front of each house. The brightly painted flowerpots were filled with tiny sprouts from the planted seeds. In some, the women had been too impatient for seeds and had transplanted some native flowering plants.

When she saw the last place and remarked, so all could hear, how beautiful she found it, the children moved forward, giggling shyly. They beckoned for her to follow them to a hut standing alone on the clearing.

"The men built it. It is our *escuela,* our school," Marta explained.

Danielle couldn't believe how well this was going, even the husbands and fathers were getting involved. She sat on one of the low benches in the bare little room while Marta put the children through one of their lessons. The ages of the children varied, but it made no difference in that none of them had ever received any formal education. She watched as Marta gave a mini-geography lesson from one of the *National Geographic* magazines.

She was startled to hear a word or two of English from the shy pupils.

"They want to learn about the United States, where you come from," Marta paused with a smile to explain.

By the time the performance was over and they went outside, Danielle felt alarm at how dark it had grown. A young couple insisted they ride home with her.

"But how will you get back? I'll ask Carlos or one of the workers to bring you home."

They shook their heads. No, they would stay overnight, with Lupe and the others, and return tomorrow.

As they began the trip back to King's Ramsom, she was glad of their company. She had never seen anything as dark as a jungle night with no moon and only the slash of the headlights to cut a buttery swath down the potholed road.

The next morning, Danielle thought she heard a car in the driveway. She wore one of the new dresses, a buttercup yellow with spaghetti straps that set off her tanned skin to perfection.

When Peter announced the Contreras brother and sister waiting in the rose garden, her elation fizzled like leftover champagne, but she couldn't very well ignore their presence.

"How lovely you look, my dear. Marriage becomes you." Raoul fawned over her extended hand and kissed it lingeringly. Peter had brought out coffee and sweet breads, so she supposed that meant she must entertain them.

"Where is Sebastian?" Teresa wanted to know.

"Out of town on business," Danielle answered. To her amusement, Teresa turned sullen, showing a decided lack of interest in the conversation after that.

Which wasn't saying much, as there was very little conversation. Raoul made small talk, they drank the coffee, he devoured her with his eyes, and she couldn't think for the life of her what she had ever found attractive about the man in the beginning.

"Surely you will attend the harvest fiesta," Raoul said. Her attention wandered from the roses to what he was saying.

"Harvest fiesta?"

"Yes. Sebastian has always escorted me," Teresa said, finally joining the conversation. "That is what I came to ask, when he will go."

"Teresa, my sweet sister, are you blind? He would be a fool not to take his lovely wife."

"No one mentioned a fiesta," Danielle said to stop the coming argument.

"Ah. Everyone from plantations miles around comes to see the fireworks and drink and dance. It is quite provincial, but charming in its own way. To celebrate the end of vanilla harvest."

He could never miss a chance to act the grand *patrón*, something Sebastian never did.

"Oh, I'm sure we'll go. If Sebastian is here then."

"Will you ride with me this afternoon?" Raoul asked.

Danielle shook her head. "No. I can't, I have—ah—things to attend to." It wasn't that Sebastian had warned her off, but only that she didn't trust Raoul.

After they left, she sat in the garden a while, soaking up the essence of hundreds of rose blossoms. As soon as Sebastian came home, she would tell him all about the project. Surely he couldn't object when he saw how happy the children were to learn.

But for now, it was time to look for that outside doorway to the underground passage. She ran upstairs to change into jeans, scrounging an older-looking shirt from Sebastian's dresser. She held it to her cheek a moment, smelling the residual earth-and-vanilla smell that always lingered when he entered a room.

Downstairs, she saw with satisfaction that the household was winding down, toward siesta time. No pots and pans rattled in the kitchen, no raucous laughter as she passed the door.

If only Ramon was resting, too. He was all over the yard, and it was impossible to do anything with him around.

She found a pair of leather gloves lying near some rose cuttings and borrowed them. Then she began her search.

CHAPTER EIGHTEEN

From one corner of the rambling old house to the next, Danielle steadfastly continued to search. Down on her knees, crawling behind bushes, she hurried, glancing at her watch often, knowing Ramon and the yard workers would soon be coming back to work.

She was almost half the way around the back when she saw what could be the door to the underground passages. Pushing aside the rosebush, her leather gloves protecting her from the thorns, she paused to look at the ground in front of it. Whoever used this entrance tried to keep it from becoming trampled, but she could see the crushed grass and broken twigs at the side of the bushes close in.

The door was exceedingly well hidden. Without knowing about it, few people could have spotted it. No wonder Ramon and his helpers had never noticed. Or did they know about it? Ramon could even be a party to whatever was going on, for all she knew. Trust no one, her grandmother had admonished.

Brushing aside the last branch hiding the door, she tried all her keys and then sat back with disappointment washing over her. What did she expect? The person who had stolen the key wanted this outside access, obviously.

Now her only recourse was to watch from the back window of her grandmother's wing. It would look down just over this area. Some night the culprit would either bring in more sacks of vanilla or take some away.

She had to find out who was involved and why.

Danielle stayed close to the house the balance of the day and through the early evening. There were papers to return to Marta; the teacher needed help organizing a curriculum, but according to Concheta, the new school was going well.

She must have dozed off, for the familiar sound of Sebastian's voice from downstairs woke her. She sat up, pretending to read, hoping he would stop by her opened door. Nothing prepared her for his anger when he strode into the room, standing, legs apart, glaring at her. He looked so handsome, she feared he could hear her heartbeat from across the room.

"What's the matter?"

"You ask me that question?" He slammed the bedroom door shut behind him. "Do you wish to explain how you go off into the jungle alone at all hours of the night to meet your lover? To send him messages and permit him to visit you here in my home."

"*Your* home?" Right away, the defensive barrier she had always put up against hurt rose between them. "And what are you talking about, meeting my lover? I never did any such thing."

"Don't look at me with those great amber eyes and pretend innocence. I warned you that discretion was important..."

"Who told you those lies? I suppose you are referring to Raoul as my so-called lover. How could you believe such a thing of me?"

"Peter and Carlos told me that you took the truck out last night. This has happened before and no one will say where you go. What else am I to believe? Do you deny it?"

For a moment they stared at each other. Sebastian's expression entreated her to tell him differently, but his eyes, those beautiful sea eyes were gray now and cold. A part of her felt elation at his obvious jealousy. He had to care for her if he felt so strongly. But it was so unfair for him to jump to these outrageous conclusions without talking to her first.

She stared at him, the fire banked inside her bosom, her eyes cold to meet his. "Think what you want. I won't dignify your accusations with admission or denial. I am not Teresa, it is time you learned the difference."

He turned to leave and she wanted to cry out to him, but she would not. She flung her paperback book at the closed door. A weary sigh escaped her as it fell to the carpet.

That evening, she dressed with extreme care for dinner. As the clinging dress fell down around her shoulders, she straightened it, looking in the mirror. The dress, a pale turquoise, complemented her hair and pale complexion.

Sebastian was already seated. Danielle missed their earlier, tentative friendship and knew it was partly her own stubbornness and secret-keeping that stood between them.

"Are you going to the fiesta?" she asked, sipping the fragrant, strong coffee.

"We are expected to put in an appearance. You would find it interesting, from a foreigner's point of view."

Oh, so now she was the foreigner. That hurt. She turned aside, not wanting him to read the pain in her eyes.

"The harvest fiesta lasts three days, doesn't it?" What a perfect time for someone to begin working with the stored vanilla. It was a time to be very vigilant.

"Yes, the first day, the plantation owners let all the household staff as well as the outside workers off to go. The second and third days are mostly for the field workers and they attend after their workday is finished. I have a short trip to make, but I will return in time to take you."

She toyed with her fork. Did he make an unusual number of out-of-town trips? she wondered. None of the servants seemed to think it unusual, but being so loyal, they would never say anything to her, anyway.

"Teresa said she usually goes with you."

Sebastian's dark eyebrow shot up and his mouth curled into a wide grin. "I am an old married man now. It would be unthinkable to go with anyone but my wife."

She wished he was telling the truth.

Upstairs that night, she sat in her bedroom and looked around sadly. Sebastian had told her he would now sleep in his own bedroom. It was so depressing to realize that this bedroom had been created for them—apparently as window dressing. She lay back on her bed and wondered what Sebastian dreamed while he slept in his room, alone.

If she had let him make love to her on the beach when he wanted to, would everything be different? In what way? she wondered. It was a curse, her mother had had it, too, of self-examination. It put her at a disadvantage against those who never bothered to look too closely at themselves. Was Sebastian one of those?

If only he had said he loved her that sunny afternoon. Wanting her wasn't good enough, but she hoped she would never be tested, her will was wearing down thin with her need for him. Whenever she was close to him, her heart thudded in her breast like a caged bird, surely he must feel it.

Yet, she wouldn't be left alone like her mother, discarded like excess baggage. Her mother had never complained, never showed bitterness, but the hurt was there, always.

The next morning she went into the kitchen, looking for someone to talk to.

"Did the *señora* sleep well?" Lupe asked.

The other women and Concheta sucked in their breaths, alarmed at the cook's brazenness. Everyone knew Don Sebastian and his new wife slept in separate rooms last night.

"I understand your concern," she answered. It wasn't any business of theirs, but they were one big family. "Sebastian had to go to work early and didn't want to disturb me." Just to be on the safe side, she added, "We decided to sleep separately, until the harvest is finished."

That seemed to satisfy the women. They changed the subject to the vanilla grove and the new school.

"Does Don Sebastian know yet?" one of the maids asked.

She shook her head. "I wanted to tell him, but the time hasn't been right. It shouldn't matter one way or another to him, should it?"

"But of course it matters!" Lupe was shocked. "Everything that happens here matters to him. King's Ransom is his lifeblood, his *querencia*."

"*Querencia?* A pretty word. What does it mean?"

All the women spoke together at once, trying to figure ou how to explain the word in English.

Finally, Lupe shrugged wide shoulders, her ample boso swaying with the effort. "I do not know how to say it. Yo have no words to explain. It means a place of longing— place of the heart—where you feel most at home more tha anyplace else in the world."

"A place where you wish your soul to reside even whe your body is no more," Concheta added, her pretty fac serious.

"Thank you. I think I understand. I'll tell Sebastia about the school very soon. I promise."

They nodded and went back to work.

When the day of the fiesta came, all of the help left. Bot Lupe and Concheta wanted to stay until Sebastian returne from the city, but she wouldn't hear of it. He promised to t here in time to take her to the fiesta, didn't he? She woul wait for him.

As the day progressed, the house became quieter an quieter. It was the first time since she had arrived that n servants bustled about with their chores or no racket of po and pans accompanied by Lupe's singing came from th kitchen. Even Peter was away; he took this time for a v cation in the city.

She located a place in the garden to conceal herself. A soon as it was dark, someone was going to come to th hidden doorway, they had to. It would be the perfect tin with all the servants away. And of course, Sebastian w conveniently gone again.

Danielle dozed and woke with a jerk. Her neck poppe and she feared anyone could hear the sound in the heav stillness of the night. Alert now, with every sense shar ened to the quick, she crouched and leaned forward, n knowing what had awakened her.

The door was open! Someone was inside the unde ground room! She leaned back on her heels, wondering the best thing would be to confront them. Since it wasr dope smuggling, it couldn't be a matter of life or death. No one would harm her, would they?

She couldn't bet her life on it. Danielle stayed back in the shadows and waited.

A shadowy figure emerged from the doorway, bent over to get through the passage. Someone tall. She leaned forward, almost out of her nest of branches, and still couldn't tell who it was. Her throat tightened as the person stood up and stretched. Was it . . . No, it wasn't Sebastian! Relief washed over her as she recognized Manuel. He went back inside and dragged out two canvas sacks, shouldered them and, as if he had all the time in the world, headed down the path toward the stables.

Now what should she do? She still didn't know if Sebastian, Teresa and Raoul were all in this together. Why would Sebastian steal from himself? The books, manipulating the books, some insurance scam, but Danielle couldn't— wouldn't believe Sebastian could be so mean, so petty to be a party to whatever was going on here. He always did things on such a grand scale. He was a man of integrity—he had proved that. She made up her mind then and there. He was not involved.

That settled, she waited, knowing Manuel would come back to the opened door. As she tried to make herself more comfortable, whispered voices penetrated the night air. At once she recognized Teresa coming up the walkway.

Where was Raoul? Had they left him out of their plans?

It was all Danielle could do to keep from leaping out and confronting them, making them tell her what they were up to, but if the bluff didn't work, they might spirit all the evidence away before Sebastian returned. It would be her word against theirs.

She leaned back against a tree and closed her eyes, struggling with the need for physical action. She had to have help, she couldn't do anything alone. As hard as it was to wait, she had to.

On the second night of the fiesta, she watched from the second-story window overlooking the garden but saw no movement. Maybe they were waiting until the third and last day or maybe they were finished doing whatever they had planned to do.

During the day, she had gone into the tunnel, into the room at the end and discovered the bags of vanilla still there. It did look as if some had been moved away. Where was Sebastian? She had to stop them somehow.

On the last day of the fiesta, Danielle had become so restless, she paced the floor. The house was silent as a tomb, the garden felt empty without Ramon's click of the trimming shears. Sebastian had given them extra time off, since he was not home, anyway.

What if Sebastian had gone to the fiesta without her? What if Teresa had prevailed upon him, one last time to take her? It hurt to think of it, but King's Ransom was the important thing now, she had to let Sebastian know what was happening here.

Just as dusk approached, she moved impatiently from her bench in the rose garden, toward the stables. She made up her mind to go to the fiesta now.

She hadn't expected to see anyone at the stables, but Carlos stood up when she entered.

"Carlos! I thought everyone was at the fiesta."

"No, *señora*. Don Sebastian asked me to stay until he returned. I was not to leave you alone."

"That's silly," she protested. "You're missing all the fun." Had Carlos seen Manuel bringing out the sacks of vanilla or was he involved, too?

"It's very quiet here. Have you seen anyone—any of the other workers around? Surely you're not the only one left here."

"Oh, *sí, señora. El Jefe* told everyone to go. Left Carlos in charge." The man swelled up his chest and Danielle caught the unmistakable smell of liquor on his breath. He could have been sleeping or hiding with his drink and not seen a thing.

"I'm going to the fiesta. My husband may not return in time and I want to attend." *My husband.* She didn't say those words often.

"Oh, no, *señora*, I—I cannot permit you to go alone. Don Sebastian would be so angry."

"You can come with me, then I won't be alone here and you won't miss the fiesta, either."

His swarthy face lit for a moment and then he shook his head. "No, *señora*, I would like nothing better, but Don Sebastian did not give me permission."

"He told you to take care of me, didn't he? I think he did. How can you do that if I am there and you are here?"

"*Pues,* well, since the *señora* puts it that way..."

"Should we take the horses or the truck?"

He scratched his head. It was plain he still did not want to go. "I have no keys." He shrugged, pointing toward the junky pickups. "No keys for them."

Sebastian had taken the Land Rover, and the good pickup was gone. It appeared *El Jefe* didn't trust her not to leave the place in his absence. That hurt.

"No problem. We'll have to use the horses."

"Very well, *señora*. I expect Don Sebastian will be very angry."

She shrugged slender shoulders. "I'll protect you, don't worry. Saddle up and let's go."

Before he could move, they heard the crunch of a vehicle on the gravel. Sebastian had come for her! She turned and struggled to keep the disappointment from her expression as Raoul drove up in a sleek, dark car. He stopped in front of her as a cloud of dust caught up with him.

"Hello. Caught you just in time." His dark eyes mirrored his approval of her colorful full skirt and crisp white peasant blouse. Concheta had Manuel pick up the material on one of his trips to the city and she'd made the skirt and blouse for her to wear for fiesta. Danielle was very proud of the gift.

"Carlos is saddling the horses. We're going to the fiesta."

"How dreary. You will be soiled and sweaty when you arrive. I cannot believe Sebastian forgot about you."

"What do you mean?"

"Why, my little dove, he is already there. He and my sister were dancing the last time I saw them and..."

"That's impossible! He said he would come for me."

His eyes narowed at her outburst, but the taut smile stayed in place.

"Then why are you going by yourself if you are so certain of that? I'm afraid he has forgotten you. Although how that is possible is beyond my comprehension."

Danielle flushed, trying to hide the swift hurt of the picture of Sebastian and Teresa dancing close, oblivious to everything.

"*Señora—*" Carlos stepped out of the shadows of the stables. "I do not believe this. Don Sebastian is working at the banana trucks, loading. When he is finished, he will come for you as promised."

"Silence!" Raoul's lips were drawn back in an ugly sneer. "No one in my employ would ever dare speak up against me in such a manner."

"Carlos is only doing his job," Danielle defended him.

"Make up your mind. The sooner we get there the sooner we find your precious Sebastian. It will take much longer on horseback and do you really wish to arrive at your first fiesta all windblown and smelling of the stables? I assure you Teresa does not."

At this last cut, Danielle turned decisively to Carlos. "I am going to join Sebastian. If he is not there, the fiesta is where I wish to be, anyway. Please stay and watch as he told you to."

Carlos stood, plainly unhappy, as she slid into the velvety softness of the luxurious car. The moment the door thunked closed and the locks clicked, she felt as if she had made a dreadful mistake. She refused to look back at the watching Carlos as the car purred out of the driveway.

When they had gone a distance, neither speaking, Danielle finally broke the silence. "Aren't you afraid of ruining your beautiful car, driving on these rutty roads?"

Raoul laughed softly. "Certainly not. When this car no longer serves me, I will get another."

It was beginning to grow darker when Raoul slowed down.

"What's wrong? Why are you driving so slow?" A creeping fear slid up her backbone, but then she tried to relax. She could handle the situation, couldn't she? An overzealous Don Juan, she would set him straight in a minute if he tried anything. Yet Sebastian had hinted at a more sinister side to this man, an insinuation she had discounted.

"There is a place, just an instant off our route, I'd like to show you before darkness shuts it away."

"It's already dark," she protested.

"Nonsense. That is only the effect of the tinted windows." Just then he braked the car and slid out from behind the wheel, waiting. "It will only take a moment, Danielle. I must show you these orchids, they are like nothing else you have ever seen."

"Oh, all right," she said crossly. "But Sebastian might come back for me and . . ."

"Ah, my sweet, I fear he has other things on his mind at the present."

Raoul's persistent needling was having the opposite effect on her than he probably hoped for. It was beginning to annoy her beyond words.

"Follow me—slowly now. There are exotic birds that feed upon the nectar of this orchid. If we are lucky, we will see one of them also."

He turned away from the road, wading carefully through some tall grass toward a huge tree.

There was nothing else for her to do but follow.

When they reached the tree, he pointed upward. There, hanging delicately from the lowest branches, intertwined with the leaves, grew exquisite flowers, beautiful beyond her wildest imaginings. She drew in a deep breath, staring as a colorful little bird the size of a large hummingbird drew up and hovered.

Only the arm creeping around her waist startled her from watching in openmouthed wonder. Raoul was standing behind her, his arms tightly encircling her now, like one of the big snakes Sebastian was forever warning her about. He bent down and nuzzled her neck.

She struggled to pull his hands away. "Raoul! How dare you touch me!" Outrage flooded through her body, giving her extra strength to break out of his caress. She kicked back with her foot; he yelped with pain as she connected with his shin.

Still he didn't release her, but turned her around to face him. His hands felt like bands of steel on her arms.

"Ah, *cariña,* you do not disappoint. I love a good fight."

His hands tightened and she could tell by the excited, questioning look in his eyes that he wanted to know when she felt pain. Now she began to realize why Sebastian had warned her not to be alone with this man, why the kitchen gossip had it that no village girl would go with him.

"Sebastian will kill you for this."

Raoul laughed, teeth flashing white in the gloom of dusk. "Your Sebastian has enough on his hands, with my sister. She is determined to be mistress of King's Ransom, you must know that."

Danielle pushed back for breathing space, hoping to calm him so that she could talk some sense to him, get him to let her go. "How? Sebastian chose to marry me."

"Ah, that is only a temporary setback. Teresa believes the old lady came back from the grave to arrange your marriage."

"What?"

"I know, it's something you would not understand. Teresa went to visit the old woman many times at night, trying to put a curse on her. The old one was strong."

"Yes. She told us—or tried to tell us—that Teresa came to her bedside at night. I doubt anyone believed her. Your sister came to my room, too, I saw her." Why was he saying this to her? Did it mean Raoul knew nothing about the hidden vanilla? Otherwise, he wouldn't dare tell about Teresa snooping around King's Ransom at night.

He shrugged, his grip never loosening. Her arms were beginning to numb but she didn't want to call attention to his hands, hoping he would relax if only a moment.

"I don't know about that. I warned her to leave you alone, but she said Sebastian knew everything she did."

"I was almost killed, someone loosened the stairs to the attic when I was up there."

"Ah. That sounds like my dear sister. If I want something, I am more direct, let me assure you." He bent closer and nuzzled his lips into her hair, as if inhaling her essence.

She relaxed a moment, to put him off, and then lunged to the side, tearing out of his grasp. She ran back to the road. The lights of his car lit it as in daylight, for it had turned nearly dark.

Danielle heard his low cursing behind her, closer and closer. She broke through the brush, ran past the car, breathing hard. Her long skirts hampered, the light, flimsy sandals were worse than nothing in the hard, rutted trail. As Danielle ran, she knew Raoul wouldn't give up so easily. Waiting for the headlights to penetrate the gloom, she realized he had turned the car and was following slowly behind her with the lights off, enjoying the cat-and-mouse game.

Now she could hear the steady purr of the big car, but still he stayed back, waiting. She thought of breaking into the jungle but he would know where to look for her. She heard her heart pounding in her ears now, her side ached and her legs were numb.

She stumbled over what felt like a good-sized rock and bent to pick it up. When she straightened, headlights loomed directly in her pathway. Danielle stopped running and waited. Fear coursed through her body but she gathered her strength, clutching the rock in her hand until the sharp edges bit into her flesh.

She was not giving up without a fight. He must have managed to get in front of her, though she had no idea how. With the rock raised in her hand, she stepped out into the glare of the headlights as strong arms encircled her, taking what breath she had away.

She struggled, trying to lash out with the rock, kicking all the while. "Don't touch me, you bastard! Sebastian will—"

Then she was lifted off the ground and shaken so that her head bounced on her neck. The fight died out of her.

"Danielle. Stop it! Are you all right? Has he hurt you?"

Blessed relief oozed through her as the blood receded to where it belonged. She slumped against Sebastian's broad chest, her heart pounding. The rock slipped out of her limp fingers.

He turned her head gently with his finger and tilted her chin to look into her eyes. "I asked you, *mia vida,* are you harmed?"

She shook her head. "He's back there. Waiting for me."

"No. I saw him turn the car around. He's gone. Raoul will not dare challenge me."

He held her for a moment and then picked her up, carrying her to a grassy knoll beyond the side of the road. He deposited her gently and knelt beside her. She could smell the crushed grass beneath her, the moon was just coming in full behind the tops of the trees along the road.

"Now tell me what happened."

She looked into Sebastian's eyes, dark now with the light behind them.

"Nothing happened. I just . . . he told me you were at the fiesta with Teresa."

"And you believed him?"

"The jealous part of me believed him, but deep down, I knew he was lying. I should have waited for you, Carlos begged me to. But my pride got in the way . . . Oh, I don't know what I believe anymore!" Tears welled up in her eyes and she brushed them with the back of her hand.

He smoothed the tears away with his thumbs, his fingers trailed onto her cheek, touching the tears. "Yes. Carlos told me you had left with Raoul. My first thought was to let you go. Until Carlos told me the lie Raoul said to get you to go with him." His voice was steady, his mouth grim. "I was sure you didn't know what you were letting yourself in for. I tried to warn you." Sebastian's eyes held a glint of steel. "I asked you before, did he harm you?"

She shook her head, unable to speak for the rush of feeling that came over her now at his closeness.

"I haven't been to any fiesta, Danielle, I have just come from the banana fields." He gestured at his dusty trousers and muddy boots. As he talked on, she could feel the anger building up in him. He had a right to be hurt, she acknowledged that. He had certainly warned her enough times not to go with Raoul anywhere alone. If only he had said why, but then, would she have believed him?

She reached up and tenderly brushed her small hand along his jawline, feeling the tight muscles held in check. 'Sebastian, will we ever trust each other? There has been so much misunderstanding between us. I wish we could start over again from the beginning." Had Raoul been telling the truth, that Sebastian knew about Teresa's schemes to scare her away, to discourage her from staying at King's Ransom? No! It couldn't be true.

He groaned and reached for her hand to bring it to his lips. He pulled her back onto the fragrant grass and leaned on his elbow, looking deep into her eyes. She waited with stilled breath as he bent closer and began kissing her, at first fiercely demanding and then gentle, as his lips moved down to her throat.

Her hand reached for the back of his head, to pull him closer. *I love you, I love you,* her inner voice rang out. Surely he must know. She felt the stirrings of a buried passion that she had never felt before.

"Oh, God, how I've wanted you so long, *mi corazón*. I can't get you out of my mind." His lips roamed over her eyes, her nose and settled on her mouth once again.

His leg rested against her thigh and she felt the hardness of his body through her light clothing. She had almost said she loved him. Would that have been a mistake?

She lay back, her heart still beating in irregular spasms as he put his hand against her breast and touched the buttons of her blouse.

Abruptly he pulled away, his eyes reflecting his reluctance. "What am I thinking? You've had a scare, we must go home now."

Home. That sounded good.

He held her close again for a moment, nuzzling his lips into her neck. Then he kissed each eyelid and placed a light one on her mouth.

"Ah—I'm okay now, Sebastian."

"Nonsense, I feel your heart tripping like it's going to run away on you. If he had hurt you..."

It isn't that man who makes my heart beat so, she wanted to tell him. But he had spoken in words of passion; she couldn't speak out in words of love. It didn't work that way. Once said, the words could not be reclaimed.

She could feel his warm breath and smell the vanilla...

The *vanilla!*

She told him everything she had been holding back.

CHAPTER NINETEEN

When they were almost back to King's Ransom, he cleared his throat and began talking.

"I wanted to tell you about Raoul ever since you came here, Danni. I tried to, but as time passed, I assumed you had heard the gossip and made up your own mind."

"Yes, I've heard things. Hard-to-believe things, even after tonight."

He sighed. "They are a strange pair, Teresa and Raoul. All anyone really can say is that when the union troublemakers showed up from the city, the Contreras place was the only one that was burned. Some of the ringleaders were tracked down later and denied setting the fire. That was to be expected, of course, and proves nothing."

"But that's a terrible thought, that they would allow a helpless man to die in the fire."

"Maybe. They didn't like him. Teresa told me many times how he didn't deserve to inherit the plantation. I still can't think she had anything to do with it."

Of course not. Danielle made a wry face in the dark, feeling in the core of her being that Teresa probably was the leader—she was much smarter than Raoul.

She didn't say anything for a moment. "Well, in light of everything, I'm sorry I was gullible enough to go off with him, but he said..."

Danielle knew Sebastian was waiting for her to finish. Did she want him to know she was so wildly jealous at the thought of him and Teresa being together at the fiesta that she had to get there under any circumstances? She shook her head. No, she didn't think so.

"He said you were already there. I just thought you had forgotten me and I had to tell you what was happening at King's Ransom with the vanilla."

"I almost didn't come after you. You've been so secretive lately, and your visits to the Contreras plantation didn't help. Peter told me..."

"I haven't... There is something I should tell you. You see—"

He braked the car and touched her lips with a finger. "Shh. I don't want to hear it. You don't owe me your life. You are mixed up in a crazy arrangement that has taken up more of your time than it should. For that I am sorry. You have a life, you should get back to it." He started up the car again.

"That's a surprising observation," she said. "I thought a woman shouldn't have anything on her mind but pleasing some man."

"Ah, sarcasm. I don't blame you, though. But your charge is unfounded. You see, I have been learning since you arrived—I no longer think of a woman as merely an extension of a man. I never think of you that way."

Great. That part was great. But he had the other part all wrong. "I never went to the—" she began again.

"Ah, here we are. It's been a rough day."

Ever since they had climbed into the Land Rover, he hadn't said a thing about the underground room and what she had seen. Had she been wrong to tell him?

He helped her up the wide steps into the house; one of her sandal straps had broken.

Once inside, she pulled on him to get him into the study. "Sebastian, sit for a minute. You're not talking about the vanilla. I want to know—"

He put a calloused finger lightly against her lips and leaned forward to whisper in her ear.

"Shh. The walls have ears. I've got to think this out."

"But there's no time! I have a feeling they will move everything out tonight."

He nodded. "You are probably right. It is only that I wanted you upstairs, in your bed, out of harm's way."

"Well, of all the nerve! You wouldn't know about this if it weren't for me and—"

He silenced her the only way he knew how, with a deep, lingering kiss. When it was over, she leaned close, absorbing the warmth of him. It didn't change his mind though.

"I want to help, Sebastian. You can't do this alone. It won't be dangerous. They could have harmed me anytime if they had wanted to."

His eyebrow shot up into the curve of dark hair. "Do you forget so soon about the stairs?"

"The stairs? I thought you didn't believe me."

He pulled her down to the couch and sat close so that they could whisper. "Why do you think I made sure someone was watching you at all times? I knew something strange was happening. It had to do with the books. The vanilla wasn't coming out in the amount of kilos it should have. But I just couldn't piece it all together."

She wasn't sure the broken stairs had anything to do with the vanilla. The stairs were more Teresa's doing; she still wanted to be mistress of King's Ransom. When Teresa saw it might never happen, she took matters into her own hands, or maybe it was just a simple matter of revenge.

He stood up. "Okay, if we're partners, come on. Show me the rooms."

"But you can't—Peter said you don't go down below the ground since—"

He sighed. "I know, I never have. That was quite a scare for a kid, but it's time I left it behind with a lot of other ghosts. Show me."

She pushed against the desk and watched in amusement as his eyes widened at the swinging bookcase and the door appearing from nowhere.

"My God, you have been busy!" he exclaimed. "Does anyone else know about this—other than Teresa and Manuel?"

She shrugged. "I've no idea. Maybe Teresa heard about it from your grandmother, somehow. Peter knew the rooms were here, but he apparently didn't know where or how to get to them."

She fitted the key in the lock and picked up the flashlight from the desk. "Ready?"

He nodded, swallowing hard. She reached for his hand as he bent over to go through the door. He needed her now, even as he put on a brave front. It couldn't be easy to go backward through a traumatic event in a child's mind.

They made their way down the passageway, walking single file at times, she leading the way. As they neared the end room, they heard voices.

"Teresa!" Sebastian's whisper of surprise came as a shock to Danielle, it was as if he hadn't believed her story.

"What do we do now?" she asked.

He motioned for her to stay as he crept closer to the last turn in the tunnel. She didn't stay there. She was in this, too, whatever happened.

As she stepped up next to him, the two figures didn't notice anyone else in the chambers, they were so busy arguing.

Teresa was livid with rage, and Manuel looked as if he might hit her any moment.

"I tell you it's not the time to move everything out. Leave it and we'll get more," Teresa said.

"No! We cannot be greedy, Sebastian will begin to suspect if we take too much at a time," Manuel tried to reason with her.

"I don't care! I am not doing this as you are, to make a petty little profit for myself. I want to ruin him, as he has ruined my life, made me an object of ridicule by marrying that...that..."

"You will ruin yourself and me, too, with your bitterness. I thought you and I..."

Teresa's laugh was high-pitched, bordering on hysteria.

"That's enough. Both of you. We need to hear no more." Sebastian stepped out of the shadows with Danielle at his side.

Manuel and Teresa swerved to face them, their expressions identical ones of dismay and surprise. *"Dio mio!"* Teresa breathed.

In two strides, Sebastian stood in front of Manuel.

"How could you do this? Why? I pay you well. I trusted you."

Manuel recovered his dignity, or what he had left of it. "You pay me well, but she—she offered more." He turned to Teresa. "She said we could go away together, buy our own plantation, if we stole enough vanilla from King's Ransom."

Teresa's full lips pulled back into a sneer. "*Estupido!* I did not care about the money, only my revenge on Sebastian and this witch who came to steal everything from me. But I had planned so well! I made copies of the necessary keys so I could come and go in the house and search for the key to the door of the tunnel. When we were children, Peter had once spoken of the underground passage. I was so careful—"

"Danielle—go upstairs to our room immediately and wait for me," Sebastian ordered, his tone as cold as ice. At her hesitation to leave him alone, he said, "Go! Now!"

Danielle watched the three for a moment and then turned to go. She had done all she could to help Sebastian and King's Ransom. From now on, it was up to him what he decided to do about it. She only hoped he'd be safe.

She had lain awake for hours until she'd dropped off into a restless sleep. She awoke, unrefreshed and more exhausted realizing that Sebastian had not come back last night.

Standing on the terrace, she looked out over the gardens for a sign of him. The air felt heavy; dark clouds hovered low in the usual brilliant blue sky. Was it the start of the rains?

Concheta knocked softly on the door and entered.

"Good morning, Concheta. Tell me, did you see Sebastian this morning?" she asked, holding her breath and praying Concheta had seen him.

The maid nodded, her smile wide. "Oh, *sí*, he left early in the truck."

Danielle breathed a sigh of relief and Concheta went on. "I met a man at the fiesta—a new worker who came here

from another plantation. They all hear how well Don Sebastian treats us."

"That's good." Danielle was happy for her but preoccupied, her thoughts on the happenings of last night. Obviously, no one knew about Teresa and Manuel. How would
this affect poor Concheta? Hadn't she had enough trouble
in her young life?

"We all looked for you. Even Lupe, but you were not
there, nor was Don Sebastian. Did you just choose that time
to stay home so you could be alone?" Mischief lit up her
dark eyes.

I wish, Danielle thought morosely. "Tell me about your
new friend," she urged, wanting to change the subject.

"Ah, he is *magnifico!* So strong, such a good dancer. We
danced until we could not put one foot in front of the other.
All of the others were jealous of my good fortune," Concheta gloated.

"Well, I'm glad someone had fun," Danielle said. She
was both happy and sad for the girl, as she watched Concheta go about her morning tasks singing under her breath.
Life could be so simple, why did it have to grow so compli-
cated?

Outside in the rose garden, Danielle sat to regroup her
thoughts. This wasn't working out. She loved this place as
much as her grandmother had hoped she would. She loved
Sebastian. But it was plain he didn't love her.

Though Danielle had suspected as much, it was easy to see
that her grandmother's strategy included more than keeping Teresa from Sebastian—she'd meant to force them together, hoping she and Sebastian would fall in love. Well, it
had worked on Danielle's side, but not for Sebastian. You
old schemer, bless your heart for trying.

"Ah, *señora,* I am so happy to find you." Ramon walked
up behind her, scuffing his boots so as not to startle her.

"Buenos días." She smiled at the earnest young man.
"Would you like some coffee?" She patted the bench for
him to sit down and he did so gingerly, hat in hand, as if he
might jump up at any moment.

"Oh, no, I do not have time for coffee, *gracias*. I bring a message from the women in the vanilla compound. They wish you to visit today—if you can spare the time."

Everyone knew how she spent her time, wandering around the garden or sitting in the study reading. "Then you know about the—my visits there?"

"Of course. Most of us do. This gift of self-respect you give the women—our people—we did not expect it of anyone, much less a stranger."

"Ah, Ramon, sometimes it takes a stranger to see things clearly."

"Then you will come?"

"I don't know if I can get away. I must speak to Sebastian, and I don't know when he'll return." She didn't want to have any more secrets between them; she wanted to tell Sebastian everything before she went again to the compound.

"He left early in the truck. He looked angry, I did not ask him where he went. Do you forget? This is Sunday, the women and children will be in the camp today. By late tonight, I think the rains will start."

"I'll ask Concheta to come with me. We could ride the horses."

"No, that would not be wise. The sky does not look good, you should take a truck. If you go soon, I will drive," Ramon offered.

Concheta was happy to go, and Danielle was grateful for their company to take her mind off the events of last night. Where had Sebastian gone? What did he do about Teresa and Manuel?

Thunder rolled across the sky, still far away, but threatening with a heavy smell of moisture in the air.

"The season of *el chaparron,* the pouring down of water, is coming early this year. First come the clouds, then a hot wind, then the rains."

"Do you hate it?"

Ramon shrugged, laughing. "How can one hate the wind or the rain, *señora?* It is just there."

By the time they arrived at the vanilla grove, the long, shady rows looked strange, eerie without the flashes of bright dresses mixed with the noisy confusion of women laughing and singing, children playing. It was like entering a giant cathedral with vanilla as the incense.

As they made the last bend that led to the workers' compound, Ramon gave a piercing whistle between his teeth.

Gaily colored streamers hung from every tree and across the entrance a large homemade banner.

"El Día de la Chaparrita," the sign read in bold black letters. She slid from her seat in the truck looking up, tears filling her eyes and running down her cheeks.

Women and children ran toward her, gathering noisily around, laughing and pointing. Suddenly they were quiet, noticing her tears.

"Is the *señora* angry because we call her *La Chaparrita?*" Ramon asked anxiously. "I, myself, I tell them just because Doña Mercedes permitted that familiarity does not mean the new *señora* would, but women, they do not listen."

No one spoke, even the children hushed, waiting.

She smiled, turning to look at all of them crowded around her. *"Estoy feliz, muchisimo gracias toda.* I am so happy, a million thanks to everyone for the honor you have paid me."

They all cheered and laughed. Concheta, in her happiness, cried and hugged Danielle until she realized what she was doing and backed off in dismay. With tears in her eyes, Danielle hugged her back. Marta stood next to her and held up her hand for quiet. "From this day forward, we celebrate the second day of the fiesta dedicated to you, in your honor."

Danielle thought of what she had decided on her way here today. Her secret choked off her air, suffocating her, but she did not relinquish it. Could not.

Sensing a protest, Ramon interrupted her. He scuffed his boots, as if suddenly aware that he was the only adult male in the vicinity. All the men were probably still on the fiesta grounds, sleeping off their hangovers or in the village.

"These women did not even offer this high regard to Doña Mercedes," he explained.

"Then I accept, with gratitude." What would they think—later? She couldn't worry about that so far ahead.

She went into each small house to see the improvements, what each woman had done with her materials and to sample some little delicacy made especially for her.

Finally, in desperation, she held up her hands.

"Please, I can eat no more. Does being named *Chaparrita* mean one must be as round as one is tall?"

For a moment, they did not understand her joke and when the buzzing started with some of the women explaining, they all broke out in wild laughter.

After that, the children put on a program and Marta and the mothers stood by proudly while they went through their paces. They acted out a little skit in her honor; she surmised it had to do with the discovery of America, make-believe ships, Indians, pilgrims, turkeys and their own vivid imaginations at work. She struggled to keep a smile from her expression; they were all so serious.

Danielle felt a thrill of accomplishment tinged with sadness. If only Sebastian could have shared this with her, but would he have understood what had happened here? To give the women something to delight in of their own, to dignify their narrow lives with pride of home and to answer their need for beauty. To offer them the hope that their sons and daughters could have the opportunity for change, if they wanted it? Or would he have seen her efforts as mere meddling?

At last the ceremony seemed over. Marta and one of the women brought out a large, square package and put it on one of the boxes used for desks.

"Oh, no! I cannot accept another thing from you. All of you have been so generous to share with me. I need nothing else."

"You will make them very sad," Marta warned as she handed over the package.

Shrugging with resignation, Danielle unwrapped it as willing little hands reached out to help. She unfolded the exquisitely embroidered bedspread.

"Every one of us, even the little ones, sewed on this," Marta explained.

A lump of gratitude stuck in Danielle's throat and she had a hard time swallowing past it. "We do not have that kind of bed, but..."

"Concheta tells us that someday you will have that kind of bed," Marta said, laughing. "And when that time comes, you *will* be as round as you are tall." As the words were repeated through the crowd, everyone laughed at Danielle's fierce blushing.

Behind her laughter and wide smile, Danielle felt a thick, encroaching fog of emptiness, for now, at last, she was certain what she had to do.

Later, when they pulled up in front of the gateway of the big house, she looked at it with sorrow. A lovely old place, a home that would age gracefully—Sebastian's soul-place.

There was no place for her here. She did not belong. Her promise to her grandmother had been fulfilled, and her husband did not love her.

If she hurried, she could still make the city tonight. The plan was simple, take the Land Rover, leave it in town, at the hotel. If she didn't go immediately, tomorrow might be too late. The servants were talking excitedly about a flood on the highway, a downpour in a village the next valley away. That's the way it started, isolated deluges of rain until it poured everywhere at once.

She wished she could have been here to see one monsoon season, she loved thunder and lightning and rain.

Upstairs, she packed feverishly, hurrying now to beat Sebastian's return. She wanted no arguments about her leaving—or worse, that cold steely look from him that said he didn't care either way. He would never love her; it was unfair to keep him trapped in this marriage.

When she left, he could tell everyone she'd gone on an extended trip home, and when the necessary months had passed, claim desertion, and the property would revert to him.

She sat on the bed for a moment, looking around her. Sebastian had his mark on everything. Closing her eyes, she impressed the image of the large, airy room and all of the work he had done for her—but she wasn't even allowed that belief. He had done it to remind everyone of their marriage, of course.

Rifling through the closets, she touched the beautiful clothing she would never wear. She came with two small suitcases and would leave the same way, with her original possessions.

She took just enough money from the envelope on the dresser to pay for her flight. When she arrived in the States, she could draw from her savings. Now came the hard part, writing a note to Sebastian.

Danielle held the pen to her teeth for a moment, thinking and then shrugged. Make it short and to the point, that was the best way.

> Sebastian,
> I have no place here, it belongs to you with my blessings.
>
> Danielle

She took out another sheet of paper and wrote that she freely relinquished any right or claim to King's Ransom or any of its properties and granted all such interest to her husband, Sebastian Beaumont. Certain that he could legally claim the property without this note, she thought it better to tie up any loose ends. She needed a witness to her signature and took it down to Lupe, hoping not to see Concheta, but they were both in the kitchen.

"I need to sign this in front of witnesses, would you two do it for me?"

"Of course," Lupe said immediately. "But, señora, you know we do not read English."

She knew that, and was grateful. Now came the hard part, the big lie. "I'm going to the coast for a few days. Don Sebastian knows all about it. I need a little change of scenery."

Lupe and Concheta nodded. Doña Mercedes had gone away sometimes, and although her grandmother had been a widow, not a married woman, they made no comment. She hugged them both, struggling with her tears, for they mustn't guess she wouldn't return.

She hadn't reckoned on Peter, barring her way in the foyer. He looked at her suitcases and back at her face.

"Madam, Sebastian said nothing about your going to meet him. As a matter of fact, the errand he is on is very delicate, perhaps dangerous. There are two work gangs who..." He broke off when he saw her frown.

"I am not going to hunt my husband down in the jungle," she assured him, needing to hear the phrase "my husband" one more time out loud. "I am only taking a short vacation in the city." So, he confided in Peter but couldn't bother to tell her what he was doing with the vanilla thieves. It was apparent to her from the beginning that more than two people were involved. Probably those strangers from the village. Doña Mercedes had been right in being worried. Too bad no one had paid any attention.

"But we cannot possibly allow you to go alone!" Peter's earnest voice interrupted her thoughts. "The weather is unpredictable now. Doña Mercedes never went out during monsoon and if she had to, she always took someone to drive—to accompany her. He would be furious if I permitted you..."

"Permitted me? I should think you'd be delighted to have me out from underfoot. You haven't been especially friendly."

He shook his head, plainly deciding whether to speak or not. Habit was too great in the old man; he was used to saying what he thought as part of the family. "No, and I did not like you at first. Only because I dislike change. And because I thought you not good for Sebastian."

He drew himself up with dignity and continued, "King's Ransom is the only home I've known for most of my adult life and Sebastian is like a beloved nephew. I was here the day he came, all dirty and ragged. I was afraid you'd throw our ordered lives all asunder, turn it all topsy-turvy."

"I guess I did that," she admitted.

"Yes, indeed." He smiled. "Sebastian told me how you investigated the theft of the vanilla when no one would listen to you. You may have saved King's Ransom from financial disaster. Lupe and the others told me what you did for the people at the vanilla compound. They also said you have not told Sebastian. Why not? He would be delighted, once he assimilated the idea."

"Now that it's started, it doesn't have to stop. There are more things that need doing here."

"I don't understand. The people are happy in the camp, I have heard it is a very good place to live."

"Maybe so, but it could be better. For instance, they need someone trained in the basics of first aid; medicines on hand for emergencies; a woman paid to watch over the children in camp so they don't have to tag along with their working mothers; something to keep the men there instead of at the village; maybe a few treadle sewing machines. It shouldn't stop now."

"It needn't stop, ma'am. When you return from your vacation, I'm certain Sebastian and you will have a lot to talk about. If I can be of any help, you can count on me."

"Thank you, Peter." It was good to know he was no longer against her, even if it was too late. "I'll be gone a day or so and then we'll see what we can do." The lie stuck in her throat, closing it so she couldn't say anything more.

"As I've said, the roads are very treacherous at this time of year, the weather is unpredictable. Please, allow someone to drive and wait for you."

"Thank you for your concern, but I need the time alone. I don't want the feeling of anyone waiting for me." She shook hands with the old man, which plainly puzzled him, and walked down the steps, past the rose garden without looking. She didn't dare.

At the stables, Carlos turned difficult.

"But, *señora,* Don Sebastian say no one use Land Rover but him."

"I can't very well go in the old truck, can I? He has the truck with the automatic shift." She had watched him with the Land Rover enough to know how to shift the gears, she felt sure of that. Those ancient trucks were something else.

"The roads, *señora,* they will be difficult." He looked up into the sky as if expecting a deluge any moment.

"Nonsense, it hasn't rained in weeks. Now give me the keys," she said with stern dignity.

He did so, but the obvious reluctance in his expression made her feel guilty. She was leaving with a cloud of lies and deceit over her head. She hated that but there was no help for it.

"I will write a note to Don Sebastian and explain that you could not stop me. He will not blame you." It cost more precious time as she scribbled out a note, and she began to listen for the crunch of Sebastian's wheels on the gravel. He might return any moment and catch her. Carlos thanked her and put the paper carefully in his back pocket with his wallet.

Hurry! Hurry! she wanted to shout at him as he slowly put her suitcases in the rear of the vehicle. Just before she slid behind the wheel, Concheta came running down the grassy incline waving a basket. Lupe had prepared lunch for her.

Tears welled up in Danielle's eyes as she whsipered her thanks and hugged the girl's slim body close for a moment. Concheta looked deep into Danielle's eyes, and that was when she knew that no one was fooled. They all knew she wouldn't be back.

Concheta's dark eyes filled with tears, spilling down the smooth skin of her cheeks, her small lips trembled.

"*Vaya con Dios, Chaparrita,* you will always live within our hearts." Then she ran back up the hill toward the house.

Suddenly Danielle was alone, with the big Land Rover waiting like some huge beast of prey, ready to devour her. How silly, she thought, you are just getting overwrought, with all this business of leaving. She put the vehicle carefully in gear so Carlos would not cringe, wherever he was hiding.

"*Vaya con Dios, mi alma,*" she whispered as she moved through the big iron gates without looking back.

CHAPTER TWENTY

As Danielle started out, the skies had looked threatening, but the downpour didn't begin until she passed the firs bridge. She gunned the powerful vehicle, traveling as fast as possible, the danger of skidding uppermost on her mind.

A blast of thunder hit the skies, bouncing back and fortl for what seemed like minutes, then the shafts of fierce lightning struck, making her flinch. She remembered then were four bridges, and as she passed the third, the dark wa ter had risen higher on the banks. One more to go! The headlights cut a swath through the rain that was as thick as a curtain in front of her. The windshield wipers barely kep up and the constant *thunk-thunk* of them drowned out some of the sky-noises.

As she neared the last bridge, her heart swelled in he throat, so that it was hard to breathe. Water gushed over the bridge already. If she didn't make this last one, she was trapped, unable to go back or forward.

She gunned the engine of the big vehicle, tromping on the accelerator and holding the wheel for all she was worth on the slippery mud beneath. All it took was one slide and . . She shivered with a quick chill, in spite of the warm rain striking her face like needles from the open window. Open to catch a glimpse of a road that was a blur from behind the windshield and the hardworking wipers.

Right in the middle of the bridge, the Land Rove coughed, a small cough, but one that turned her blood to ice. "Come on, old girl, you can do it. Please." She kept he foot down on the accelerator, and with a bucking jump like an angry horse, the car leaped the last feet of the bridge jus as a wall of water swept across behind her.

"I've heard of burning bridges behind you, but this is ridiculous." The sound of her voice was somehow reassuring. Tears of relief shrouded her eyes for a moment and she wiped at them with the back of her hand. No time to dillydally, there still could be problems between here and the city even without bridges to contend with.

By the time she reached the outskirts of the beach city, Danielle was exhausted from the ordeal. The streets were dark. The few lights made barely a crack in the dense rain that fell from the unrelenting sky.

She hoped she remembered how to get around in the city and to the beach and the hotel. What if it closed for the rainy season? She needed one last comfort—to stay in their same room for one last time.

Remembering her, the manager and most of his staff rushed out to welcome, fuss over her, as gentle hands divested her of wet outer garments. If they wondered why she came alone, no one asked, there was not even a raised eyebrow.

Upstairs, she listened to the downpour on the windows, watching from the terrace. She was dry, clothes changed, and very restless. She opened Lupe's generous basket of food, but lacked an appetite; the desolate and empty bed haunted her. She recalled waking up and finding him next to her that one time.

So easy to imagine his dark head against the white of the pillow, the hard planes of his chiseled face, his eyes, fringed in dark lashes that made them look unfathomable, like the sea in a storm. And yet they could be so gentle, so perceptive.

Staying in the same room was a mistake, she could see that now. What could she have done to change things? Should she have been more aggressive—pursued him? She held her bottom lip between her teeth, squinting her eyes closed tightly to keep away the tears. She would not cry, could not, or she might never stop.

They were from two different worlds, and while, for a time, she thought they both might change enough to blend, it was impractical, wasn't it?

She had changed in many ways since coming here, deep
ened and matured from the brittle, frightened girl who ha
held herself so in control for fear of being hurt. Yet in he
inner self, where the real Danielle hid, she still had feared t
take the chance that her mother had taken—and lost.

During the night, the storm had abated and by morning
the sun shone brightly through banked clouds. She stood i
her nightclothes at her balcony, overlooking the white beac
and noisy, cresting waves. The desk clerk had made reser
vations for her flight early this afternoon. She had time fo
a walk.

Dressing in her bathing suit beneath a thin sundress, sh
headed out for the sand, turning in the direction that sh
and Sebastian had walked together.

Walking slowly along the beach, half in, half out of th
rushing white water, she bent from time to time, picking u
shells to look at, then discarding them. No baggage, tha
was the way to go through life, she supposed. It wasn'
turning out to be the easiest way, but it was her way.

The water felt warm on her bare feet. A few scattere
couples walked arm in arm past her, causing feelings of bit
tersweet self-pity to intrude.

Focus on New York, she scolded. You have a career t
pursue, a new one to start. She couldn't go back to work i
the old place—not with Howard there. Some of what sh
had learned was never to settle for second best. The ne
Danielle would demand life on her terms, not wait for wha
was handed to her as if she deserved nothing better.

Would she always compare every man she met with Se
bastian? She knew she would. And she knew she'd neve
love anyone else.

She had walked for so long that, without realizing it, sh
had reached Sebastian's secret cove. Should she go inside
relive the painful memories of Sebastian's closeness
Looking back toward the hotel, not a human silhouette wa
in sight.

She needed this time to say goodbye. Ducking her head
she crawled into the dim coolness of the grotto, feeling th

varm, soft sand against her skin, as the thin sundress slid
up. She leaned back against the bank, closing her eyes. Behind her eyelids, scenes from the passing months slipped by
as if played on a video cassette.

After a while, tears spilled over her cheeks, and this time
he let them fall, hoping they would cleanse her mind and
motions.

"Don't cry, my Danni." Sebastian's deep voice filled the
heavy silence after the last wave's booming. It was so real,
he knew it only came from her terrible need.

Her eyes flew open as his strong hand wiped the tears
gently from her face and he leaned forward to kiss her lips.

He was real, no doubt of that.

He knelt in front of her, his broad shoulders blocking out
ght from the cave entrance. "I hoped to find you here, I
was afraid I had missed your plane and would have to fol-
ow you to New York."

"You would have done that?"

"*Mi vida, mi alma*—my life, my soul—of course I
would."

"But how did you—I thought I saw the last bridge go out
behind me..."

"No, the bridges are like the people, they don't break with
bad weather, only bend. Anyway, I rode Diablo here."

Her eyes widened as she held him away, staring. That was
possibly the most foolhardy, dangerous stunt he could have
pulled, riding the big stallion through the flooded marsh-
land.

"Why have you come? You don't need me, you have
ing's Ransom. Isn't that what you wanted?"

"Ah, *querida,* no one has entered my thoughts since the
first time I saw you. No one will ever own my heart again.
Surely you must have guessed my feelings, they were so
strong."

"Guessed? How would I guess?"

"Peter and Lupe and Concheta all jumped on me, told me
about what you'd done in the camp. Why didn't you tell
me?"

"I thought you would consider it interference, mec dling. Then when I wanted to tell you, this vanilla thin came up and...what about that? What happened wit Manuel and Teresa?"

He leaned back and looked out at the pounding ocean. ' saw to it that Manuel and Teresa will get what they deserv Reporting them to the police would have been useless— have no tangible proof of their guilt, other than hidde sacks of vanilla. I have in my own way made sure that bot of them will be quite uncomfortable in their future."

"Oh." That was all she could manage to say. She didn care about Manuel and Teresa—she only cared about Se bastian.

"Remember what you said—it seems like a lifetime ago that you wished we could start new again? I, too, wis that," Sebastian said as he turned to caress her with his eye "I need you here. We need you. You have touched all of with your generous spirit. There is much for you to do King's Ransom."

"You want me to stay?"

"You belong to King's Ransom as much as I, it's in you blood, I saw that in the beginning. Perhaps that was wh drove me wild, thinking you belonged there more than *She* saw it, too, and planned for this to happen. Can y believe it? Between her and Paul LeFarge, I don't know wh maneuvered us the most, but they did it and we fell for it.

"I thought that might be true. But I still have reserv tions about Teresa and Raoul. Would they leave us peace?"

He frowned, the muscles in his cheeks turned rigi "They'll have to. I have blackmail to use against them i need it, although I don't think Raoul was involved with t vanilla scheme. I had quite a talk with him and would li to break him in two for what he tried to do to you. Th could go to prison for a very long time, should they ev come near you or us again. I would see to it."

She knew he would.

"No more talk. I've other things on my mind," he said he began to kiss her eyelids, her nose, leading down to h outh. When he pushed aside the flimsy straps of her dress, e gasped as his hot mouth found her throat and led kisses ' fire down to the swelling of her breast.

She slid her hands from beneath his shirt and raked her ils lightly over his taut stomach, moving up to feel the rd little buttons of his nipples beneath her fingers. He oaned and held her close for a moment, neither of them oving.

He pressed her gently back and as she lay facing him. He did her belt and slipped the dress down around her an-es.

"You are so beautiful," he whispered, burying his face in r satin skin. He reached behind her and undid the bra rap to her bathing suit. "Oh, my love, I knew you would : this splendid." He leaned down and with exquisite care, d his tongue around on her breast as if savoring every inch flesh. When his teeth softly surrounded a rosy nipple, she ched her back and took his head in her hands, winding her ngers in this thick hair.

She pulled him upward, needing to feel his mouth fuse th hers, needing to feel his heartbeat against her own. ney kissed, long and slow, breath mingling with breath. ne familiar sweet vanilla smell of him lingered in the closed ace.

As if regretting to lose his place on her lips, he pulled vay gently, moving down her body, lips trailing kisses of e down, down until she could stand it no longer. His ong, calloused hands gently cupped her breasts, his umbs rubbing her nipples until they were taut and strain-g.

Suddenly nothing mattered but his lovemaking. She felt erished, precious to him, his patience and gentleness in the ce of his need showed that. He loved her, mere words ren't as important as knowing and trusting.

"Make love to me, dear heart. Now," she whispered.

His control frayed to the breaking point, he slid up to et her body, their hearts beating as one. He entered her refully, and she felt herself closing around him and she ched under his hips, arched to meet his hard body, to meet

every thrust until—until she gasped with surprise as t
lights exploded behind her closed eyes. He moaned an e
dearment as they collapsed, trembling and exhausted,
maining close together.

He kissed her forehead, pushing back the damp hair fro
her face with his lips.

As they lay together, only the boom of the crashing wa
and the screams of the gulls flying overhead could be hea
beyond their own heartbeats.

"Sebastian, when did you begin to—to care for me? W
didn't you tell me?"

He groaned and rolled on his back, facing upward. S
missed the warmth of him, but wanted so desperately
know.

"I guess I must have loved you from the moment I s
you standing on the steps of King's Ransom. You look
both lost and totally in command, an attitude that h
driven me wild from the beginning and probably alwa
will. I have learned to adore that in you." He reached to ta
one of her hands, to bring it to his lips.

"But if..."

"I know it sounds crazy, fighting against what I felt
you. That's why I had to stay away so much. I began to l
control because of my need for you. That made me ang
I've never lost command of my feelings before. I j
couldn't understand it."

"I understand. I had the same feelings at first. I did
want to lose control. We didn't trust each other."

"You can't know how much it hurt to think that Do
Mercedes discarded me for a stranger in her last days.
reject me for someone of her own blood, it was a knife in
heart."

"But she didn't do that! She...."

"Shh! Sweetheart, I know that now. I realize the n
ment she saw you, she loved you too, and wanted Kin
Ransom for both of us. It took us so long to see that."

Danielle nodded. *You longer than me*. She smiled. He h
said he loved her. Her body was still aflame from th

lovemaking, and now he'd said the words she'd longed to hear for so long.

He moved back and, turning her chin in his hand, looked deep into her eyes. In the dim light, she felt immersed in his gaze. Slowly, he began caressing her again, this time without the frenzied passion of need, but with a knowledge beneath his fingers, a knowledge of her body and how it would respond to him.

She kissed his shoulder, nibbling at his hard muscle, making soft little cat-bites of pleasure. They didn't have to hurry this time, for she knew they had the rest of their lives to be together.

*   *   *   *   *

He staked his claim...

HONOR BOUND

by
New York Times
Bestselling Author

previously published under the pseudonym Erin St. Claire

As Aislinn Andrews opened her mouth to scream, a hard
hand clamped over her face and she found herself face-
to-face with Lucas Greywolf, a lean, lethal-looking
Navajo and escaped convict who swore he wouldn't hurt
her— *if* she helped him.

Look for HONOR BOUND at your favorite
retail outlet this January.

Only from...

where passion lives.   SBHB

SILHOUETTE.... Where Passion Lives

Don't miss these Silhouette favorites by some of our most popular authors!
And now, you can receive a discount by ordering two or more titles!

Silhouette Desire®

#05751	THE MAN WITH THE MIDNIGHT EYES BJ James	$2.89	❑
#05763	THE COWBOY Cait London	$2.89	❑
#05774	TENNESSEE WALTZ Jackie Merritt	$2.89	❑
#05779	THE RANCHER AND THE RUNAWAY BRIDE Joan Johnston	$2.89	❑

Silhouette Intimate Moments®

#07417	WOLF AND THE ANGEL Kathleen Creighton	$3.29	❑
#07480	DIAMOND WILLOW Kathleen Eagle	$3.39	❑
#07486	MEMORIES OF LAURA Marilyn Pappano	$3.39	❑
#07493	QUINN EISLEY'S WAR Patricia Gardner Evans	$3.39	❑

Silhouette Shadows®

#27003	STRANGER IN THE MIST Lee Karr	$3.50	❑
#27007	FLASHBACK Terri Herrington	$3.50	❑
#27009	BREAK THE NIGHT Anne Stuart	$3.50	❑
#27012	DARK ENCHANTMENT Jane Toombs	$3.50	❑

Silhouette Special Edition®

#09754	THERE AND NOW Linda Lael Miller	$3.39	❑
#09770	FATHER: UNKNOWN Andrea Edwards	$3.39	❑
#09791	THE CAT THAT LIVED ON PARK AVENUE Tracy Sinclair	$3.39	❑
#09811	HE'S THE RICH BOY Lisa Jackson	$3.39	❑

Silhouette Romance®

#08893	LETTERS FROM HOME Toni Collins	$2.69	❑
#08915	NEW YEAR'S BABY Stella Bagwell	$2.69	❑
#08927	THE PURSUIT OF HAPPINESS Anne Peters	$2.69	❑
#08952	INSTANT FATHER Lucy Gordon	$2.75	❑

	AMOUNT	$	_____
DEDUCT:	10% DISCOUNT FOR 2+ BOOKS	$	_____
	POSTAGE & HANDLING	$	_____
	($1.00 for one book, 50¢ for each additional)		
	APPLICABLE TAXES*	$	_____
	TOTAL PAYABLE	$	_____
	(check or money order—please do not send cash)		

To order, complete this form and send it, along with a check or money order for the total above, payable to Silhouette Books, to: *In the U.S.*: 3010 Walden Avenue, P.O. Box 9077, Buffalo, NY 14269-9077; *In Canada*: P.O. Box 636, Fort Erie, Ontario, L2A 5X3.

Name: _____

Address:_____ City:_____

State/Prov.: _____ Zip/Postal Code: _____

*New York residents remit applicable sales taxes.
Canadian residents remit applicable GST and provincial taxes.

SBACK-OD

Silhouette

Relive the romance...
Harlequin and Silhouette
are proud to present

by Request™

A program of collections of three complete novels by the most requested authors with the most requested themes. Be sure to look for one volume each month with three complete novels by top name authors.

In January: **WESTERN LOVING**   Susan Fox
                                  JoAnn Ross
                                  Barbara Kaye

Loving a cowboy is easy—taming him isn't!

In February: **LOVER, COME BACK!**   Diana Palmer
                                     Lisa Jackson
                                     Patricia Gardner Evans

It was over so long ago—yet now they're calling, "Lover, Come Back!"

In March: **TEMPERATURE RISING**   JoAnn Ross
                                    Tess Gerritsen
                                    Jacqueline Diamond

Falling in love—just what the doctor ordered!

Available at your favorite retail outlet.

REQ-G3

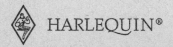 HARLEQUIN®    *Silhouette*

Christmas Classics

Share in the joys of finding happiness and exchanging the ultimate gift—love—in full-length classic holiday treasures by two bestselling authors

JOAN HOHL
EMILIE RICHARDS

Available in December at
your favorite retail outlet.

Only from 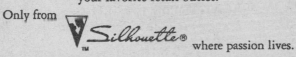 *Silhouette*® where passion lives.

**Silhouette Books
is proud to present
our best authors,
their best books…
and the best in
your reading pleasure!**

Throughout 1993, look for exciting
books by these top names in
contemporary romance:

DIANA PALMER—
The Australian in October

FERN MICHAELS—
Sea Gypsy in October

ELIZABETH LOWELL—
Chain Lightning in November

CATHERINE COULTER—
The Aristocrat in December

JOAN HOHL—
Texas Gold in December

LINDA HOWARD—
Tears of the Renegade in January '94

When it comes to passion,
we wrote the book.   BOBT3

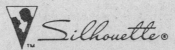

**Fifty red-blooded, white-hot, true-blue hunks
from every State in the Union!**

Look for MEN MADE IN AMERICA! Written by some
of our most poplar authors, these stories feature fifty of
the strongest, sexiest men, each from a different state in
the union!

Two titles available every other month at your favorite
retail outlet.

In January, look for:

DREAM COME TRUE by Ann Major (Florida)
WAY OF THE WILLOW by Linda Shaw (Georgia)

In March, look for:

TANGLED LIES by Anne Stuart (Hawaii)
ROGUE'S VALLEY by Kathleen Creighton (Idaho)

You won't be able to resist MEN MADE IN AMERICA!

To welcome you to Silhouette's newest series, here is a spine-tingling offer just for you.

In this hair-raising short-story volume from Silhouette Books, three of your favorite authors tell tales perfect for a spooky night in front of the fire.

ANNE STUART
"Monster in the Closet."

HELEN R. MYERS
"Seawitch."

HEATHER GRAHAM POZZESSERE
"Wilde Imaginings."

And it's yours absolutely FREE with 6 coupons plus $1.50 for delivery.

Take a walk on the dark side of love.